Royal Target

OTHER BOOKS AND AUDIO BOOKS
BY TRACI HUNTER ABRAMSON:

Undercurrents

Ripple Effect

The Deep End

Freefall

Royal Target

a novel by

TRACI HUNTER ABRAMSON

Covenant Communications, Inc.

Cover images (left to right): *Silver Semi Auto Handgun* by ThePropShoppe, courtest of iStock; *Aged and Weathered Crown* © Roy Konitzer, courtesty of iStock.

Cover design copyrighted 2008 by Covenant Communications, Inc.

Published by Covenant Communications, Inc.
American Fork, Utah

Printed in Canada
First Printing: October 2008

14 13 12 11 10 09 08   10 9 8 7 6 5 4 3 2 1

ISBN 13: 978-1-59811-628-1
ISBN 10: 1-59811-628-2

For Diana, Christina, Lara, and Luke
May you each find your happily ever after.

acknowledgments

My sincere thanks goes to Rebecca Cummings for helping me begin this adventure and for helping me through the long editing process. Thank you to the many others who helped make this novel what it could be, especially Nikki Abramson, Lynn Gardner, and Jennifer Spell.

Thank you to the CIA Publication Review Board for reviewing this novel . . . twice . . . to ensure that I stay out of trouble and for your continued timely support.

As always, I want to express my appreciation for the wonderful people at Covenant who continue to afford me the opportunity to do what I love and for their constant support. My special thanks goes to Kat Gille, Rachel Langlois, Robby Nichols, and Kathryn Jenkins for your many efforts in the editing and marketing processes.

Finally, thank you to my family and friends, who continue to encourage me in my pursuits. I don't know what I would do without you.

chapter 1

Janessa Rogers stepped into the plush lobby of the Marriott hotel in Caracas, her stomach jumping with anticipation. She still couldn't believe she was here. The welcome dinner for the annual World Trade Summit was one of the most important social events of the political world. She had mingled with her share of dignitaries during her three years with the Central Intelligence Agency, but never before had she attended an event of such magnitude.

Her ability to speak several languages had resulted in her invitation. Officially she was just a guest, one who could help facilitate communications if an additional translator was needed. Though she knew the US ambassador to Venezuela liked to send her to social events to help reinforce her cover, she suspected the invitation had also been a peace offering of sorts. Thoughts of the Rominez tragedy flashed in her mind, and she struggled to push the images aside.

She wasn't going to think about that now, she decided as she listened to the myriad of languages being spoken in the lobby. She moved past the seating area and check-in counter, her eyes sweeping the area in a subtle analysis. She could hardly wait to tell her family about the event—she was already taking mental notes so that she could describe everything in detail.

Janessa stepped into the elevator and smoothed her gown of vivid green. When the doors slid open, she glanced at her watch, seeing that she was only forty-five minutes late. While her new superior at the embassy would likely frown on her tardy arrival, she knew that arriving any earlier would make her stand out as an American. After being in the country for more than a year, she would rather have

Donald yell at her than to ignore the social customs she had long since adapted to.

Janessa showed her invitation and passport to the security officer at the ballroom door, grateful that tonight she would be just another face in the crowd. Those acquainted with her would recognize her as a representative from the US Embassy, but only a select few knew that she was actually an intelligence officer.

When she stepped inside, her smile was instant. The air hummed with salsa music, though it was barely audible over the multitude of voices. Stunning women shone like gems among the crowd made up of high-level government officials, heads of state, and a few splashes of royalty.

Janessa turned to scan the room, awed by the familiar faces—faces that before now she had seen only on television and in newspapers. Reminding herself that she was supposed to blend in, she struggled not to be intimidated. Growing up, she had always known she wanted to travel and experience life away from her family's farm in Iowa, but she never expected to be standing in the same room with so many of the world's influential politicians.

She took a calming breath, hoping that she looked like she belonged. Her rich, flame-colored hair was swept up in a complicated twist, and her ivory complexion left little doubt that she was a foreigner. Still, Janessa knew from experience that her talent with languages often caused people to mistake her for a European rather than an American.

Janessa spotted Donald across the room, looking very uptight and distressingly bureaucratic in his three-piece suit. Maybe all those years serving in Washington, D.C., had kept him from appreciating the finer benefits of working for the government, like enjoying a great party.

Donald noticed Janessa as well and motioned for her to join him. She gave a barely perceptible nod before starting to work through the crowd laced with friends and acquaintances. After taking only two steps, she saw someone she knew and stopped to chat. During her third conversation, she passed the bar and lingered long enough to order a soda. She finally emerged next to her boss twenty minutes later.

She sipped her drink as she took her position next to Donald.

"Do you have any idea what time it is?" The creases in his face deepened into a frown. The thirty extra pounds he sported from working behind a desk for the past fifteen years were concentrated around his middle, and his dark hair was peppered with gray.

Janessa ignored his tone and refused to look at her watch. Instead, she glanced at the waiters hovering nearby. "I imagine dinner will be served shortly."

Clearly annoyed that she'd deliberately misunderstood his question, he lowered his voice. "You do realize that you were supposed to be here an hour ago."

A sigh escaped her. She really hated breaking in new bosses. "I realize that the invitation said the party would start an hour ago." She glanced toward the door where a steady stream of guests continued to arrive. "I also realize that if you arrived at that time, you were the only one here."

His breath came out in a little huff. "Regardless, there has been a change of plans. The Meridian government asked for some help with their security tonight for Prince Stefano and Prince Garrett. The ambassador requested that you help out. Levi will give you the details."

Janessa ignored the little tug of disappointment she felt as she prepared to shift into work mode. César Navas, the police chief, and his wife, Felisa, made their way to her side before she had the chance to look for Levi. Janessa slipped into Spanish as she greeted them and introduced them to Donald.

A few minutes later, Janessa excused herself to go about her duties. She had yet to see either of the princes, but she followed her instincts and headed for the edge of the dance floor where a crowd had formed, including several photographers.

She expected that the photographers in the room were in heaven with the numerous politicians and celebrities mingling in the crowd. She had certainly seen plenty of pictures of both the Meridian princes over the years in newspapers and tabloids, so she had a good idea who she was looking for. She glimpsed Prince Stefano on the dance floor with a princess from Sweden. At age thirty-two, he was every bit the handsome European prince, tall and dark—and he didn't seem the least bit disturbed by the hovering press.

Turning back toward the crowd, she spotted Levi and stepped beside him. Like Janessa, Levi Marin was adept at fitting in with the crowd. He was just under six feet tall, and his dark hair and olive complexion made him look more like a native of Venezuela than the United States.

Janessa glanced around the room once more before asking, "Where is Prince Garrett?"

Levi simply nodded to the crowd. "He's been cornered since he got here."

Janessa caught a glimpse of him between two women who were probably in their late twenties. Prince Garrett was twenty-nine and a bit taller than average. His naturally athletic build was more noticeable in person, though the paparazzi had certainly made every attempt over the years to exploit his unforgettable good looks and the intrigue that invariably surrounded the royals.

He smiled and chatted with the women nearby, his rigid posture giving him an air of arrogance and indifference. He looked perfect. Too perfect. She imagined he was accustomed to having people cater to his every whim and wondered if he had any real understanding of what life was like for the commoners of the world.

Janessa studied him a moment and concluded that underneath the polished sheen and flawless manners, he was about ready to die of boredom. "What's the layout?" she asked Levi, referring to the location of the other security personnel.

"Their security forces are covering the perimeter, and each prince has two bodyguards nearby. Basically, you're an insider."

Janessa nodded, understanding perfectly. Her responsibility was simple. Look like everyone else, act like everyone else, and eliminate any threats that got past everyone else. She looked over at Prince Garrett again, her sympathies stirred as he tried to tactfully put some distance between himself and the woman to his left.

"That's Monique Cuvier, the French ambassador's daughter," Levi said, following her stare. "She's been coming on to him all night."

"Perhaps you should introduce me to the prince," Janessa suggested.

Levi nodded. He worked his way through the crowd surrounding the prince with Janessa close behind. They emerged in front of Prince Garrett just as the French ambassador put a hand on his daughter's arm and began escorting her away from the prince and across the room.

Levi spoke in English, setting the tone for the conversation. "Your Highness, this is the friend I was telling you about. Janessa Rogers, this is Prince Garrett of Meridia."

"Your Highness." Janessa gave a deferential nod, acknowledging his royal presence. The stiffness was still there but now with a hint of curiosity. The intensity of his stare surprised her as his eyes locked on hers. His eyes were the color of dark chocolate and were set in an aristocratic face with sharp cheekbones and a fall of dark hair across one side of his forehead.

"Miss Rogers, I am delighted to make your acquaintance," Prince Garrett greeted her, his English perfect, his voice rich and smooth with the cadence of a Meridian accent. He took her hand in his and studied her openly. She struggled not to fidget under his stare which was both direct and unnerving.

Someone in the crowd pushed forward, and Janessa barely managed to keep her footing. Uncomfortable with the crowd surrounding the prince, Janessa went with her instincts. Her eyes still on his, she tilted her head toward the dance floor. "Would you care to dance?"

The prince looked from Janessa to Levi and back again, apparently surprised by her directness, but he gave a slight nod and said, "It would be my pleasure." With her hand still in his, he led her to the dance floor.

Janessa's eyes swept the area as she and the prince moved forward, and she nodded her approval when Levi positioned himself close by. She noticed Prince Stefano still dancing a few yards away and turned to gauge where his security detail was positioned. Then Prince Garrett turned her into his arms, and her mind simply clicked off for a very dangerous moment. She settled her hand on his shoulder and found herself staring up into those dark eyes.

She reminded herself that she was one of many who had been in this position and focused once more on her responsibilities. "I'm sorry to be so forward, but you looked like you needed some space."

His dark eyebrows lifted, and surprise lit his eyes. "Did it show that much?"

"Only from a distance." Amusement laced her voice. "Dinner should be served shortly. If you have a preference of whom you would like to sit with, I'm sure it can be arranged."

"Excellent. Now then, do I understand correctly that you work for your government?"

Janessa nodded, and the aloof expression on his face was quickly replaced by delight. The smile transformed his features, making him more real somehow.

"In that case, perhaps I should sit beside you for dinner." With the grin still on his face, he leaned closer—close enough for her to see the little gold flecks in his eyes. "For protection."

"If you wish." Janessa returned his smile as a camera flashed nearby. She reminded herself that this man was routinely photographed with women all over the world, though rarely with the same one twice. Remembering that he had been attending law school in the United States, she turned the conversation to that. "Have you already graduated from law school?"

He nodded. "Two weeks ago. I'll leave for Meridia after the trade summit."

"I imagine you're anxious to get home."

Before he could answer, the music ended and the announcement was made that dinner was being served. Round banquet tables were covered with baskets of bread and a variety of traditional Venezuelan side dishes. Uniformed waiters circulated the tables carrying trays of meat ready to be carved.

Prince Garrett took Janessa's arm and guided her to a nearby table as she once again checked the location of his security forces. She took her seat, finding herself sitting across from César and Felisa Navas and next to Donald.

Janessa made the proper introductions, barely managing to suppress an annoyed sigh when Monique Cuvier sat on the other side of the prince. Janessa's eyes quickly swept over the woman. Once she was satisfied that Monique didn't have any place she could easily conceal a weapon, Janessa glanced at Prince Stefano, who was seated at the next table. She noted the heavy security stationed nearby for him and some of his dining companions, and then she turned her attention back to the man beside her.

She wondered briefly what it would be like to be royal, and she shook her head at the thought of the extremes that must exist in such a life—the incredible wealth married with the constant imposition of the press and public. Even now more than a dozen security personnel were scattered around the room to ensure the safety of both Prince Garrett and his brother.

Prince Garrett shifted in his seat as Monique slid closer to him and hooked an arm through his, despite the fact that he was trying to eat the salad that was now before him.

Sensing his tension, Janessa leaned closer and lowered her voice. "I can have her moved to another table if you wish."

Garrett's grin flashed unexpectedly, and he whispered back, "I have a better idea. Do me the favor of playing along."

Janessa didn't have the chance to ask what he meant. Monique began speaking to the prince in French. "You will have to save me a dance after dinner."

"I would love to," he responded in her native tongue, "but I'm afraid my girlfriend is the jealous type."

He then slid his hand over to Janessa's, lacing his fingers through hers as he lifted her hand to his lips. He spoke in English now as he turned to face Janessa. "Darling, how is your dinner?"

Janessa had barely managed to keep from laughing when he kissed her hand. She knew this was simply his way of dealing with a difficult situation and decided it wouldn't hurt to help him out. "It's delicious, thank you."

As Donald and the Navases cast speculative glances her way, Monique sent Janessa a frosty stare before releasing the prince's arm. Prince Garrett gave Janessa an appreciative look as he leaned closer and whispered into her ear. "I told her you're my girlfriend. Hope you don't mind."

"I'm here to serve." Janessa lifted a shoulder, noticing that he'd left out the part about her being jealous. Unless Donald had read her file, no one at the table would have any reason to suspect that French was one of several languages in which she was fluent.

For a moment, insecurity washed over her as she saw herself as an insignificant commoner pretending she belonged among royalty. Annoyed at her train of thought, Janessa turned her attention to the dinner in front of her, determined to enjoy herself as she engaged in conversation with the prince and the Navases.

Numerous questions were directed at Prince Garrett over the course of the meal, and Janessa could see him stiffening degree by degree as his posture once again became rigid and formal. She thought she could feel his impatience with the tedious conversation, but each time she looked at him, she saw only his perfect manners and an air of formality. Between dinner and dessert, a waitress arrived and served after-dinner drinks.

Janessa looked at the red liquid in the glass that was placed in front of her. It was possible this was a fruit drink, but since it was in a glass commonly used for wine, there was a good chance it was alcoholic. She turned to César and asked in Spanish, "What is it?"

"You'll like it," he told her absently.

Though she worked undercover for the CIA in many different settings, her religious standards were one part of her cover that never changed. The chief of police was aware that she was a Latter-day Saint, and in the past he and his coworkers had gone out of their way to serve her drinks that were in keeping with her beliefs. Yet she couldn't help feeling wary of the drink in front of her. She asked César again, "But what is it?"

"Sangria."

Leaning forward, Janessa spoke quietly. "Doesn't it have alcohol in it?"

"You must drink with us," César insisted, nudging her glass toward her.

Janessa shook her head, instantly aware that the prince was staring at her. Still, she spoke calmly to César, her voice low. "You know I don't drink."

"This is different. It's for a celebration." An edge came into his voice.

Felisa Navas leaned across her husband, her words slurring a bit as she added sternly, "You must drink. It is an insult if you do not."

Janessa looked from Felisa to César, realizing that Felisa had already had too much to drink. Hoping to shift the attention away from herself, she was about to initiate a conversation with the prince when Felisa reached across her husband and pushed the drink closer to Janessa.

"You must drink with us." Felisa's voice raised another decibel.

Donald leaned forward, clearly becoming upset by the scene unfolding. He lowered his voice and demanded, "What are you doing?"

"I'm Mormon. It's against my religion to drink, and I'm not going to get pushed into it," Janessa told him in hushed tones. She sensed the prince's surprise and wondered if he was familiar with her faith.

The Navases made one more attempt to convince Janessa to drink with them. César was calm, trying to explain that she was breaking custom, but Felisa was clearly angry. All the while, Prince Garrett looked on silently.

Finally, Janessa pushed back from the table and spoke in Spanish, her voice low in the hopes that she could avoid drawing any more attention to herself. "I am sorry if I have insulted you by not drinking this." She waved a hand at the sangria. "But please understand that it is an insult to me that you would expect me to set aside my religious beliefs for a drink."

Felisa gasped at her words, but Janessa turned away, intending to have Levi cover for her until she could trade places with someone working outside of the ballroom. To her surprise, Prince Garrett stood as well.

"I'll escort you home." He took her hand in his before turning his attention back to those at the table. "I hope you all enjoy the rest of your evening."

With that, he motioned toward the door and accompanied Janessa out of the room.

chapter 2

Garrett stepped into the hall and studied the petite redhead beside him. Her cheeks were flushed with color, her posture rigid. He couldn't help but admire her for standing up for her beliefs, especially now that he could see how shaken she was. His mind was still trying to wrap around the news that she was Mormon as he laid a hand on her shoulder and asked, "Are you all right?"

Janessa nodded, turning to face him. "I'm fine. I can trade places with one of the others on security detail so you can go rejoin the party."

"Are you kidding?" Garrett tugged at his collar to relieve some of the pressure from his bowtie. "You just saved me from another two hours of boredom. I owe you."

Her posture relaxed somewhat, and she managed a small smile. "Would you like me to arrange for your car to take you back to your embassy?"

Garrett considered what she was offering, the peace and solitude he had wanted all evening. Suddenly, he wasn't sure he wanted to be alone after all. "Perhaps you can suggest someplace else we can go. I don't think I'm quite ready to call it a night."

Janessa tensed, and Garrett could sense her reservations as she asked, "What did you have in mind?"

"Perhaps you know of someplace where we can get dessert," he suggested.

Now Janessa relaxed and gave him the gift of a genuine smile. "I think we can manage that." She stepped closer to one of his security guards that had followed them into the hall. She spoke in Italian, instructing the guard to inform Prince Stefano of his brother's departure and to request a small contingent of guards to accompany them.

Garrett looked on, surprised at her easy use of his language. "Where did you learn to speak Italian?"

"I went on a mission for the Mormon Church to Italy." Janessa motioned down the hall to the elevators. "We'll take my car so that your brother can leave when he wants."

"I imagine he will be here for some time. For some insane reason, he actually likes these events."

Janessa just nodded as she stepped into the elevator. A few minutes later they emerged from the service entrance and were met by a member of Garrett's security force. Janessa's driver was already waiting for them outside, along with another car filled with security personnel.

Janessa's driver opened the door to let Janessa and the prince into the back seat. He then climbed behind the wheel as Garrett's personal bodyguard slid into the passenger seat. Janessa leaned forward, informing the driver of their destination.

Garrett expected her to choose some high-end restaurant nearby, but when the car approached one of the popular night clubs, he wondered if he should have gone back to the embassy after all. While the press often painted him as a man who spent his time clubbing, few people realized that he didn't like crowds. To his relief, the driver continued down the street and pulled into a parking lot a mile later. He studied the glass-fronted ice cream shop, pleased with its simplicity and lack of clientele at this late hour.

Out of habit, he stayed in the car until his bodyguard opened his door and indicated that the security sweep had been completed. Janessa escorted him inside, apparently comfortable in the simple setting despite the fact that she wore an evening gown and her escort was in black tie.

Showing an unexpected warmth, she greeted the proprietor by name and led the way to a booth in the corner. Garrett slid into the seat across from her, somewhat surprised at how easily her professionalism had melted away. He nodded in the direction of the owner. "I gather you come here often."

She carelessly lifted a shoulder. "Once or twice a month."

"How do you know the owner?"

"I introduced myself to him the first time I came in." Janessa passed him a menu. "After you taste the ice cream here, you'll see why."

Two of Garrett's bodyguards stood by the exits, even though the place was nearly empty. A trio of girls occupied a booth in the center of the restaurant, and on the far side six teenagers were eating out of an enormous bowl filled with various flavors of ice cream.

Garrett motioned across the room. "I hope all of the portions aren't that big."

Janessa shook her head and laughed. "After the dinner we just ate, I think one scoop will do it for me tonight. The challenge is deciding what flavor."

Opening his menu, he began to understand what she was talking about. Over three dozen flavors were listed inside. He was still deciding when the waitress came over to take their order, and he finally chose something at random.

As soon as the waitress left them, he turned his attention back to Janessa. "I gather you are stationed here in Caracas?"

Janessa nodded. "I've been in the country just over a year."

"I have to admit, you don't look anything like the security officers I've had in the past."

"Appearances can be deceiving," Janessa said as the waitress approached with their dessert. "By the way, thanks for helping me out tonight. I didn't expect to get cornered like that by my friends."

"It was my pleasure. Like I said before, you likely saved me from hours of boredom." Garrett leaned forward as though telling her a secret. "And you also saved me from a rather awkward situation with Monique."

"Does this mean we're even?" she asked with a smile.

"Absolutely."

Janessa picked up her spoon and scooped up a little of the ice cream the waitress had set before her. "You said earlier that you plan to return home after the summit. Do you know what you'll do once you get there? Do you have duties waiting for you, or can you sort of carve out your own future?"

Garrett stared at her for a moment, more surprised by the fact that she thought to ask such a question than by the question itself. Reminding himself that he barely knew this woman, he kept his response neutral. "I'm still considering my options."

She nodded sympathetically. "I imagine being royal is difficult, trying to balance the doors that are open to you with the limitations your title creates."

"Not many people recognize the limitations," Garrett stated simply. He took a bite of ice cream, and a slow smile crept over his face. "I can see why you chose this place."

"I try to stop by every time I'm in this part of the city." Janessa smiled.

"Where else do you suggest I visit while I'm here?" Garrett asked, relaxing back into his seat.

"Well, you probably don't have time to go to Canaima and visit Angel Falls." Janessa shrugged a shoulder. "That's one of my favorite places, but there's a lot of history right here in Caracas."

Garrett continued to enjoy his ice cream while he listened to the charming redhead talk about the city and some of her favorite sights. She seemed at ease with him, reminding him of the friends he'd left behind in Washington, D.C.

When the waitress approached with their bill, Janessa glanced down at her watch. "It's getting late. Would you like me to take you home?"

Garrett laughed as he lifted his hand and motioned for one of his bodyguards to take care of the bill. "Isn't that supposed to be my line?"

"Not tonight."

* * *

Janessa couldn't figure him out. Prince Garrett leaned back in his seat as they made their way to his embassy, somehow looking comfortable despite the tuxedo he wore. He chatted amiably about his country, then asked about her family. He was acting so incredibly normal that the whole scene seemed surreal.

Even more surreal was the fact that she was sitting beside him, somehow keeping up her end of the conversation. The stiffness she had first noticed in him had faded, and his demeanor was now friendly and relaxed. In fact, he seemed to have completely forgotten that she was present as a member of his security force, treating her instead like a casual acquaintance he had chosen to spend time with.

Janessa slipped back into work mode when the Meridian Embassy came into view along with a half dozen reporters waiting outside the main gate. She leaned forward and instructed her driver to circle the block to give the prince's security forces sufficient time to eliminate any potential threats.

Prince Garrett waited until she turned her attention back to him and asked, "Can I expect to see you tomorrow?"

"I don't know if I'm on duty tomorrow."

He grinned. "Perhaps I should pull a few strings. Being royal does have its advantages."

Janessa laughed. "You just want to make sure that Monique sees us together so she'll leave you alone."

"I'm a man who knows how to use his resources well."

"Of that I have little doubt." Her smile stayed put as she noticed that they were approaching the embassy once again and that his security detail was now in place. "Thank you again for helping me out this evening."

"The pleasure was entirely mine," Prince Garrett said as the driver opened the car door. "I'll see you tomorrow."

Janessa responded automatically. "I look forward to it."

Then, with a spree of flashbulbs, he climbed from the car and disappeared behind the embassy gates. As the driver pulled away, Janessa glanced back over her shoulder, realizing that she really was looking forward to tomorrow.

* * *

"Your behavior was completely unacceptable." Donald drummed his fingers on his desk. "Imagine my surprise when I found out that this was not the first incident you'd been involved in."

Janessa watched Donald open up her personnel file, afraid of what he might find there. She had thought the early morning summons to Donald's office was to tell her she had been requested for Prince Garrett's security detail. Instead, she found herself once again defending her beliefs. She held back a sigh, deliberately keeping her voice free of emotion. "I can explain."

"I don't even want to know what happened at the bathhouse in Japan. Obviously you caused a major stir if you were reassigned after only two weeks in the country." Donald skimmed over the papers in her file. "And then you punched the ambassador's aide in Paris."

"He's the one who made a move on me." Janessa held up a hand as she made her point. "I tried asking him nicely to stop. He just wouldn't listen."

"You broke his nose!"

Janessa nodded, trying to look remorseful. A touch of humor still laced her voice when she spoke. "That was unfortunate."

"This string of *unfortunate* incidents leaves me little choice." Donald shuffled the papers on his desk, standing when he located the one he wanted. "Here are your travel orders to go back to Washington. Your flight leaves first thing in the morning."

Sighing heavily, Janessa snatched the travel orders from Donald's hand, muttering as she left his office. "So much for religious freedom."

chapter 3

The weeklong World Trade Summit had concluded several days before, but such events held no importance for the two figures clad completely in black. Soundlessly, they slipped through the darkness outside the gates of the US Embassy in Meridia. Thick clouds overhead blocked any light the moon might have provided, and together they ducked behind the row of cars parked along the street.

Security cameras were perched in several strategic locations on the outside of the building, but they were blind to the two stealthy figures. The security guards inside would see nothing but darkness and parked cars. At least, they would see nothing until it was too late.

A dog barked in the distance, causing them both to slow for a moment. Once satisfied that the animal was not a threat, they continued on in their hunched-over positions. The person in the lead came to a stop behind the car that had been chosen hours earlier, a car that had the size and positioning for their objective.

Squatting down, they unloaded the contents of their backpacks and went to work. Several minutes later, one of them reached under the car and activated the bomb that would send their message to the world.

* * *

Prince Garrett Fortier walked down the cavernous hallway of the palace, his footsteps sounding on the tile floor. His ancestral home had been standing for over four hundred years, and, at its core, the palace remained very much the same as it had been at the time of its construction. Generations of Fortiers had ruled from this palace and would continue to do so for generations to come.

From the windows on the west side, Garrett could see the ruins of the castle that had housed his ancestors throughout the Middle Ages. The demise of the castle had come in 1598, when the French civil wars had spilled over into Meridia. Garrett hesitated a moment before turning his gaze from the ruins. A fight for religious freedom had been the underlying cause of the destruction of the grand structure and had nearly forced his family from power.

He thought of Janessa, remembering the brief battle she had waged in defense of her own religious freedom. He had been so tempted to confide in her about his plans. She had seemed so unassuming, and he sensed she could be trusted. Still, his upbringing had taught him not to trust easily, and ultimately he hadn't been willing to risk sharing confidences with a woman he barely knew.

His inquiry about Janessa's availability to work on his protection detail in Caracas had revealed that she had returned to the United States. He hoped that a country that boasted of so many liberties wouldn't penalize one of its citizens for exercising her religious beliefs, but the fact remained that Janessa was no longer in Venezuela.

His impression of Janessa during their brief time together was that she would fight for her rights regardless of the consequences. Deliberately lifting his chin, Garrett knew he had to follow her example.

Ignoring the nerves balled in his stomach, Garrett turned the corner toward his father's office. Whether or not he could make his father understand his own need for religious freedom, he had to at least take a stand. He knew the risks, and he understood the weight of his decision. He would be the first in the family to leave the Meridian Church to embrace another in over a thousand years.

Anticipating the battle to come, Garrett ran a hand through his thick, black hair. He had arrived from Caracas only two days before and already he felt crowded by the heavy security and the constant presence of the household staff. His three years attending law school at George Washington University in DC had given him a taste of what he often craved but rarely attained: privacy and freedom.

He had enjoyed the duality of his life in the states, both the endless variety of his official duties and those moments he had managed to blend in with the crowd. His best friend and study partner, Tim O'Donnell, had given him a glimpse of middle-class America and so much more—he had given him a Book of Mormon.

Garrett had started reading the book out of curiosity, more because of his fascination with history than any desire to find religious significance. He couldn't say that he had ever been very religious in the past, never having found the need for such things, but many passages of the Book of Mormon seemed familiar, as though he had read them before.

The sense of discontentment he had always struggled with had melted away, but he didn't recognize the source of the change. When Tim got married at the end of their first year of law school, Garrett had been shocked and angry to find that he wasn't allowed to attend the wedding inside the temple. While he was waiting in the shadows of the temple, his temper faded and he realized that it was the first time anyone aside from his parents had told him he couldn't do something.

Ironically, being subjected to rules that made no allowances for his royal status gave Garrett a new respect and admiration for the Mormon Church. He soon found himself asking Tim more and more questions. The religious discussions they shared sparked something in Garrett, and before long he became a regular fixture at Tim's house each Sunday. On occasion he even managed to attend sacrament meeting with Tim without being tailed by the paparazzi.

Garrett continued to read the Book of Mormon and slowly came to terms with the understanding he found within its pages. His conversion had been so gradual he had hardly realized it was happening, and when Tim had challenged him to be baptized, panic had shot through him. Despite his newfound understanding of the gospel, his choice was anything but simple. Would his family still permit him to function as part of the royal family if he chose baptism into the Mormon Church?

As demanding as his duties could be at times, he couldn't imagine what it would be like not to function as a royal. He had enjoyed his independence while in the United States, but he knew that he could never live life as an ordinary man. He hadn't been born one. He wasn't destined to rule Meridia, but he would always be expected to play an active part in the politics and protection of his country. In truth, he wouldn't want it any other way.

He was still amazed by how subtle his conversion to the gospel had been, just as he was surprised at how much he wanted it to be a part of his life. As the time to return home had drawn closer, Garrett had started contemplating what he would do if his father denied him what he so dearly wanted. For the first time in his life, he knew he was prepared to go against not only his father's wishes, but against the king's.

The door to his father's office was open when he arrived, and his older brother Stefano was seated inside. Though it was barely nine o'clock, the paperwork in front of Stefano indicated that he and their father were already several hours into their work day. Not for the first time, Garrett was grateful he wasn't the eldest. As heir to the throne, Stefano was already entrenched in the everyday affairs of Meridia, from military concerns to the country's diplomatic corps.

Hoping to speak to all of his family at once, Garrett asked, "Where's mother?"

"She is visiting down at the hospital." King Eduard Fortier IV glanced up at Garrett. "A car bomb went off outside of the US Embassy here this morning. At least a dozen people were injured, and one of the embassy drivers was killed."

Tension settled quickly on Garrett's shoulders. "Do we know who's behind it?"

"No one has come forward to claim responsibility, but we think it must be terrorists."

"The United States has long been a prime target." Garrett sat in one of the chairs opposite his father. "And our negotiations with the US, allowing them to build a naval base here, have caused a lot of tension—perhaps some extremists among the opposition are now resorting to violence."

"Unfortunately, there's more. The threats against our family have also increased over the past two weeks." Eduard lifted a paper off of his desk and handed it to Garrett. "This is a copy of the threat we received this morning."

Garrett looked at the page and read the note: *Keep the US out of Meridia, or a member of the royal family will die.*

The words appeared to be cut out of the local newspaper. Just below the message was a news photo of the king, his head cut off of the photo and pasted at his feet. Garrett looked up at his father, unwilling to think of him as anything but invincible.

Stefano spoke up. "Surely you aren't concerned with a security breach here at the palace."

Eduard shook his head. "The palace, no, but I do worry about the chateau. The summer gala is less than two months away. We need to fortify our security there before the gala takes place."

"Can we move the gala here to the palace?" Garrett asked.

"The economic reports have not been good over the past few years. Bellamo needs the gala to help stir its tourism industry," Eduard told him. "We must act quickly against these terrorists to show the world once and for all that terrorism will not be tolerated in Meridia."

"What can we do that hasn't already been done?" Garrett asked.

Stefano spoke now. "Father, I think you need to consider the proposal from the Americans."

"What proposal?" Garrett looked from his brother to his father.

Eduard straightened slightly in his chair. "The United States has offered some of their military and intelligence officers to help us investigate the bombing and maintain security while we finish negotiations for the naval base."

"Do you really think that's necessary?" Garrett asked. "They have enough to worry about, trying to provide security at their own embassy."

"Regardless, they have offered to help. And since our alliance may be the source of these latest problems, I think it best to allow them a limited presence here while the negotiations are completed." Eduard handed a file to Garrett. "Garrett, I want you to oversee the security and preparations for the gala."

Garrett's eyebrows lifted. "Father, I'm hardly equipped to meet with florists and caterers."

Though Garrett had been speaking to his father, Eduard's sharp tone told Garrett that Eduard was responding as the king. "I need someone I trust to ensure your mother's safety."

"Of course, Father." Garrett's voice was immediately respectful, even as he noted that as the second son, his safety was of lesser importance to the royal family.

"I will find someone to help oversee the hostess duties, but I want you at the chateau, where you are easily accessible to Martino," Eduard continued, referring to the chateau manager.

Garrett nodded and stepped toward the door. "I'll go meet with our chief of security and inform him that I'll be staying at the chateau."

As Garrett left the room, he thought of the Book of Mormon in his nightstand drawer. He suppressed his frustration that he had been unable to share his new understanding with his family. It wouldn't be an easy subject to broach, and considering the possible outcomes, Garrett didn't feel good about adding any more drama to the king's already long list of stresses. Once again he wondered if he really could balance duty with religion.

* * *

Tim O'Donnell checked his watch for the third time in as many minutes. He had already completed the first two phases of applying for the FBI, and he was now anxiously awaiting the phone call that would tell him if he was headed on to the next phase.

Tim had spent two years as a police officer in Maryland before deciding to go to law school. During his first year, he had considered pursuing a career as a prosecutor in the hopes of helping keep criminals off of the streets. By the time he had reached his third year, he'd realized he wanted to get back into law enforcement. With his police experience and his new law degree, he now hoped to fulfill his secret lifetime dream of becoming an agent for the FBI. The woman he had spoken with the day before had assured him that he should expect a call by the end of the work day.

The front door opened, distracting him momentarily. His wife, Lauren, stepped through with a bag of groceries in each arm.

"Let me get those." Tim crossed the room to relieve his wife's burden. "You shouldn't be lifting so much."

Lauren rubbed a hand over her newly expanding stomach. "I promise you that when this little guy arrives, I'll let you do all of the grocery shopping for a month."

"Just one month?" Tim teased.

"Okay, maybe two." Lauren sat down in a living room chair and watched Tim set the bags on the kitchen counter. "Have you heard anything yet?"

"Not yet." Tim shook his head. "I don't know what I'm going to do if I don't get accepted."

"You could always go back to being a cop," Lauren suggested with a shrug.

Tim looked up and grinned at his wife. "Or I could be a lawyer."

"Even worse," Lauren teased just as the phone rang.

He plucked it up, praying for good news. To his surprise, his friend Garrett was on the other end instead of his potential employer.

"Hey, Garrett." Tim opened the refrigerator to put the cheese away. "Did you tell your parents yet?"

"I'm afraid that conversation won't be happening in my near future," Garrett told him. "My duties have taken an unexpected turn."

"In what way?" Tim asked, and Garrett relayed the conversation he had had with his father and brother that morning.

"I'm sorry about the embassy—I didn't realize it would impact you directly. I heard about it earlier today," Tim told him before redirecting the conversation once more. "You don't think your parents will really disown you for joining the Church, do you?"

"I don't know." A hint of anxiety came over the line. "I like to think they'll accept it, but it's hard to say. If it does come to that, at least I spent the past few years learning to live as a commoner."

Tim started to disagree but decided he would let Garrett keep his illusions that he understood what real life was like for most people. Instead he said, "All I can suggest is that you keep praying about it."

"Yeah," Garrett agreed and then promptly changed the subject. "Anyway, I just wanted to warn you about what's going on over here. I wasn't sure if you and Lauren would still want to come for the gala, especially now that she's expecting."

"I've seen how much security you have following you around, so I'm not too concerned about me, but I'll talk to Lauren." Tim shrugged. "Hopefully things will settle down in the next couple of weeks. Who knows, you might even capture whoever bombed the embassy."

"Let's hope so."

chapter 4

Janessa looked aimlessly out the window of her sister's living room at the evening traffic filtering by, still feeling latent frustration from being sent back to the States again. She had been looking forward to attending the rest of the trade summit and watching history unfold, even if it was only as a member of Prince Garrett's protection detail. Instead, she had spent the past week and a half pushing papers in a tediously dull office job. She took some measure of comfort in the fact that this current job was only temporary until the Agency decided what to do with her. She wasn't terribly worried about being let go. After all, she had already completed her trial period with the Agency, and except for the three incidents Donald had mentioned, her work record was excellent.

Don't think about it, she told herself, then turned to Mary. "You never finished giving me the latest gossip from back home. Is Jake going to marry that girl he brought home last Christmas?"

Mary shook her head. "He broke up with her a few weeks ago."

"Why?" Janessa asked, glancing down at a framed photo of her family, taken the last time she was in Iowa. "She seemed perfect for him."

"I thought so too." Mary shrugged. "I think he's afraid of commitment."

"Maybe," Janessa commented, not sure what to think. She couldn't claim to have any real experience with serious relationships. She had made the decision long ago that she would marry in the temple, but it had never occurred to her during her teenage years that she might not find the opportunity. Too often she felt as though being single meant she had failed somehow.

She knew that twenty-seven really wasn't old, but she wasn't exactly tripping over men who were potential husband material. As her travels overseas continued to limit her contact with single members of the Church, she had all but given up on the possibility of marriage. Fortunately, most of the time she was happy just being herself, even if she was destined to live alone.

When the doorbell rang, she motioned for her very pregnant sister to stay seated. "I'll get it."

Janessa pulled open the door, surprised to find a courier on the doorstep so late in the day. She signed for the envelope addressed to her and then tore it open. An embossed invitation was clipped to a stack of papers. She scanned it, wondering why she would be receiving an invitation to Meridia for a party. She thought of her evening with Prince Garrett, but she couldn't imagine that the few hours they had spent together would warrant a royal summons. Then she thought of her friend in security who was fond of practical jokes. "Supposedly I've been invited to Meridia by the royal family."

"Are you serious?"

"It's just a joke." Janessa dropped onto the couch in her sister's apartment. She flipped through the privacy agreement attached to the envelope, shaking her head. "I'll have to compliment Alan on his originality this time. He can't resist rubbing it in every time I get into trouble."

"How can you be so sure it isn't real?" It was obvious that Mary was itching to call home to tell their parents and four younger siblings about the letter her sister had received.

"Be serious, Mary." Janessa lifted the embossed invitation. "'You are cordially invited to the summer home of King Eduard Fortier of Meridia for the annual Independence Day gala.' There's no way this could be real. Royalty doesn't invite Iowa farm girls to their summer homes. Besides, only the people from work know that I'm staying with you."

"Which means anyone in the government could probably track you down."

"True." Janessa sighed. "I hate my job."

"You love your job," Mary countered easily. She rubbed a hand across her swollen belly, smiling when the life within her gave another kick.

"I loved my old job." Janessa pouted. "I'm a linguistics specialist. I don't want to sit around Washington, D.C., all day long and translate for boring politicians."

"So you would rather sit around some third-world country all day long and translate for boring politicians?" Mary asked.

A giggle escaped Janessa at the accuracy of her sister's words. "Well, yeah. I can't tell you how exciting it is to live in another culture, to really get to know it."

"You can always go places on vacation."

Janessa sighed. "It's just not the same."

* * *

Alan Neisler was engrossed in his surveillance plan when Janessa entered the security office. He didn't notice her presence, so Janessa simply leaned against the doorjamb, watching him. His skin was a shade darker than molasses, and his features still had a baby-face quality about them, though he was only two years her junior at twenty-five.

The tip of his pencil broke, and he reached for another without looking up. Amused that his concentration was so unbreakable, Janessa walked into the room and sat down on the corner of his desk. Still, he continued writing until Janessa took his work and slid it out from under his pencil.

His eyes followed the surveillance plan, and a confused look crossed his face. He looked up, seeming more surprised that his work had escaped him than to find Janessa sitting on his desk, feet crossed at the ankles.

Alan lifted one eyebrow, a skill Janessa had always admired. "Did you want something?"

"This one was actually pretty funny." Janessa dropped the thick envelope on his desk.

"What?" Alan studied the contents of the envelope with his typical intensity. He read the invitation, set it aside, and moved on to the privacy agreement. For several minutes he remained absorbed in the text. Finally, he looked up and spoke. "Is this a joke?"

"Of course it's a joke." Janessa laughed. "When did you find time to come up with this?" She fingered the gilded invitation. "I mean, the bubble bath after the little incident in Japan was funny, and of course the rubber nose after that problem in Paris, but this really takes first prize. I guess that's what I get for telling you that I met a prince."

Alan leaned back in his chair. His lips curved into a smile that slowly moved over the rest of his face. "I didn't send this to you. I think it's real."

"What? It can't possibly be real."

Turning to a computer, Alan punched a few buttons to pull up the recent cable traffic from the overseas stations. He focused in on the cables from Meridia, finally finding the one he wanted. "Read this."

She stepped behind him, reading over his shoulder. She had heard about the bombing at the US Embassy in Meridia just two days before. Her eyes widened as she saw King Eduard's request for military and intelligence assistance.

Janessa stepped back and studied her friend. "This is insane."

Alan's grin stayed in place, and mischief flashed in his eyes. "I've never met any royalty before. Can you get me some autographs?"

"I thought you were headed to London next week. You'll be tripping over royalty in no time."

"Oh, come on." Alan continued. "The only way I'm going to see royalty in England is if someone plants a bomb in Buckingham Palace." He pulled out a pad of paper. "Here, you can use this for an autograph book."

"Stop it." Janessa laughed, despite the absurdity of the situation. "There's no way I'm going."

"Of course not." Alan tried to keep a serious face. "Insult Venezuela last week, insult Meridia this week. For you, it's par for the course. By the way, you're supposed to go see personnel. You really are getting a new assignment."

Janessa stood, shaking her head. "I'm leaving now."

"What about the autographs?" His laughter followed her into the hallway. She made her way to the personnel office to find out where she was going to be posted next. Surprisingly, the receptionist handed her a message that told her to report to the director's office.

Confused, Janessa headed upstairs to the recently remodeled offices. She announced her arrival to the director's personal secretary, deliberately not wringing her hands together. Surely the problem in Venezuela wasn't bad enough to have gained the attention of such a high-level government official. She was surprised when the receptionist immediately showed her into Director Palmer's office.

The man sitting behind the huge mahogany desk motioned her in. Janessa had seen photos of him before, but this was the first time she had seen him in person. He was thinner than she had expected, though she had heard through the grapevine that he was adamant about exercising every day. His charcoal suit fit him precisely, the color nearly matching his hair.

Determined to appear professional, Janessa sat in the chair he indicated across from him. She clasped her hands together, wishing her first meeting with the director were under better circumstances. Undoubtedly, she was going to be reprimanded for the most recent of her blunders.

Director Palmer leaned back in his seat. Just a hint of humor laced his voice. "I reviewed your personnel file for the first time today. I have to admit that it's quite colorful, considering that you've only been with us for three years."

"The incident in Caracas was simply a misunderstanding. I'm sure that if I had been allowed to stay I could have worked it out."

He held up a hand to stop her explanation. "As I looked over your incidents, I noticed that all the explanations have a common thread. It seems your religious beliefs were somehow insulted each time." He paused and closed the file. "In fact, it appears that when it comes to your religious beliefs, you tend to act first and think later."

Janessa remained silent, unsure how to respond.

"I made a call to the president of your church."

"You called the *prophet*?" Janessa's eyes widened.

"The president wasn't available, but I spoke to someone at your church headquarters." He continued, drumming his fingers on the file in front of him. "I was concerned that your beliefs might cause a problem during your next assignment." He lifted up an identical copy of the privacy agreement that had accompanied her invitation to Meridia. "The man I spoke to assured me that while you will undoubtedly remain true to the teachings of your church, there should be no conflicts that would prevent you from accomplishing your duties in Meridia."

"You want me to go to the gala?" Surprise crossed Janessa's face.

"Are you aware that our government has been negotiating for some time with the king of Meridia to build a naval base in his country?"

Janessa shook her head.

"While King Eduard does not oppose the presence of our armed forces in his country, finding a suitable location has caused some significant roadblocks. The bombing yesterday will undoubtedly throw up a few more," Director Palmer told her. He tapped a finger on her file as he added, "I was also informed by the man at your church headquarters that they are about to break ground for a temple in Meridia."

"Really?" Her eyebrows lifted at the news that yet another temple would be built in Europe.

"Apparently so. If only we could be so lucky in our own negotiations for land."

"Um . . . I still don't understand how all of this affects me," Janessa admitted, fiddling with the silver CTR ring on her right pinkie. "I certainly wouldn't have any effect on these negotiations just by attending a party."

"You would hardly just be attending a party. Since neither Prince Stefano nor Prince Garrett is married, the only hostess in the royal family is Queen Marta. In the weeks prior to the event, she would normally be making plans and arrangements on-site at the chateau in Bellamo. Understandably, King Eduard does not want his wife anywhere near Bellamo until her safety can be guaranteed."

"So if I understand what you're saying, you want me to secure the chateau and also throw in some hostessing duties?" she said dubiously.

"That's right. But there's more."

"More?"

"You are going to be engaged to Prince Garrett."

"What?" Janessa leaned forward, her jaw dropping. "You can't be serious!"

"It's just for show," he assured her. "You wouldn't have to do anything more on that front than a few public displays of affection, an interview or two with the press, and the usual social functions. The reason for the charade is that as his fiancée, you would have complete access to the grounds and the staff of the chateau. You would also be privy to all of the security arrangements being made. Basically, you would be our inside man."

"So you want me to go undercover," Janessa said, finally seeing some logic behind the request. "Let me ask you one thing. Why me?"

"The king didn't name names, but he asked that we send the woman best suited for the job, and I believe that's you. The fact that Prince Garrett requested you to continue on his security detail in Caracas weighed in. Besides that, you have integrity, and you speak the language." He shifted the file on his desk before his eyes met hers once more. "You need to understand that in essence you are this team's leader. From this moment on, everything you do has to be consistent with your cover story."

Director Palmer stood now, and Janessa followed his lead. "You have your first briefing in the morning on Meridia's culture, the royal family, and the plans for the naval base. My secretary will give you the details."

Janessa nodded and followed him to the door. When he opened it, she turned back to face him. "Well, it was nice meeting you, sir."

"The pleasure is mine," Director Palmer said, the corners of his mouth quirking up into a smile. "Rogers, try to stay out of trouble."

Her smile was instant. "Sir, I always try."

chapter 5

"I still can't believe I was chosen for this job," Janessa said as she followed Levi Marin into the conference room where they would receive the first of several briefings.

"I wish I could see Donald's face when he sees pictures of you and Prince Garrett plastered all over the tabloids." Levi grinned as he sat down at the conference table across from her. "The security on this assignment is so tight, not many people are going to know your engagement isn't real."

A sense of unease settled over Janessa as she considered the enormity of the difficulties she was about to face. "I don't know if I can really pull this off, especially once the press gets wind of the engagement."

"That's why I'm coming too," Levi pointed out. "I'll work the technical end of the chateau's security, and you size up the people we're dealing with. The US ambassador to Meridia has been instructed to give us any assistance we need."

Janessa gave a reluctant nod. "Will anybody else know who I really am, besides the ambassador and the royal family?"

"The chateau manager, Martino, and the chauffeur, Enrico, are aware of your true identity," Levi told her. "Both have been with the royal family for years and are trusted."

"Will they both know about you?"

"Martino knows who I work for, because he made the arrangements for me to work with the chateau's security staff," Levi said. "Everyone else will only know that I have been hired to help improve the security for the gala."

Levi slid a paper across the table to her. "Here's the latest report on the embassy bombing. So far neither government has managed to find any solid leads as to who is behind it. All we know is that the attack is consistent with the MO of several known terrorist groups."

"But we have no idea which one," Janessa finished for him.

"The staff at the embassy will continue to work on the investigation." Levi shifted some papers in front of him and then passed a stack to Janessa. "Here's what we are more concerned about. Threats against the royal family have been arriving with some regularity over the past several months. These are the ones that have been received over the past few weeks."

Janessa looked at the top page and was shaken when she saw the computer generated image of Prince Stefano and Prince Garrett hanging from a tree. The next one was directed at the queen. A picture of a gun was aimed at the queen's head. Nearly a dozen threats were in the stack, all of them threatening that one or more members of the royal family would die.

"I'll never understand what drives someone to even think up this kind of stuff, much less follow through." Janessa flipped through the threats again. "Do you think these are from the same person who bombed our embassy?"

"There's no way to be sure." Levi shrugged. "But one way or another, it's our job to make sure no one gets the chance to follow through."

* * *

"Father, you can't be serious." Garrett paced across his father's office.

"I am serious. The invitation has already been sent." Eduard leaned back in his massive chair and watched his son pace.

Garrett dragged a hand through his dark hair. "Doesn't it seem ridiculous to you for me to get engaged to a woman I've never met before?"

"This is the only way she will have full access to the chateau," Eduard insisted. "I can't let your mother go to Bellamo until we're sure it's safe. Someone has to oversee the caterers and their employees to make sure that whoever is behind these latest threats doesn't try to get someone inside during the gala."

"Can't she go undercover as a servant or a guest?"

"As a servant she would not be able to interact on an equal basis with those who will provide services for the gala, and guests don't have full access to the chateau." The king shook his head. "The only way she will be able to take over your mother's duties is if she is considered part of the royal family."

"But won't my engagement to an American aggravate the anti-American sentiment here in Meridia?"

"We are hoping that the union will actually have the opposite effect."

Garrett's mind whirled as he tried to come up with another alternative, any alternative. "Surely you know that the attention we'll get from the press will make security even more difficult."

"We've considered that, but your brother feels that this will help pull the attention away from the embassy bombing and let the press focus on something more positive."

"So I'm a distraction." Garrett shook his head in frustration.

"You know that publicity is only one factor that has been considered. I realize you are not always comfortable in the spotlight, and I'm sure the press will thrive on the story both when your engagement is announced as well as when it is broken. Regardless, I am concerned with the safety of this family, and I believe this is the best way to fortify our defenses at the chateau."

Garrett sighed with resignation. "Who is she, and when do I meet her?"

"She should be arriving on Tuesday. Since your duties will likely keep you here at the palace until then, the driver from the chateau will pick her up from the airport and take her to Bellamo to get settled in," Eduard told him. "We will officially announce the engagement here at the palace the following Monday."

"Why wait?"

"Stefano thought it would be more believable if you were seen with her a few times before we made the announcement." He held a photograph out to Garrett. "Her name is Janessa Rogers. She was handpicked by the director of the CIA."

Garrett snatched the photograph from his father's hand, his eyes widening as recognition dawned. "She was on our security detail in Caracas."

"Good, then she will be familiar with our security procedures."

Garrett took a step toward the door, his attention still on the photograph. "If you'll excuse me, I need to make some phone calls."

"Garrett . . ." Eduard waited for his son to turn back to him before continuing. "I appreciate the sacrifices you are willing to make for the family."

Somewhat mollified, Garrett nodded and slipped out the door.

* * *

Garrett stood on the balcony of his room, looking out into the darkness. A crisp ocean breeze ruffled his hair as he dialed the phone number.

He wasn't sure why he was calling except for the simple reason that he wanted to talk to her. His confidence suffered a blow when a man answered the phone.

"May I speak with Janessa Rogers, please," Garrett asked formally.

"Just a minute," the man on the other end said.

A moment later Janessa picked up the phone. "Hello?"

"Janessa? This is Garrett Fortier."

She hesitated for the briefest moment before responding. "Your Highness, what can I do for you?"

"I hope that wasn't a jealous boyfriend who answered the phone," Garrett started, half seriously.

As he had hoped, Janessa laughed. "No, that was my brother-in-law, Kevin. I've been staying with my sister since I came back to Washington."

"That's a relief. I would hate to find out my fiancée was dating someone else already."

"Your Highness . . ."

Garrett cut her off before she could continue. "Call me Garrett. After all, we are going to be engaged soon."

"Okay, Garrett," she managed. "Can I ask you something?"

"Of course."

"Do you always work this fast?" Humor filled her voice. "After all, a week and a half ago I went from a woman you'd just met to a jealous girlfriend in a matter of minutes. And now we're talking about getting engaged."

"It's amazing what can happen after one date. You obviously made quite an impression on me." He smiled and felt some of his anxiety easing. He was glad he hadn't been saddled with a harsh, business-only woman for this imaginary engagement. As nice as Janessa was, though, he wondered whether she really could do much to help augment the chateau's security. But at least he would be relieved of the duties typically carried out by his mother. "I actually called to see if you have any questions about where you will be staying here or what you need to bring."

"I probably have more questions than you have time to answer." Janessa laughed. "I've only had one day of briefings, but I don't have any real information about what my duties will be there."

"During the day you will have a number of business meetings to help arrange for various services for the gala, and I'm afraid you can expect a lot of formal dinners in the evenings."

A sigh came over the line. "So you're telling me I need to bring business suits and evening gowns."

"Basically." Garrett grinned. "It wouldn't hurt to bring a swimming suit along too. Our beaches are beautiful."

"I'm looking forward to that part of the assignment," Janessa admitted.

"A driver is scheduled to meet you at the airport when you arrive. Let me give you my cell phone number in case you have any questions before then." Garrett rattled off his phone number and then, as an afterthought, gave her his private numbers at the palace and the chateau.

He had planned on ending the call then, but when she jokingly asked how things had gone with Monique after she left Caracas, he found himself telling her the highlights of the trade summit. They chatted for nearly an hour before he finally hung up.

Moving back into his bedroom, Garrett set down his phone and thought back to the night he had first met Janessa. More than once during that evening he had nearly forgotten that she was assigned to his security detail, especially with the way she was so easy to talk to. Tonight's phone conversation hadn't been any different.

He could only wonder if she would still be the same down-to-earth girl after her photograph was splashed all over the world and her name was linked with his.

chapter 6

Janessa stepped off the turboprop airplane onto the tarmac. She had decided to treat her soon-to-be-announced engagement as just another assignment. One that would be overridden with press and annoying inconveniences. The phone conversations she had had with Garrett over the past several days confirmed what she already suspected—the press was going to be intrusive and at times would likely be an obstacle to overcome in performing her duties.

She still couldn't believe that a prince had been calling her so casually, but she had talked to him a dozen times as she prepared for her trip. On a few occasions she'd had to remind him that she had work to do to prepare for her trip, but when they spoke each evening she felt like she was talking to a friend rather than an assignment. In fact, they had spent nearly two hours on the phone the night before while she packed. She smiled as she thought of his last request—a box of Krispy Kreme doughnuts. She glanced down at the two boxes she carried.

Her smile stayed in place as her gaze fell on the nearby village. White buildings with red tiled roofs lined the hillside in no apparent order. Lush, green flora fought its way out of the craggy gray cliffs that dropped off into the Mediterranean. The airport itself was a modern structure made of steel and glass, an anomaly amid the fairy-tale setting.

Janessa lifted the handle of her carry-on bag and fell into step with the other passengers as they deplaned and headed inside. Nerves fluttered in her stomach as she worried about seeing Garrett in person again. Despite their lengthy phone conversations, she still wasn't sure how she was supposed to act in public. She also wasn't sure how Garrett felt about this whole façade. Though he often joked about her being his fiancée, he never really said anything about how all this was going to impact his life for the foreseeable future.

Levi Marin had arrived at the chateau the day before and was already working with the chateau manager and the security staff to identify where they needed to augment the current system with new safety measures. From their briefings earlier in the week, Janessa expected that she wouldn't see much of Levi unless she sought him out.

As she stepped inside the airport, she spotted a uniformed chauffeur near the entrance holding a sign with her name on it. He was not terribly tall, and his build was comfortably rounded. His otherwise dark hair was peppered with gray, and his dark eyes were scanning the crowd.

"Signore, I am Janessa Rogers," she said as she stepped in front of him, automatically speaking in the country's native Italian.

He lifted an eyebrow at her use of Italian. "You are American?"

"That's right."

He nodded his approval. "I am Enrico Saldera." Before she could object, he took her carry-on bag, leaving her with only the doughnuts to carry. Ten minutes later, they walked out of the airport to the waiting limousine. A porter followed behind with her luggage and efficiently loaded it into the trunk.

Enrico opened the door to the back of the limousine. Janessa glimpsed the plush inside but turned to Enrico rather than getting in. "Would you mind terribly if I rode up front with you? I'll feel silly sitting back there by myself."

The initial surprise that passed over his face was quickly replaced with a genuine smile. "Of course, signorina."

As soon as they were both settled in the front of the limo, Enrico found himself bombarded with questions. Janessa started out asking about his family. Yes, he was married. His wife, Patrice, served as the cook for the royal family at the chateau, and he happily told Janessa about his two sons and his daughter. Janessa learned that Enrico's family had been serving the royal family for generations and that his father, Paolo, still managed the stables.

As they drove, the conversation turned to questions about life in Meridia and the royal family. Enrico gave Janessa far more information about protocol and the kingdom of Meridia during their hour drive than she had received in several days' worth of briefings. She learned that though the primary language was Italian, several areas of Meridian culture were strongly influenced by the French, particularly food and fashion. Enrico also confirmed what she had already suspected: The royal family was loved unconditionally by their subjects. The press loved them as well and particularly enjoyed exploiting the activities of Prince Stefano and Prince Garrett.

As they entered the town of Bellamo, Janessa was beginning to feel more comfortable with the prospect of spending the next several weeks in this tiny country nestled between France and Italy.

Her thoughts were interrupted as the royal chateau came into view. Built of weathered native stone, the grand structure sprawled over the green hillside, a unique combination of turrets, towers, and balconies. The Mediterranean glistened below in a mirror image of the cloudless sky. Flowers spilled from pottery urns on the balconies, and the courtyard was alive with the color provided by a dozen kinds of roses.

They pulled up in the driveway, which circled a gushing fountain. Janessa stepped from the car and looked at the coastline. Pristine white beaches stretched for several miles to the west, interrupted by impassable rocky cliffs, which provided a natural defense. To the east, the beach was visible until the land curved out of sight. A Meridian naval base was situated at a point where the beach jutted out half a mile into the ocean, a strategic location to protect the royal vacation home as well as the resort villas that lay beyond.

Janessa watched a destroyer coming into port and wondered idly if she would be allowed a tour of the base.

"I will have your bags taken upstairs for you." Enrico put his hand on her elbow to lead her up the steps. He gave her arm an encouraging squeeze and motioned to the front entrance. "Welcome to Meridia."

* * *

Janessa stood in the doorway of the parlor and stared for a full minute. The room was five times the size of her parents' living room, yet it still managed to feel welcoming rather than overwhelming. Couches, love seats, and chairs were arranged to create intimate conversation areas, the upholstery comfortably faded from the light streaming through the tall windows. Janessa moved forward just as a man walked through a doorway on the other side of the room. He appeared to be in his fifties, but his dark hair did not show a speck of gray, and his lean frame indicated he was still active.

"Signorina Rogers." His voice was formal with a hint of disdain humming through it, but he moved forward and took her hand in his. "I am Martino. I am the manager of the chateau," he said in English.

"I'm pleased to meet you." Janessa shook his hand then took the seat he indicated. With a smile, she continued in Italian. "Please don't feel you have to speak to me in English. I'm happy to speak your language."

"Very well," Martino said stiffly, now speaking Italian. He sat down across from her and opened up the portfolio he held. "I understand you will be taking over the hostess duties until Queen Marta arrives from Calene."

"That's correct." Janessa nodded. "I need to take some time tomorrow to acquaint myself with the chateau, and I would like to meet with the caterers early next week."

"I will make the appointment with the caterers," Martino insisted in a superior tone. "This evening, you will dine with Prince Garrett and his guests, and then tomorrow afternoon you will accompany His Highness into Bellamo."

Refusing to be affected by Martino's cold tone, Janessa slid a pocket organizer from her purse, along with a pen. "What time is dinner this evening?"

"Seven o'clock," Martino told her.

"I'll need a copy of the guest list for tonight." Janessa let her voice take on an edge of authority.

"I will bring that up to you shortly. Now, if you would like me to show you up to your rooms, Prince Garrett should be arriving within the hour."

Rooms? Janessa thought, but all she said was, "Thank you." Determined to keep an open mind, Janessa followed Martino up the curving staircase, hoping that he would warm up to working with her before too much time passed. Her next thought was that she shouldn't expect everyone to like her. Even her own siblings reminded her often enough of her flaws—"bossy" being at the top of their list.

A few minutes later, Janessa stepped out onto her balcony and breathed in the sea air. The view was incredible, almost too perfect to be real. To the right, a swimming pool was nestled among Mediterranean palm trees and climbing roses, and to the left, the expansive gardens swept along the back of the chateau all the way to the seawall that separated the chateau from the beach just beyond.

A short flight of stairs led to the beach from the swimming pool, and another flight of stairs mirrored it, descending from the gardens. The Mediterranean Sea glistened beneath the midday sun, and a few boats were visible on the water. She leaned on the railing, wondering if she had ever seen such perfection before. She had always imagined that the coastal regions of Italy would look something like this, but on her mission she had never served near the water.

The sitting room behind her was nearly as large as her entire apartment in Caracas, and her bags had already been delivered and were currently on the floor in her bedroom. Yes, Martino really had meant *rooms,* plural. She was afraid she would get spoiled if she stayed here very long.

Her mind turned to the man she would soon call her fiancé. She had read his bio several times over the past few days, trying to reconcile what was on paper with the man she had met so briefly in Caracas. He had graduated college when he was twenty-one and then served for four years in the Navy. She had been surprised to find that his military training had been rather intensive and that he had spent nearly two years working with naval intelligence. After his time in the service, Garrett had spent a year working with his father before attending law school at George Washington University in Washington, D.C.

Janessa smiled as she thought of the irony of it all. Garrett had just spent the past three years in her country while she had spent most of that time living outside of it. Still, Prince Garrett had popped up in the newspapers and glossies with regularity, with a different woman on his arm almost every time. The last thing she recalled seeing about him was his breakup with some actress, though she couldn't remember ever actually seeing them photographed together. She had meant to ask him about it the last time he called but had never found the opening.

When a knock came at the door, Janessa stayed where she was. "Come in." She turned, expecting to see Martino in her open doorway. Instead, Prince Garrett stepped through.

For a moment they stared at each other. Reminding herself to follow Meridian protocol, Janessa dipped into a curtsey. A strand of her thick, red hair caught in the breeze. Self-consciously, she brushed it out of her face and moved from the balcony into the sitting room.

"I hope you find your accommodations acceptable," Garrett said as he moved into the room and closed the door to ensure some privacy.

"I was just admiring the view. It's spectacular," Janessa replied. She wondered if he had chosen to speak in English out of habit or if he had forgotten she spoke Italian.

Garrett motioned for her to sit down, settling himself in a chair once she was seated. "My father asked me to thank you for agreeing to assist my country during this difficult time."

"It's my pleasure," she responded, somewhat surprised by the formality of his tone.

"Now that you are here and I don't have to worry about anyone eavesdropping on our conversation, can you tell me a little about what you do for your government?" He shifted in his chair. "The information my father gave me was rather vague."

Janessa smiled. "I'm not even sure *I* know what I do for my government."

Garrett's eyebrows rose. "I thought you were some sort of security officer."

"Officially, I'm a linguistic specialist." Janessa shrugged. "Unofficially, I use my knowledge of languages to gather information."

"You're a spy?" Garrett laughed.

"Not exactly." Janessa replied, not at all offended by the prince's reaction. "When I was working as a linguist for the State Department in Madrid, I happened to overhear an important conversation. A few weeks later the Central Intelligence Agency recruited me."

"Forgive my laughter, but I find it hard to picture you as an intelligence officer."

"Which is exactly why I'm good at my job," Janessa stated confidently.

"I hope so, for all of our sakes." Garrett stood now. "I'll let you get settled in. Dinner is at seven."

"Oh, I almost forgot." Janessa stood as Garrett started toward the door. She moved into the bedroom for a moment and returned carrying both boxes of doughnuts. Holding them out, she smiled. "Enjoy."

Surprise followed by humor lit his eyes. Then he grinned, and the formal air melted away. "I didn't think you would actually bring them."

"Then why did you ask?" Janessa laughed, for the first time feeling like she was talking to the same man who had called her on the phone. "One dozen for you, and another dozen to share."

Garrett was still grinning when she shifted the boxes into his arms. "Did you want one?" he asked.

She shook her head and patted her stomach. "I'd better not." She lowered her voice as though sharing a secret. "There were three boxes when I got on the plane."

Garrett's laughter rang out. "I'll see you tonight."

Janessa's smile stayed in place as she watched him leave the room. Then she turned from the door and focused on the pressing matter of what to wear.

chapter 7

Janessa studied the other guests while listening halfheartedly to the woman standing next to her in the parlor. The excitement level in the room was high, as this was the first official function at the chateau for several months.

Uniformed waiters moved through the room carrying trays of hors d'oeuvres and glasses of champagne. Every lesson in protocol and etiquette ran through Janessa's mind as she accepted a miniature quiche and declined the champagne. She tried to convince herself that she belonged here amid the wealth and glamour, but she couldn't help feeling a little out of her league. Still, she hoped that the last few years of pretending to be something she wasn't would help her appear comfortable in this formal setting.

Across the room, Prince Garrett stood near the terrace doors greeting several of his guests. Laughter rang out as a young woman moved closer to Garrett, laid a hand on his arm, and held on.

Three women clustered behind her spoke of the latest tabloid article about Prince Garrett. Though Janessa had never read more than an occasional headline, she was well aware of Garrett's many exploits during his naval career. Of course, his presence in the United States over the past few years had made his social life even more interesting to the American people. Even though she didn't put much stock in anything printed between the covers of gossip magazines, she doubted that Prince Garrett was anything like the good LDS boys her parents and siblings kept throwing in her path.

Already she was having trouble reconciling the man across the room with the man she had spent hours talking to over the past few days. He looked the same as the first time she had seen him—formal and a bit aloof. On the phone he had been so . . . normal. She had already started to think of him as a friend rather than an assignment, something she knew was against both of their best interests. Still, those phone conversations had given her so much insight into what to expect as well as a comfort level with the assignment she never would have had without Garrett's help.

She thought of their meeting earlier. She realized that he wasn't sure she could protect his family. And despite her confidence in her own abilities, Janessa wasn't sure she could either. The Rominez assassination had proven what she knew all too well: Even the best security could be breached under the right circumstances. She just had to make sure those circumstances were highly unlikely over the next five weeks.

The model-thin woman clinging to Prince Garrett leaned in to whisper something in his ear. With an inward sigh, Janessa excused herself from her current conversation and crossed the room. She had to start playing the part of Garrett's girlfriend sometime.

She moved slowly across the parlor, taking a moment to gauge what language was being spoken. Though several scenarios crossed her mind, she opted for a subtle solution. When she reached Garrett, she lightly ran a hand over his shoulder as she spoke in French to the woman clinging to him. "I can't believe Garrett hasn't introduced us yet. I'm Janessa Rogers. I'm a guest at the chateau for a while."

When the woman saw Janessa's extended hand, manners demanded that she release Garrett and extend her own. She was several inches taller than Janessa, standing about five foot nine, and she took the time to look down her nose at Janessa. "Isabel Dumond."

"I am so pleased to meet you." Janessa flipped through her mental file of the evening's guests. "You must be Pierre's daughter. I understand your father has headed the museum in Bellamo for many years now."

"Yes," Isabel said. She smiled coyly at Garrett before continuing. "My family has enjoyed a close association with the royal family for some time."

Before Isabel could cling to Garrett once again, Janessa resolved the problem. Stepping neatly between Isabel and Garrett, she angled her head toward Isabel. "Have you met Mademoiselle Poratte?"

Eyes narrowing, Isabel shook her head.

"She just arrived from Paris last week and would love to gain your perspective on life here in Meridia." Janessa laid a hand on Isabel's arm and motioned across the room.

Isabel lifted her chin a bit higher. "I'm sure someone else can help her with that."

"Perhaps, but there are so few of us here that are close to her age. I would love to help, but I haven't been here long enough yet." Janessa gave her a subtle nudge as she turned to Prince Garrett. "If you will excuse us."

"Of course, Janessa." He nodded and turned to speak to the French ambassador as the two women crossed the room.

Janessa introduced Mademoiselle Poratte to Isabel, deliberately ignoring Isabel's annoyance. If she guessed right, Isabel had set her sights on Garrett and was determined to get her way. Janessa breathed an inward sigh of relief when Isabel's father joined them a moment later and introduced himself. He reminded her a bit of her own father with his open, intelligent expression, sturdy build, and dark hair peppered with gray.

"I understand you are staying here at the chateau," Pierre commented, his voice welcoming.

"Yes, I only arrived today, but I'm looking forward to exploring a bit tomorrow."

"There are days I would like to do the same thing. The history and artwork here make me feel like I'm in a museum disguised as a home." He lowered his voice fractionally. "One that has the best cook in the province."

Janessa took another miniature quiche from a servant's tray and nodded her approval. "I'm definitely going to have to compliment the chef."

A few minutes later dinner was announced. When everyone moved into the dining hall, Janessa stopped at the entrance and absorbed her surroundings.

Three elaborate chandeliers were evenly spaced over the enormous table. The wooden floors were freshly polished, and Janessa imagined that the wood itself was centuries old. She guessed the room could easily seat a hundred people, though only half that many would dine here tonight. A bit intimidated by the size of the room and the formality of the setting, Janessa forced herself to move forward. After a quick search, she found the place card with her name on it and was surprised to see she hadn't been seated next to Garrett.

As Janessa sat down, a waiter moved to fill her wine glass. Janessa held the glass out to him, speaking quietly as she explained in Italian that she didn't drink and asked if he might give her a glass of water instead. The waiter nodded in agreement, removing her glass and returning a moment later with a goblet filled with water.

Janessa thanked him and took a sip as the rest of the guests filtered in. When Prince Garrett entered, she moved to stand as protocol demanded. Noticing her already at the table, he caught her eye and smiled, then changed his course so he would pass her as he moved to his own seat at the head of the table.

He leaned in to kiss her cheek and whispered, "Having fun yet?"

She whispered back, "Probably as much as you are."

He smiled and moved on, leaving Janessa wishing they had been seated more closely. The guests at tonight's party were dignitaries from the French Embassy along with selected family members and a few prominent French citizens working in Meridia. The conversation was tedious and single-minded as the French ambassador continued to express his concerns over an upcoming trade summit. Thankfully, the delicious meal more than made up for the lack of interesting conversation.

At the head of the table, the prince smiled and chatted with those around him. He evaded some questions and answered others, every time responding politely to each of his guests. His voice was sincere, yet his posture remained rigid throughout the evening, and he never seemed to really relax.

His eyes were dark and just a little mysterious, as though he didn't want anyone to pierce through to the man beneath the polished sheen. He managed to take a bite of his meal occasionally, but several of his dinner companions failed to recognize that they were there to eat. Every time Prince Garrett moved to take a bite, someone else would ask him a question.

As Janessa ate her dessert, something sinfully chocolate and airy, her sympathies went out to the prince. He never even got a chance to pick up his spoon.

When the meal finally concluded, everyone moved back into the parlor. The open terrace doors invited the night air in. Garrett introduced several people to Janessa. He then spent a few moments socializing with Isabel and two other young women in attendance before he excused himself to go get a breath of fresh air. Rather than give him the few moments alone he so clearly needed, those chatting with him decided some fresh air would benefit them as well.

Garrett's manners were impeccable, and only a flicker of annoyance flashed in his eyes before he quickly concealed it and smiled at the women who escorted him outside. One of the dignitaries shifted to follow them, and Janessa glanced around the room. Some of the guests had settled down to have an after-dinner drink, but many others were preparing to leave.

Realizing her job was basically done for the night, Janessa checked with Martino before excusing herself. She moved out of the parlor and past the dining room, pleased when she found the kitchen. Janessa knocked on the door as she pushed it open. She spotted a slightly rounded woman with graying hair she guessed to be Enrico's wife, Patrice.

"I just wanted to compliment you on a wonderful meal," Janessa said in Italian. She moved forward and extended her hand. "I'm Janessa Rogers."

"Patrice Saldera." Patrice's eyebrows lifted even as she shook Janessa's hand. "Everything was satisfactory?"

"Everything was delicious." Janessa smiled.

Patrice sighed, waving a hand at the counter where a tray of desserts lay, most of them untouched. She spoke Italian with a thick French accent. "I thought maybe they didn't like it."

"I think too many of them are on a diet." Janessa shrugged. "I'm afraid they didn't give the prince a chance to eat his either. He may appreciate it if you save some for him."

Patrice nodded. "Signorina Rogers . . ."

"Please, call me Janessa."

"Very well. Gianessa," Patrice corrected herself, using the Italian version of Janessa's name. She waved at the platters of leftover food. "Did you get enough to eat?"

"More than enough." She patted her stomach and nodded at the dessert dishes. "Mine is the empty one."

Patrice chuckled and nodded her approval.

"Good night. Thank you again for a wonderful meal." Janessa turned to leave just as the door opened behind her.

"Oh, I beg your pardon." Prince Garrett stopped just inside the door. Surprise flickered in his eyes. He looked from Janessa to Patrice and then back to Janessa. "I hope you didn't get lost."

Janessa shook her head, her lips quirking up in the beginnings of a smile. "No, not at all." She motioned to the food behind her. "You must be hungry. I'll get out of your way so that you can eat."

"We just ate."

"*I* just ate." Her smile broke free. "*You* entertained. Try the dessert. It's magnificent."

Clearly surprised by her observation, he turned to see Patrice smiling at him. "She's right. My boy never eats enough at these dinners," Patrice said in a matronly tone as she waved toward a doorway on the other side of the kitchen. "Go sit down. I'll fix you a plate."

All formality melted away as Garrett grinned and crossed to kiss Patrice on the cheek. "You're too good to me." He kissed her other cheek. "And you're still the best cook in the province."

"You just want me to make you fresh strawberry pie."

Garrett chuckled. "That too." His grin was still in place when he turned to Janessa and asked, "Will you join me?"

Janessa's eyebrows rose. "I thought you would appreciate some time alone."

Garrett shook his head. "I don't like to eat alone, and Patrice doesn't ever sit down until the dishes are done." He winked at Patrice and gave Janessa a boyish smile. "If you don't eat with me, she might put me on dish duty like when I broke the breakfast room window when I was twelve."

Now curious, Janessa followed him into the breakfast room. "How did you manage that?"

"Home run." Garrett shrugged as he pulled one of a dozen chairs out for her. "I guess we should have been trying to hit away from the chateau."

"Lesson learned." Janessa laughed. She sat down at the square table, amazed at how quickly Garrett had shed his formal air and become once again the man she had spent so many hours talking to on the phone.

Garrett waved in the direction of the kitchen. "Did you get enough dinner? I can have Patrice fix you a plate too."

"I had more than enough. As I told Signora Saldera, I don't think I can eat another bite." She watched Patrice put a full plate in front of Garrett and then a dessert in front of each of them. She laughed despite herself. "Okay, maybe just one more bite, but I'm going to have to schedule time to run tomorrow."

"I think that can be arranged." Garrett took a bite as Janessa swirled her spoon in her dessert. "From what I understand, nothing is scheduled tomorrow until lunchtime."

"Martino mentioned an outing tomorrow afternoon."

Garrett nodded, his eyes meeting hers with a directness she wasn't accustomed to. "You did well tonight. I hadn't realized that you spoke French."

"I told you I'm a linguistics specialist," Janessa reminded him. "Romance languages are my specialty."

"I should have realized that when you mentioned being a jealous girl-friend." Humor danced in his eyes. "How many languages do you speak?"

"Six, if you don't include Japanese." Janessa pushed her half-eaten dessert away from her and leaned closer as though sharing a secret. "And trust me, my Japanese tends to get me into trouble."

"I guess it's a good thing we don't have any pressing engagements with Japan in the near future." Garrett laughed. "And thank you for your help tonight with Isabel."

"I gather she's admired you for some time."

"She has admired my title for some time," Garrett corrected. "It often makes for an awkward situation."

"Like the one in Caracas." Janessa smiled. "Maybe being engaged will help keep you out of awkward situations for a while."

"I hope so," Garrett agreed, leaning back in his chair.

They continued chatting while Garrett finished his dinner until finally a servant interrupted. "Excuse me, Your Highness. Your father is on the phone and wishes to speak with you."

Garrett pushed back from the table and smiled at Janessa. "Thank you for joining me."

Janessa nodded and stood as well. "I'll see you tomorrow." She watched him follow the servant out of the room and then stacked the dessert dishes on Garrett's plate. Moving into the kitchen, she set the dishes on the counter and turned to Patrice. "Thank you again for a wonderful meal."

With that, she left the kitchen and ascended the stairs to the rooms she would call home for the next five weeks.

chapter 8

Garrett paced across his sitting room, flipping through the file in his hand. After his conversation with Janessa the evening before, he had asked his father to send him a complete background on her. He had expected to see a simple dossier outlining her various assignments and perhaps an evaluation or two. The thick file in his hand not only surprised him—it intrigued him.

She had been honest with him when she'd summarized her work experience—sort of. She had indeed worked for several months for the State Department, but she had been overly modest about how she had come to the attention of the Central Intelligence Agency.

The important conversation she had mentioned overhearing had actually been that of three men preparing to plant a bomb at the US Embassy in Madrid. Janessa had had the presence of mind to use her cell phone to take pictures of the three men, write down their conversation, and follow them to where they were preparing the explosives. The men had been in the process of moving the bomb when the police had arrived to take them into custody.

The rest of the file was filled with similar incidents. Some were simple undertakings, like recruiting various household staff of high level officials to share information with her or recognizing valuable information in seemingly meaningless conversations. Others were more complicated, like helping the Venezuelan government identify the route Columbian drug dealers were using to ship cocaine into their country.

Janessa's training with the CIA had been extensive, which explained why she had been assigned to his security detail. Basically, she was a jack-of-all-trades. She had spent nearly a year working in different areas of the CIA, learning about everything from weapons to security.

Even with her file in front of him, he couldn't quite picture Janessa as an intelligence officer. Then again, he wasn't accustomed to working with intel officers who were women. The night before, Janessa had followed protocol precisely, yet she had done so with an air of casualness that suggested she might choose to stop at any time. When he had questioned her abilities, she had not seemed the least bit offended, nor had she found it necessary to detail her previous successes.

Her attire at the dinner had been simple and elegant, and several men in attendance had made a point to make her acquaintance. Garrett couldn't say he blamed them. The highlight of the past several days had been his conversations with Janessa. Not surprisingly, he had awoken this morning with a sense of anticipation at the thought of spending time with her. If nothing else, her company would help break up an otherwise tedious day filled with meetings.

He hoped the press and public would warm up to her the way his guests had the night before. Janessa was beautiful in an understated way, but she was definitely someone who would be remembered after the evening was over. Even the women seemed to like her, surprising considering that Janessa was an American, a nationality occasionally looked down upon by the French.

He read through the file for several more minutes before realizing that his guests the night before might never have been informed of Janessa's nationality. He looked out the window across the room, staring as he replayed the evening's events. He remembered hearing her speak with Martino briefly in Italian. Her accent hadn't been Meridian, but neither was it American. When speaking to Isabel, she had spoken in French, again without a discernable accent. Garrett couldn't recall her ever speaking in English except to him.

When he came to the part of Janessa's file that listed her religious preference, he could only smile at the irony. At times he still couldn't believe that the woman who had been chosen as his fiancée was a member of the church he was determined to join. For a moment he let himself wonder what would happen if their engagement were real. What would his family do if he announced he wanted to marry someone of the Mormon faith, or that he wanted to marry in the LDS temple?

Again Garrett shook his head, reminding himself that this was all an act. For now he had to focus on what mattered most—playing a role that would help keep his family safe.

* * *

The early morning breeze dragged at the ends of Janessa's hair as she stepped outside onto the terrace. The sun was still low in the eastern sky, and she had not noticed anyone stirring within the chateau walls except for some of the kitchen staff. Though she had considered a morning run on the beach, she wasn't quite sure if that would be considered acceptable in her situation.

Deciding that a walk was the best she could do at this early hour, Janessa had dressed comfortably in jeans and a button-up cotton shirt. She stood for a moment and took in the view. The Mediterranean glistened beneath the rising sun, and a few boats were already out on the water. She drew a deep breath, amazed that she was standing here in the shadows of the chateau. Even more amazing was that somewhere inside the walls was a prince whom she was beginning to think of as a friend.

The fragrance of jasmine scented the air as Janessa passed by the expansive gardens. She continued to wander away from the chateau, past the gardens and up a well-trodden path. Another more familiar scent lingered as she stepped over the rise. A large white building was situated at the center of the paddocks and fenced pastures that checkerboarded the area. Janessa identified the building as the stables, guessing that it could house at least two dozen horses. Several horses were grazing in the grassy fields behind split-rail fences.

Enchanted by the setting, Janessa closed the distance to the stables, stopping near the door when she noticed a young foal frolicking around his mother. The mare lifted her head from grazing when Janessa rested a foot on the bottom rung of the fence. As though only half interested, the mare slowly walked toward her, the foal close at her heels.

Because the setting seemed to call for it, Janessa spoke in Italian as she ran her hand down the mare's soft nose. "Aren't you a pretty thing." Her laughter rang out when the foal edged closer and nipped at her shoelace. Janessa wiggled her toe, laughing again when the foal startled, running and bucking the length of the pasture.

"That one is afraid of his own shadow." An elderly man stepped from the stables carrying a bundle of hay under one of his burly arms. He tossed the meal-sized clump of hay over the fence at the mare's feet.

"I think his mother is happy to have him distracted." Janessa smiled as the foal cautiously approached her again. She reached out and stroked the soft muzzle, unconcerned when the foal nipped at her shirt.

"You know horses," the man stated. "You will ride now?"

Janessa turned to him, beaming. "I would love to."

"The horses need exercise," he said and extended one of his weathered hands. "I am Paolo Saldera."

"Gianessa Rogers." She shook his hand, remembering that Paolo was the father of Enrico, the chauffeur. Though he moved with agility, Janessa guessed that Paolo was past seventy. What little hair he had was snow white, and his face was deeply creased with laugh and worry lines. "Are you done feeding?"

"Just finished." Paolo nodded. "Come, I'll show you around, and we'll find a horse for you to ride this morning."

Grinning, Janessa followed him inside. The horses were well tended, and nearly all of the stalls were occupied. She thought briefly of her riding boots that were currently in her parents' attic and decided that her tennis shoes would have to do. Twenty minutes later, Janessa guided her mount down a trail to the east.

She rode over rambling hills through dense trees for nearly an hour before she emerged onto the beach. She glanced back to the west and could see the chateau. A breeze lifted off the water, pleasantly cooling the overly warm morning air. Turning to the east, she studied the naval base in the distance, noticing that the beach was completely deserted as far as she could see.

Impulsively, she turned east and urged her horse into a gallop. She laughed out loud as she met the wind head on, the sand kicking up behind her. Her hair whipped in the wind, and she tasted the sea air even as she urged the gelding beneath her to give her more speed. She hadn't surrendered to this kind of reckless freedom in years.

As the horse beneath her began to breathe heavily, Janessa slowed to a canter and then finally to a walk. She continued down the beach, edging closer to the naval base. She thought back on her conversation with the director of the CIA. Though she could understand her country's need for a naval base in this area, she hated the idea of more of these pristine beaches being destroyed to accommodate such an undertaking.

The Meridian naval base was more expansive than she had first imagined, curving around the jut of land to the other side. The docks were well maintained, but many of the buildings stood in various states of disrepair. She glanced back at the beach behind her, perfect except for the tracks her horse had left. An idea began to take shape. Perhaps she could help accomplish what her government needed without asking the royal family to compromise any more land for its defense.

She turned her horse back toward her temporary home and once again enjoyed the freedom and beauty offered where land and sea joined.

chapter 9

Garrett descended the main staircase, wondering if Janessa remembered their date. Martino had already leaked their plans to the local press to make sure Garrett and Janessa would be noticed while they were together in the village. First they would have lunch at one of the popular restaurants in Bellamo, and then they would take a walk through the shopping district.

He glanced at his watch just as he heard heels clicking on the tile floor. When he looked up, he simply stared. Her thick, flame-colored hair hung down her back in ringlets, and her eyes were an even more vivid green than he had remembered. Her dress was pale blue, falling just below her knees. It was simple in cut and line, nipped at the waist, and had a modest neckline.

"I hope I didn't keep you waiting," Janessa apologized as she crossed the entryway. "I'm afraid time got away from me this morning."

"You're right on time." Garrett opened the door and escorted her outside to the waiting limousine.

"Hello, Enrico," Janessa greeted their driver as she descended the front steps.

"Good afternoon, Signorina Rogers." Enrico pulled the door open and nodded to Garrett as they approached. "Your Highness."

As soon as they were settled in the back and Enrico slid into the driver's seat, Garrett asked, "Enrico, you know where we are going?"

"Yes, Your Highness."

With a nod, Garrett closed the window between them and turned to Janessa. "I thought we might want to take a minute to talk about our history before we appear in public together."

"Let's see." Janessa shifted in her seat. "We met three years ago when you moved to Washington to attend law school. We then crossed paths several times, first while I was working in Paris and then again when I returned home to the States. And, of course, I saw you in Caracas."

"And now you're here at my invitation to attend the gala."

"One question though," Janessa began. "What happens when the women you were really dating see our story in print? Won't they challenge our story?"

Garrett shook his head. "I never dated anyone more than a couple of times while I was in the States."

"Too many girls impressed with your title?" Janessa asked.

"Something like that," Garrett acknowledged, relaxing enough to smile. "What about you? Any old boyfriends I need to know about?"

Janessa shook her head. "Apparently I was holding out for you."

"That's good to know." Garrett's eyes sparkled mischievously as the car came to a stop and the door opened. He stepped out and turned to help Janessa out of the car. He reached for her hand, a little surprised by how natural the gesture felt. Her hand was warm and smooth, and he kept it in his as they crossed the sidewalk to the restaurant.

He noticed the spree of cameras flashing behind them, and he expected that by the time they finished their lunch, the number of reporters outside would double. He had been honest with Janessa about his recent dating expeditions. Most of his socializing during law school had centered around study groups and public functions. Only when protocol demanded it did he bother to mess with individual entanglements. He supposed he could consider this date a result of protocol, but he had to admit that he had been looking forward to this outing all day.

The maitre d' showed them to a table overlooking the sea. Garrett glanced out the window, appreciating the view of the crisp blue sky over equally blue water. A white sailboat crossed into his view as he took his seat across from Janessa. He wondered how she had remained single for so long. Clearly she was attractive, but beyond that was her intelligence, sense of humor, and, if he wasn't mistaken, a healthy sense of adventure. Not an easy combination to resist. Then he qualified that thought. Those wouldn't be easy attributes for him to resist, but some men he knew would find them a little intimidating.

A waiter took their drink order and then left them to study their menus. Garrett glanced at his, deciding quickly what he would order. When he looked at Janessa, he saw her ignoring her menu and instead staring out over the water.

"I can't get over the view." Janessa pulled her eyes from the Mediterranean to look at him. "This is the most beautiful place on earth."

Garrett smiled. "I have often thought so myself."

Over lunch, conversation flowed easily enough that no one near them would have guessed that they had met just weeks before. Garrett considered broaching the subject of religion, but when the waiter arrived to refill their drinks, he decided that topic would have to wait until the conversation could be just between the two of them.

After they finished their meal, they walked hand in hand through the main shopping district. A window display caught Janessa's eye, and she pointed with her free hand.

"Do you mind if we go inside?" She motioned to an elegant white afghan in the window. "My sister's baby is due next month."

"Of course." Garrett pulled the door open, trying to recall the details about her family. "You have five siblings?"

"Yes. I'm the oldest." Janessa nodded. She moved to a display of beautifully crocheted blankets, turning when the shopkeeper approached. Garrett noted the surprise and awe in the shopkeeper's expression as he greeted them.

"Good afternoon." He bowed to Garrett before turning to Janessa. "May I help you with something?"

"I was just admiring the workmanship," Janessa told him. "Are these all handmade?"

The man beamed with pride. "Yes, my wife makes them."

"She's very talented." Janessa fingered a delicately crocheted afghan in pure white. "My sister would love this. I'll take this one."

As Janessa moved to the cash register to pay, Garrett stepped forward and put a hand on her shoulder as he addressed the shopkeeper. "Please have it delivered to the chateau, and put it on my account."

"Of course, Your Highness."

Janessa started to insist on paying herself, but when she noticed Garrett's stern look she turned instead to thank the shopkeeper and then let Garrett guide her out of the store. As soon as the door closed behind them, she looked up at him. "Why didn't you let me pay?"

"It wouldn't look right," Garrett told her.

"Oh." Janessa narrowed her eyes, considering. Then, with a shrug, she fell into step beside him as they started down the sidewalk. "I'll have to pay you back later then."

"It's not necessary," Garrett said in an offhanded tone.

"Yes, it is," Janessa insisted.

He didn't respond, instead slowing when they approached the jeweler. "Perhaps we should stop in here," Garrett suggested. "After all, we'll need to shop for a ring at some point in the near future."

"I guess I never thought about that," Janessa told him. She glanced at the reporters hovering down the street and noted the position of Garrett's security. "Though it would make an interesting story—Prince Garrett ring shopping."

"That's true," Garrett agreed as he ushered her inside. He called the jeweler by name, having frequented his store many times before. Of course, most of his previous visits had been at the request of his mother. "Davide, may I introduce you to Janessa Rogers."

"So pleased to meet you, signorina," Davide greeted her. "What may I interest you in today?"

"We need an engagement ring, Davide," Garrett told him, lowering his voice as he added, "A ring fit for a princess."

Davide's eyes widened, first with surprise and then with excitement. "Congratulations! Oh, I am so happy for you, Your Highness, signorina."

Garrett put his hand on Janessa's waist and guided her to a seat while Davide bustled to gather a selection of diamond rings. What had sounded like a simple venture turned out to be a major production. Davide felt that anything less than five carats was unacceptable, and Janessa thought that her hands weren't suited for such a large stone. Garrett settled the matter by choosing a simple, square-cut stone, larger than Janessa would choose for herself but small enough to suit her slight build.

Once the selection was finally made, Garrett stood and instructed Davide to have the ring sized and delivered to him at the chateau. As soon as they were outside, Janessa leaned close and whispered, "The stone really is too big."

"It suited you," Garrett said with sincerity.

She looked surprised. "Thank you."

"Come. Let's take a walk on the beach." Garrett led her to an opening in the seawall. He smiled when she instinctively toed off her shoes and carried them in her hand.

"I don't know how you managed to stay away for so long," Janessa told him as they approached the surf. "Not having this view after growing up with it must have made law school that much more difficult."

"Actually, a local artist painted a scene not unlike this one—just a small landscape of the view from my window at the palace. My father commissioned it as a gift for me right before I began my service with our Navy." Garrett hesitated a moment as he reached down and picked up a seashell from the sand. "Like you, he must have thought that this view was something difficult to live without."

"Even though I didn't grow up here, I know I'll miss it when the time comes for me to leave." Janessa stared out over the water. Her hair caught in the wind, and for a moment Garrett saw in her face a vulnerability he hadn't noticed before. She stirred in him a desire to protect, in spite of the fact that she was here to protect him.

He brushed a strand of hair from her face and then took both her hands in his. "Would it be terribly forward of me to kiss you right now?"

Both of her elegant eyebrows lifted as she answered his question with one of her own. "Does the prince often kiss women in public?"

"Princes rarely have private moments."

"That may be true, but in this case, the only reason you want to kiss me is for your public."

"You're mistaken." Garrett stepped closer. "The press has nothing to do with why I want to kiss you."

Her eyes clouded with confusion as he took another step toward her. He had intended to keep the kiss brief, but as he pulled her closer, this thought was quickly dismissed. In that moment, he forgot the reporters and cameras and the reasons Janessa was here. Instead he thought only of her.

He drew back, even more confused by his emerging feelings now that he knew how she felt in his arms.

Her eyes were wary, guarded. "I don't understand you."

"That makes two of us," Garrett managed. "Come on. We should get back."

chapter 10

Janessa leaned back against the kitchen counter as she watched Patrice kneading some kind of dough. She suspected that if she wasn't careful, she wasn't going to fit into her evening gowns for long. She said as much to Patrice and was rewarded with her laughter.

After poking around the chateau for the past few days, Janessa had concluded that, as was the case in many homes, the kitchen was the center of activity as well as the best place to pick up on the latest gossip. Patrice provided a wealth of information about the caterers and the typical guests for the gala. Many of the kitchen staff also provided gossip of a more personal nature.

She was pleased to see that the vices typically found among staff members seemed to be limited here, particularly those that would concern her the most—excessive drinking and gambling. From what she had ascertained in her first few days at the chateau, the staff was loyal and well chosen.

After snitching a croissant from a basket on the counter, Janessa headed outside and waited on the terrace. She only had to wait for a few minutes before Levi arrived under the pretense of checking the surveillance cameras.

"How is everything going so far?" Janessa asked as she kept her gaze on the gardens.

"I think we've identified the trouble spots. I'll slip my report under your door after the maid finishes in your room."

"Great," she said as he moved to check on the nearest security camera. "I actually have some ideas about the naval base I want to work on today."

"Good luck," Levi said as he started toward the next camera. "The sooner that gets resolved, the easier it's going to be for all of us."

With a nod, she turned and moved back inside.

* * *

"Politics," Janessa muttered under her breath. Her conversation with the aide to the US ambassador to Meridia had been less than useful. She had spent hours trying to get through to the embassy, and once she was finally successful she wondered why she had even bothered.

Her suggestion for the US Navy to request access to Meridia's naval base in Bellamo was such an obvious solution she was surprised no one had pursued it earlier. Meridia didn't want to give up more of its pristine coastline to development, and the United States wanted a base in the strategic location Meridia could give it. After seeing the size of Meridia's naval base, Janessa was certain that the needs of the US could be accommodated by using a portion of the existing base.

The completion time would be significantly shorter than if they opted for new construction, and sharing a base would alleviate the high threat of terrorism within Meridia that much sooner. Even the environmental groups who were lobbying against the base would likely be satisfied with this solution.

Unfortunately, the Navy's proposal was for a new base, and the ambassador's aide was unwilling to consider any other possibilities. Clearly, the military was not yet privy to the capabilities of the Meridian naval base, or someone would have already explored this option.

Janessa paced across her sitting room, working off her excess anger. If she were honest with herself, she would admit that she was as annoyed at the situation with Garrett as she was at the ambassador's aide. Unfortunately, she was inherently honest.

Since their kiss on the beach, she had barely seen him except at official functions. They had made sure members of the staff saw them together periodically, but in all settings they kept their conversation free of personal topics and their physical contact to a minimum. It wasn't until Garrett wasn't around that Janessa realized how much she missed his companionship. *Silly,* she thought to herself. She barely knew the man! But she couldn't deny that she had sensed a connection between them. She had imagined that he had felt it too, but now she wasn't sure what to think.

She wondered if their date would be easier to forget had it not been documented in the newspapers and magazines. Martino had provided her with all of the latest, including photos of them leaving the jeweler's and kissing on the beach. Janessa looked down at that picture now. The kiss should have been innocent, just a tool to convince the world that she had a right to be here. If only she hadn't felt anything.

With a shake of her head, she reminded herself that Garrett was simply playing a role to keep his family safe. No matter how nice he was, he was a prince and by default was probably very experienced in the romance department, no matter how he might try to deny it. She couldn't let herself get distracted by the illusion that he might really be romantically interested in her. Even if he was interested, any kind of relationship would be impossible. Besides the fact that she and Garrett came from different worlds, he wasn't LDS.

She ignored the sinking feeling in her stomach, instead concentrating once again on the naval base. Unwilling to give up, Janessa pulled out her laptop and drafted a letter to the director of Central Intelligence. Hopefully he would understand the benefits of her suggestion and present her idea to the Navy.

After writing and rewriting her proposal, Janessa carefully prepared the diplomatic pouch and set it on her dresser. She moved to the French doors leading to the balcony, surprised that after half a week in Meridia the view could still captivate her. Through all of her travels, she had never known that a single place could hold so much beauty.

The farm in Iowa where she had grown up had always held a peaceful, quiet beauty for Janessa—green fields of new crops, horses and livestock grazing near the barn. Yet, she had always known that she was destined to leave there to find her own place. As she looked at the scene below, she wondered if she could find a place to call her own with a view such as this.

* * *

Her gown was black tonight, accented simply with a strand of pearls. Garrett watched Janessa enter the parlor, annoyed at himself for wanting to ignore his guests so that he could be with her. She saw him staring, gave him a brief nod, and then smiled at the defense attaché to the Italian ambassador.

For the most part, Garrett had managed to avoid Janessa for the past three days. They had to keep up appearances, certainly, but otherwise he hadn't sought her out since they had returned from their date and she had insisted on paying him back for the blanket. He had tried to tell her to keep her money, and he still wasn't sure why she was being so stubborn about the whole thing. After all, it wasn't like his family couldn't afford it.

The day after their date, he had been in meetings for hours on end as he tried to acclimate back to the duties expected of him. In his free moments, he had tried to analyze exactly what was going on between him and Janessa. The kiss on the beach had been impulsive, and it had rocked him to the core. He had liked Janessa from the first time they met and had found her attractive, but kissing her had opened the door to a level of interest that took him by surprise. Now he wasn't quite sure what to do with the feelings she stirred in him.

Perhaps it wouldn't be so difficult if he didn't want the permanence that marriage and a family of his own would bring him. Too easily, he could imagine Janessa in that picture, and he was concerned that he already thought of her far too often each day. After all, he had only met her a few weeks earlier.

Garrett watched Janessa work the room for nearly ten minutes before he excused himself and crossed to her. As much for show as for his own pleasure, he leaned down and kissed her cheek. "I need a little fresh air." Garrett reached for her hand and led her through the terrace doors before she had a chance to answer.

As soon as they were outside, Janessa spoke. "You're neglecting your guests. That's not like you."

"Are you sure?" Garrett asked, leading her down the terrace steps toward the garden. "Maybe I'm not a very good host."

"I find that unlikely," Janessa stated. She glanced around to make sure they were alone and then asked, "Have you heard anything new about the bombing?"

"Nothing." Garrett shook his head. "The latest report said that a few shadows on the surveillance tape have helped pin down the time the bomb was planted, but no one has taken credit for it."

"I'm sure something will turn up eventually." She turned to admire a cluster of blue dawn flowers. "The gardens here are so beautiful."

A smile crossed his face. "No matter where we go, you find something to compliment."

She shrugged and stopped beside a vine bursting with red blooms. "It's hard not to here."

"I agree." Garrett was struck once again by how he relaxed almost instantly in Janessa's presence. He felt he could simply be himself with her. He started to move closer, but Janessa stepped back.

"Please don't." Her voice was calm but had a slight waver to it. "I have a job to do, and neither of us can afford any distractions right now."

"That may be, but I've missed talking to you the last few days."

Janessa studied him for a moment, her eyes wary. "I think you know that nothing can develop between us."

"Maybe it already has," Garrett said as a servant stepped out onto the terrace to announce dinner. "We'll talk about this later when we can really be alone."

He guided her back into the parlor, pleased that she allowed him to escort her to the dining room where many of their guests were already waiting. Though she wasn't seated next to him, she was close enough for Garrett to hear pieces of her conversation with the ambassador's aide and the defense attaché. He could have sworn he heard something about a secret vacation spot in Italy and then pieces of a lighthearted disagreement on where to find the best chocolate in Europe. A few minutes later, Garrett noticed Janessa sharing confidences with the defense attaché's wife.

She was already accepted by those who dined regularly with royalty as though she belonged now and always had. Only four days had passed since she had arrived in Meridia, yet she had already made more acquaintances than Garrett could count. He could only wonder if her ease with people was natural or just part of her training.

Kindness seemed to rest easily on her, whether she was speaking with an ambassador or a shopkeeper. After their outing together in Bellamo, he had also come to find that she photographed exceptionally well. She tolerated the intrusion of the press well, smiling on command when the situation called for it, even though he sensed she wasn't any more comfortable in the spotlight than he was.

Though the tabloids were known to be cruel, the photographs and articles about him and Janessa had been quite the opposite. The speculation was widespread about where they had met and how serious their relationship was. Even amid the speculation, she was already winning over the public without even knowing she was doing it.

As he watched her charm her way through dinner, Garrett knew that she was winning him over as well.

chapter 11

Janessa stepped to her window and breathed in the morning air flavored by the sea. The sunlight bloomed over the water, turning the sky magnificent shades of color.

A horse whinnied in the distance. Seagulls cried out as they swooped down in search of their early morning meals. The fragrance of roses wafted up, reminding her of her mother's garden in the summer. She breathed in the scent as her mind began to wander. She wondered what the chateau would be like without the constant flow of guests.

She could imagine the royal family spending time here away from the pressures of their duties to rejuvenate and relax. She wondered for a moment what Garrett had been like as a boy. Had he always been raised to think of duty first? Or had he been permitted to simply be a child when he was young? Had he ridden horses under Paolo's watchful eye or his father's?

Janessa thought of her walk with Garrett the night before, annoyed that he had been heavily in her thoughts since then. She had been slightly put off by his peremptory tone, but she knew from experience that it was a common problem among people with high social status or great wealth. She suspected that like others who had been born to power, he probably didn't even realize that his commands could be offensive. There had been no point in bringing it up then, so she had just nodded and followed Garrett inside. At the end of the evening she had managed to avoid the "alone time" he had casually demanded earlier, but she knew that sooner or later she'd have to clearly define the boundaries of their relationship.

She shook her head, trying to clear her mind. According to the headlines, Prince Garrett lived a life of ease and was prone to arrogance. After only a week in Meridia, she already knew that the public's perception wasn't anywhere close to reality. Though Garrett rarely mentioned his work, she knew from her talks with the staff that he worked long hours each day. She knew firsthand that his duties typically continued well into the night, as he was expected to attend various dinner parties and public functions.

During her analysis of the staff, she had found that those who worked for the royal family thought highly of Prince Garrett. He was considered fair and understanding. The staff seemed eager to meet his needs largely because he appreciated their service.

Determined to push Garrett from her mind, Janessa turned from the window and dressed for church. She slipped out of her room and made her way downstairs to the kitchen.

Patrice was standing at the stove, and several of the servants were eating breakfast at the table. Everyone exchanged greetings with Janessa as she crossed to the table and helped herself to a croissant. She slipped into the seat next to Enrico and waited for him to finish his morning meal.

He turned to her as he finished off his glass of milk. "You still want to go to your church this morning?"

"Please." Janessa nodded.

"Let's go then." Enrico stood and motioned for Janessa to follow him. He turned away from the front entrance, instead leading her to the private family entrance. Once outside, he crossed a section of driveway to the long, white building that housed the various vehicles maintained for the royal family's use. He punched in the code to open the first set of garage doors and motioned inside.

"Do you have a preference of which car we take?"

"Something normal," Janessa suggested, waving a hand in the direction of two luxury sedans. "Those are probably as close as we can get."

Enrico grinned and opened the front door of the nearest car for her. He then moved to a glass-encased box hanging on the wall with various sets of keys dangling inside it. He selected the ones he wanted and then took his seat behind the steering wheel.

"I really appreciate you taking me like this," Janessa began as Enrico pulled away from the chateau. "I know it's out of your way."

"For you, I don't mind," he said in a tone very much like her father's. "It's a beautiful drive to this church of yours, and you will see much more of this country than just the beaches and the stables."

They fell into easy conversation as Enrico navigated through narrow, winding roads up into the hills. The drive to the town where the church was located took nearly thirty minutes. Janessa was beginning to believe the directions she had been given were faulty as they drove through the thick, almost overgrown hills. Then, suddenly, they turned a corner and Janessa saw the church building situated in a clearing off to the side.

The building was small and was constructed of white stone that contrasted with the deep green foliage that surrounded it. Enrico pulled into the small parking lot and let Janessa off next to the entrance, promising to return in three hours to pick her up.

Janessa wasn't sure how people would react if they knew about her alleged relationship with Prince Garrett, but she ignored her nerves and walked inside. She noticed a few questioning glances cast her way, but they were accompanied by smiles. She was barely two steps inside the door when two missionaries approached her. Though the taller, lanky elder looked like he was straight out of the MTC in Provo, Janessa spoke to them both in Italian, explaining that she would be visiting for the next month or so.

As she took her seat in the small chapel, she wondered what Garrett would think of her church. She wondered if he would think it strange or old-fashioned that she was committed to not marry outside her religion. Then she chastised herself for letting herself think that it would matter.

Admittedly, she felt a spark of attraction for Garrett. That, combined with the friendship they had begun, might even develop into something more under normal circumstances. She reminded herself that these circumstances were anything but normal. In a month she would return to the States to await her next assignment, and Garrett would settle back into his normal routine. She ignored the unaccustomed tug of regret as she thought of leaving Meridia—and Garrett—behind.

At the front of the room, the branch president stood up to begin the meeting. Among the announcements was the news that the pianist had just had a baby. Immediately following the announcement was a plea for anyone who might be willing to fill in for her.

Janessa glanced around the room. Barely forty people were seated in the chapel, half of whom were children. When no one stepped forward, Janessa stood and walked to the piano. The branch president smiled and gave her a nod of gratitude before announcing the opening song.

She winced as she messed up on the very first chord, but somehow she muddled through. To her relief, nobody seemed to care that her talent at the piano was limited. After the sacrament hymn, she slid into the seat next to the piano. From her seat on the stand, she looked out at the congregation. The members of the branch were dressed simply. They did not appear impoverished, but neither did they appear to have much beyond their needs.

The meeting seemed to speed by as Janessa listened to the talks about the temple. The Spirit filled the room as the speakers expressed their appreciation for the fact that they would soon have a temple in their country. From what Janessa had been told, the Church was in the difficult process of obtaining the necessary building permits.

After sacrament meeting, the branch president introduced himself to Janessa. She agreed to fill in for the pianist during her stay, however long that might be. As the chapel transitioned into the gospel doctrine class, she moved down from the stand to take a seat before being asked to introduce herself.

"I am Gianessa Rogers. I am here visiting friends in Bellamo."

The sister who was teaching the class studied her for a moment, her eyes widening as she recognized Janessa from the various newspaper articles that had been floating around over the past several days. "You are staying at the chateau?"

Reluctantly, Janessa nodded.

"I see." The sister stared a moment longer before adding, "We're happy to have you here."

As the meeting progressed, Janessa felt numerous branch members look over at her. She told herself that she would be curious too if someone who was constantly in the newspapers showed up in her home ward. Though she was nervous about how she would be received by the other members of the branch, when Sunday School was over, three women approached with warm smiles to welcome her. One ventured to ask how long she had known Prince Garrett, but the others seemed too timid to broach the subject. Only a handful of sisters were in Relief Society, and Janessa was pleased that the small class size gave her the chance to meet all of them.

By the time Enrico arrived to pick her up, Janessa found herself looking forward to attending church the following week. She just hoped she could find some time to practice on the grand piano she'd seen at the chateau.

* * *

Where was she? Garrett stalked through the entryway and headed for fresh air. He had sent for Janessa nearly two hours earlier only to be told that she wasn't in the chateau. A member of the kitchen staff had told him that she had asked Enrico for a ride, but no one seemed to know where they had gone or when they would return.

Surely she wouldn't be so careless as to go gallivanting through the countryside while the climate toward Americans was still so hostile. She of all people should know that her association with him made her a possible target, particularly since several articles had noted her nationality.

Garrett yanked open the door with every intention of going out looking for her himself when he saw the car pull into the drive. The wave of relief was quickly swallowed up by annoyance.

"Where have you been?" he demanded the moment Janessa climbed out of the car.

Her eyebrows rose at his tone, but to her credit, she moved forward anyway. "I went to church."

"Did it occur to you that I might need to know where you are?"

"No, it didn't. I left that information with Levi. That seemed sufficient," Janessa said, irony lacing her tone. "If you have something to discuss, I'm here now."

"We have several things to discuss, actually." Garrett gestured stiffly toward the door. Instead of moving into the parlor, he led her up the stairs. "We need to speak privately."

They walked in silence, annoyance vibrating from both of them. Garrett felt the waves of irritation rolling off of Janessa, but both of them controlled their tempers as they passed by several servants and entered his private quarters. Pushing open the door, he pointed to the sitting area. "Sit down."

Her chin shot up. "I'd rather stand." She waited for him to close the door before speaking again. "In case you haven't forgotten, I am not one of your subjects. I'm here to help your family." She held his stare. "I don't appreciate being treated like a servant."

"Even guests should be courteous enough to tell their hosts when they are going somewhere," Garrett shot back before he thought to check his temper.

Janessa ignored whatever truth might have been in his statement and folded her arms across her chest. "What was so urgent that you needed to talk to me right now?"

Garrett took a steadying breath and tried to summon a reasonable tone. "My father has requested that we join the family for dinner at the palace in Calene this evening. He wants to announce our engagement tomorrow and prefers to meet you before the reporters arrive for the press conference."

"Then I guess I had better go pack." Irritation still hummed through Janessa's voice. Before she could cross to the door, Garrett took her hand.

"I was worried about you," he blurted out. "I went looking for you, and no one knew where you were."

Her posture relaxed slightly. "You already knew that I was devoted to my religious beliefs. I didn't think it was necessary to announce that I go to church on Sundays."

"A lot of people don't."

"I'm not a lot of people."

"I know," Garrett said softly. "There's one more thing."

"What?"

Instead of answering her, he crossed into his bedroom. A moment later, he returned with a jeweler's box in his hand.

Janessa's gaze remained on the box as he opened it to reveal the ring he had chosen. "I believe it's time you start wearing this."

She swallowed hard, saying nothing as he drew the ring from its case and reached for her hand. Her eyes darted up to his as he slid the ring on her finger. When Garrett lifted her hand to his lips, lingering a moment longer than expected, a mixture of confusion, frustration, and pleasure crossed her face.

To Garrett's surprise, she stepped back quickly and tugged her hand free. "I really should go pack."

"There's something else we need to discuss." Garrett waited for her eyes to meet his. "Our personal lives are about to become very public."

He stepped closer. She stepped back.

"We don't have a personal life—only the illusion of one," Janessa insisted as she tried to keep her voice controlled. "As I tried to tell you last night, nothing can develop between us. I have a job to do."

"We both have a job to do," Garrett clarified. "That doesn't change the fact that I have feelings for you."

"I'm flattered, really," Janessa managed. "But you're wasting your time. I don't want a romantic relationship with someone outside of my faith. I'm sorry, but we can't be more than just friends."

Garrett studied her silently. He could tell her everything—that he too understood her religious convictions, that he knew the Book of Mormon was true, and that he believed her church was headed by a living prophet. He also understood that if there were no barriers between them, and he continued to act on his attraction, it was possible he could distract her from her job.

He wanted to confide in her, to share his beliefs, and to take another step toward what was developing between them. He also knew it was essential that Janessa be given every opportunity to do her job to protect those dear to him. Something squeezed at his heart as concern for his family outweighed all else. With a great deal of effort, he nodded, opened the door for her, and said nothing.

chapter 12

Queen Marta tapped a perfectly manicured nail on her antique desk and made the final adjustments to the seating chart for the upcoming dinner. What had begun as a quiet family affair had expanded to include several members of the ruling council and their wives.

Only the members of the royal family knew who Janessa Rogers really was, with the exception of Martino, the chateau manager who had been assigned to assist her, and Enrico, the chateau driver. Marta had hoped for a quiet dinner and a chance to assess the woman who would be coordinating so many details for the gala. Now she would have to wait until morning to meet with Janessa privately.

Marta reached for one of the magazines her assistant had given her. On the cover, her youngest son was kissing Janessa Rogers. A sigh escaped her. She wasn't sure she wanted her son to voluntarily put his private life—however fictitious—so firmly in the public light.

Of everyone in her family, Garrett was the one who was the least comfortable in front of the press. He had been trained to handle the reporters and photographers, but he always looked forward to getting out of the spotlight. Marta understood how he felt. She could remember a time when she too had shied away from the cameras, especially during the early days of her courtship with Eduard.

As the daughter of a Meridian councilman, Marta had grown up around cameras, but they had rarely been aimed at her. But when the press learned that her childhood friendship with Eduard had bloomed into a full-blown romance, they had been relentless. She had just turned twenty-one when her photograph began appearing regularly with Eduard's.

Eduard had been protective of her when dealing with the press in those early days, but he didn't quite understand Garrett's discomfort in front of the media. Though Marta was annoyed that Eduard had put his current plans in motion before consulting with her, she understood his reasons. After nearly thirty-five years of marriage, she knew her husband was just protecting what was his. She also understood that Eduard needed Garrett to start acting more like an active member of the royal family.

He had been gone too long, first at sea and then at law school. The year he had spent at home before leaving for school had been much too brief and felt so long ago. He had always been restless, even as a child. She had hoped he would find what he was looking for in the Navy, but while four years in the service had helped him transition from boy to man, he still hadn't found his peace.

For a while, she thought that he had found contentment while at law school, but something had been troubling him since he had returned home, something she had yet to identify.

Perhaps once they moved past this current crisis, she would finally have some time to spend with both of her sons.

* * *

Janessa fiddled with the ring on her finger, still adjusting to the new weight there. She hated to admit it, but she loved how the diamond sparkled in the sunlight, even if the engagement itself was a sham. During the two-hour ride from the chateau, she and Garrett had hardly spoken a word except for a brief conversation about the upgraded security at the chateau. Their relationship had once again taken on a professional air.

Janessa could only assume that the brief interest he had shown in her had been extinguished by her revelation that their religious differences were an impassable roadblock. She convinced herself she was relieved that the spark of attraction between them was little more than an obstacle to overcome in doing her job.

She glanced over at Garrett, who was currently taking advantage of the time to review reports on the embassy bombing. He looked so aristocratic just then, his brow furrowed in concentration, his chiseled features set. For a moment she wished he wasn't quite so handsome but immediately realized that it wouldn't matter anyway. Although his looks had been one of the first things she had noticed about him, it was his kindness that she found most attractive. She hadn't expected that someone who had been raised with nearly unlimited wealth and power would be so appreciative of those who served him.

Janessa turned back to the letter she was writing to her sister Mary. She couldn't tell her much except that she was doing well. She wished she could inform her sister that the engagement which would appear in the papers so soon was not real, but Mary would never be able to keep a secret from the rest of the family, which left Janessa no choice but to avoid the subject.

Instead Janessa tried to describe the beautiful setting in which she was currently living. Palm fronds swayed alongside the road, and a glance at her watch told her that they should arrive in the capital city of Calene in a matter of minutes. Looking out the window, she noticed a rambling village on the hills above the sea. It wasn't until she saw the port that she realized the village was Calene.

They went around a curve, and Janessa got her first look at their destination. She leaned forward in her seat and moved closer to the window so she could see it more clearly. The palace could only be described as magnificent.

While the chateau was nestled right on the seashore, the palace spread across high cliffs overlooking the Mediterranean. The palace faced the water on a jut of land that fell off sharply into the sea on three sides. A short distance away, the ruins of the Fortiers' first family home was visible. Only a single stone wall still remained.

Unlike its predecessor, the palace was nearly impregnable. Attack from the sea was unlikely, as it rose high above the water, and the steep hills leading to the palace made attack by land nearly impossible. Janessa approved of the functionality of the location just as she approved of the structure itself. Turrets, towers, and battlements were constant reminders of the centuries that had come before, but the gleaming white stone looked fresh, as though the building were brand new. Situated on the highest point overlooking the village, the location afforded its inhabitants protection even as they sought to protect the village and lands below.

"It's beautiful," Janessa said softly.

Garrett looked up at the palace and then turned his gaze to Janessa and smiled. "I thought you would like it."

Within minutes, the limousine pulled through the palace gates and stopped in front of the magnificent structure. Two uniformed guards stood solemnly on either side of the massive wooden doors. Just as Garrett and Janessa got out of the limo, the front doors opened. Janessa lifted her hand to shade her eyes against the setting sun as two servants walked outside and moved to bring in their luggage. A moment later, Garrett's older brother emerged from the palace and descended the wide steps. He was slightly broader through the shoulders and an inch or two shorter than his younger brother.

"I was wondering when you were going to get here," Stefano told Garrett, his eyes shifting from his brother to Janessa.

"Stefano, you remember Janessa." Garrett glanced briefly at the servants attending to their luggage before continuing the façade. "I introduced you a few weeks ago in Caracas."

Stefano played along. "So nice to see you again." He took Janessa's hand and brought it to his lips with a great deal of charm.

Janessa smiled, but she couldn't help noticing that her heartbeat continued its normal rhythm, unlike its tendency when Garrett performed the same action. Then Garrett stepped forward and, in a possessive move, slipped an arm around her waist, and her heartbeat quickened.

Stefano motioned to the door. "Please come inside. I have to go into the village for a meeting, but Father is waiting for you both in his office."

Garrett nodded and guided Janessa inside to his father's office. Garrett rapped on the door, opening it when the command came from within.

The moment Janessa stepped inside, she felt power emanating from the man behind the oversized desk. Like his sons, his face had sharp angles, reminiscent of the aristocrats and the warriors he descended from. His dark hair was graying, giving him a distinguished look. His eyes were sharp and somewhat troubled.

"Welcome home," he said to Garrett before turning to Janessa. He stood and moved around to the front of the desk. "Signorina, welcome to our home."

"Your Majesty." Janessa dipped into a curtsey. "Thank you for having me."

King Eduard took her hand and motioned for her to sit down. "I'm afraid our quiet dinner plans for tonight have expanded considerably," he began as he sat down across from Janessa. "Several members of the ruling council will also be in attendance with their wives."

"Lord Tratte?" Garrett asked, settling onto the love seat next to Janessa.

"For one." King Eduard nodded. His eyes shifted from Garrett to Janessa. "Lord Tratte has been one of the biggest opponents to US military presence here in Meridia. I'm afraid he isn't pleased to see my son paired with an American."

"Don't worry, Father." Garrett placed his hand on Janessa's. "If anyone can handle him, Janessa can."

The king nodded, and Janessa wondered what he thought about his son's easy familiarity with her. He again directed his comments to Janessa. "Have you had time this week to analyze our security at the chateau?"

"To some extent." Janessa nodded. She retrieved a file from her oversized bag and handed it to the king. "Here is my initial report."

King Eduard opened the file and skimmed its contents. "Explain to me about these sensors you want to install."

Janessa leaned forward slightly. "The chateau is most vulnerable to a clandestine attack from the hillside behind it. We would like to install a series of motion detectors in that area to alleviate this concern. Since you already have guards stationed on the road leading to the chateau, the most likely source of trouble would then be an insider penetrating security through some type of service job."

"Our staff is loyal. I don't believe that any of them would hurt the family in any way."

"I agree. I have only found a few minor indiscretions, nothing to indicate otherwise."

Garrett asked, "What kind of indiscretions?"

"Little things." Janessa shrugged. "Lilia on the kitchen staff leaves twenty minutes early every day to go pick up her daughter so her mother can get to work on time. Ronaldo in the stables is romantically involved with both Regina from housekeeping and Maria, the assistant gardener. But nothing indicates a potential breach in their loyalty to the royal family." She turned back to the king. "I'll meet with the caterers this week. I didn't feel it appropriate to begin my research there until the engagement was announced."

Eduard nodded in agreement. "My wife will meet with you tomorrow to review what still needs to be done to prepare for the gala. She should be able to give you some additional insight as to where it would be easiest to penetrate our security."

Janessa nodded. "Also, I would like your permission to send for a dog trained in bomb detection. One of the best dogs in the world is currently in London, and he and his handler are experienced with the devices that are most common in this part of the world." She was glad her friend Alan Neisler and his dog, Max, were available for this job. She hoped the king would agree to use them.

"How do you plan to use this animal?"

"We will do daily sweeps of the chateau. On the night of the gala, the dog will be stationed at the gate to check out all of the service vehicles."

"Very well." King Eduard stood. "Garrett, please show Janessa to her rooms. Our guests are expected to arrive at seven."

"Your Majesty, is there any way I can get a copy of the guest list for tonight?" Janessa asked.

"Of course." King Eduard nodded, glancing at Garrett.

"I'll take care of it, Father."

With that, Garrett led Janessa from the office and through a series of hallways to the family quarters. "In case you need anything, that's my door there." Garrett motioned down the hall as he paused at the room that would be Janessa's for the next few days. He pushed her door open to reveal an elegant sitting room in pearl and soft blue.

Janessa stepped inside and crossed directly to the window seat. She stared at the village below and the boats on the water. "I keep thinking that I've already seen the best view in Meridia, and then I see something new."

"You are fortunate to appreciate the beauty the Lord has blessed us with." Garrett laid a hand on her shoulder, for a moment staring out the window as well.

Warmth spread through her at his touch, but she tried to ignore her unwanted reaction and turned to face him. He looked down at her, and for a moment she felt as though she were the most important thing in the world to him. *Snap out of it,* she told herself, but when she tried to speak, to say something to break the mood, she found herself speechless.

Garrett lifted his hand and caressed her cheek. Even as she told herself to move away, she watched him lower his mouth to hers for a brief kiss.

He pulled away from her. "I'm sorry," he said quickly. "I'll stop by a few minutes before seven to escort you to dinner."

As she watched him leave the room, she felt even more confused than before. She looked down at the ring on her finger, concerned that its sparkling presence was clouding her judgment. Turning away from the view and the sinking feeling in her stomach, she moved to the bedroom to prepare for the upcoming evening.

chapter 13

Janessa looked over the evening's guest list, tapping away on her laptop as she retrieved biographies on the various council members and their wives. The guest list included more than twenty guests, and she wished she had enough time to research everyone's background thoroughly.

She didn't see anything in particular that raised concerns. All of the members of the ruling council were financially secure, and none of them had any suspicious changes in either their income or their spending habits.

As she reviewed the council members' political views, she noted that Lord Tratte consistently voted against ties with the United States and had voted that way throughout his political career. Realizing that he wasn't the only council member who preferred to avoid strong ties with the US, she sighed and hoped that she wasn't sitting next to any of them at dinner.

* * *

Garrett knocked on Janessa's door at precisely five minutes before seven. He had chastised himself for giving in to impulse by kissing her earlier and resolved to keep his distance tonight. When she called out for him to come in, he pushed the door open. She stood in front of a framed mirror hanging on the wall, and for a moment Garrett stood rooted to the spot, overwhelmed by her beauty.

Her hair was swept up, leaving her slender neck exposed and making her seem more delicate. A few curls escaped to frame her face, and her eye makeup gave her a mysterious and exotic look. Diamond earrings winked from her ears, and a column of ivory silk hung from her shoulders down to her ankles. As she turned to him, he doubted anyone would question why he had chosen her to be his bride.

"Should I wear the ring tonight?" she asked as he continued to stare. "I didn't know if I should wear it in public before the engagement is officially announced."

"Wear the ring. The council members always like it when they find things out before the press does." His resolve to keep his distance melted away as he reached for her hand and lifted it to his lips. "You look exquisite."

"Thank you." Janessa looked down at their joined hands and shifted uncomfortably. "We should go."

"Are you afraid to be alone with me?" Garrett asked, at first guilty for causing her discomfort but then suddenly pleased as he realized she was less upset at his show of affection than at her own reaction to it.

"Uneasy would be a more accurate word." She tilted her head, as though studying him from a new angle. "I thought I made myself clear that this engagement is only for show. There can't be anything else between us."

"It would be simpler, wouldn't it, if you weren't attracted to me."

Her breath came out in a little huff. "Garrett."

He grinned now. "Ah, so you don't deny it." He squeezed her hand and led her to the door. "Now I just need to get you to admit it."

"It doesn't seem like there's any point. Why—"

"Maybe things aren't always what they seem." Garrett opened the door. "Besides, I like a challenge."

* * *

The main salon was wide and spacious, sectioned in half by a wide archway running through the center of the room. When Janessa and Garrett entered, Stefano was already entertaining the first arrivals over drinks. A servant immediately offered to get Garrett and Janessa a drink, and Janessa was both surprised and touched when Garrett ordered ginger ale for both of them.

Janessa only had to look around the room to understand what the evening would entail. The language was Italian, the food was French, and the conversation was all about the Americans. Determined not to lose her objectivity, she easily adopted Italian as her language for the evening as Garrett began introducing her to the guests.

Most of the council members were middle-aged, though a few were of an older generation. Garrett had just introduced her to Councilman Hennero, one of the few single members of the ruling council, when Stefano requested a moment with his brother. Janessa continued her conversation with the young council member, talking about the quality of handcrafted sailboats in Meridia. As they chatted, Janessa discovered that Hennero owned a company in Calene that had been producing some of the finest sailing vessels in the Mediterranean for generations.

"You really must go out sailing this summer. If you think the view is magnificent from the beach, you will love it from the water," Hennero told her as an older gentleman approached.

"I'll seriously consider it," Janessa replied, pausing as the older man shook hands with Hennero.

"Eric, you do always find the most beautiful women in Meridia." The man turned and looked at Janessa.

Hennero smiled, motioning to the new arrival. "Lord Tratte is just jealous, signorina."

"You are both too kind." Janessa smiled, surprised that Lord Tratte failed to recognize her from the numerous photos that had been taken of her and Garrett. "We were just discussing how perfect the weather has been for sailing. I think I may be tempted to go out myself this week."

"This is the best time of year—not too hot and not too many tourists." Lord Tratte nodded his approval. "Hopefully we won't soon have American naval vessels cluttering up our waters as well."

"You worry too much," Hennero said mildly.

"And you worry too little," Tratte replied.

Janessa bit back the temptation to try to guide the conversation. She was disappointed when the argument didn't continue. Instead, Hennero again steered the conversation away from politics. A moment later, Garrett appeared at her side.

"Lord Tratte, I see you have met Janessa." Garrett placed a hand on the small of her back, even as he shook hands with Tratte.

Before Lord Tratte could respond, Janessa said, "We were just discussing how perfect the weather is to go sailing."

Garrett grinned down at her. "If you think I'm taking you sailing so you can avoid the press conference tomorrow, you're sadly mistaken."

"A girl can hope." Janessa smiled up at him, appreciating how well he played along.

Hennero spoke now. "Your father has been somewhat elusive as to the nature of tomorrow's press conference."

"I'm afraid that's my doing," Garrett told him. He grasped Janessa's left hand and brought it to his lips to bring attention to the ring on her finger. "We will be announcing our engagement tomorrow."

"Congratulations!" Hennero shook Garrett's hand and leaned over to kiss Janessa on the cheek.

Tratte's response was more reserved, although he too offered his congratulations. "I wasn't aware you had known each other that long."

"Our paths have crossed a number of times over the past few years," Janessa told him.

"It wasn't easy to convince her that she's the only one for me," Garrett added. Then, noticing his mother walking into the room, Garrett nodded to the two men. "If you will excuse us, I need to speak to my mother for a moment."

As they approached the queen, Janessa struggled to believe that this woman was old enough to be Garrett's mother. She was a couple of inches taller than Janessa, her face was nearly free of lines, and she looked like she was in better shape than most twenty-year-olds. She exuded elegance, from the tiara situated on her dark hair to her gown of midnight blue. She smiled as she excused herself from the couple she was talking to, her voice somehow managing to be both warm and regal.

When Garrett reached his mother's side, Janessa watched as the woman before her transformed from royalty to motherhood in an instant. She opened her arms as Garrett stepped into them for a warm embrace. Love flowed over them, creating a little island of affection amid the crowded room. When Garrett stepped back, Janessa was surprised that he didn't offer any formal introductions. "Mother, I'm sorry we didn't see you this afternoon when we arrived."

"That's quite all right." Queen Marta's quiet eyes studied him for a moment before she turned her gaze to Janessa. "You look lovely this evening."

"Thank you, Your Majesty." Janessa dipped into a curtsey, appreciating the obvious affection the queen had for her family.

"I wish we had a few moments to chat, but I'm afraid dinner is about to be served." The queen motioned to the dining hall. "My husband told you I want to spend some time with you tomorrow?"

Janessa nodded. "I look forward to it."

* * *

King Eduard presided over his table, keeping a sharp eye on those dining with him. So far it appeared that everyone believed the fictionalized version of how Garrett and Janessa had come to be engaged so soon after being spotted together by the press. The talk of the US naval base had come up as had been expected, but the majority of the ruling council still remained supportive of his wishes.

Frustration over the investigation of the US Embassy bombing continued to cloud negotiations, but so far no one had stepped forward to claim responsibility, and leads were practically nonexistent.

Eduard's gaze landed on Janessa, and he smiled at the way she charmed those around her. He would have to thank Director Palmer for sending her to them. He doubted even he could have selected someone so well suited for the task at hand. As he watched Garrett lean over and whisper something in Janessa's ear, he felt the undercurrents between the young couple. His eyes narrowed fractionally as he recognized that Garrett's feelings for this young woman might be genuine.

Not sure how he felt about his son having a relationship with an American, he looked up to see his wife watching Garrett. It took only a moment to realize that she, too, was analyzing their son's true involvement.

chapter 14

Photographers and reporters shuffled on the eastern terrace, vying for the best position for the upcoming press conference. As anticipated, news of Prince Garrett's engagement had leaked out from a member of the ruling council, and the press had come out in droves for the historic announcement.

Garrett stood inside the terrace doors, waiting for his father to give the command to begin. Janessa stood beside him wearing a dress of sunflower yellow, a dress he knew his mother had helped her select from her wardrobe earlier that morning. She fingered the ring on her left hand, the only outward sign of nervousness.

"Don't worry," Garrett assured her, placing a hand on her back. "If you run into a question you don't want to answer, we'll help you out."

"I didn't expect there would be so many reporters," Janessa admitted.

Garrett nodded in agreement as he tried to quash his own nerves. He couldn't remember ever seeing so many reporters at the palace.

"Are you ready?" King Eduard asked, motioning to the doors.

Janessa took a deep breath. "I think so."

"We're ready," Garrett confirmed.

Queen Marta took Janessa's hand as she passed by and gave it a squeeze. "You'll do fine."

Janessa nodded, allowing Garrett to guide her through the doors behind the king, the queen, and Prince Stefano.

King Eduard stepped up to the podium that had been set up for the occasion. The crowd instantly quieted. "Thank you all for coming." King Eduard's gaze swept from one side of the crowd to the other. "My countrymen, my friends, I do not wish to delay in sharing with you the joy that has come into our family. Queen Marta and I are pleased to announce the engagement of our son Prince Garrett Eduard Fortier de Meridia to Janessa Rogers of the United States."

A ripple of excitement shot through the crowd, and a few enterprising photographers began snapping photographs of the young couple. Before the questions could start, King Eduard continued, relaying the story of how they had met several years ago and had been in loose contact since that time. He provided enough details to keep the press from asking difficult questions about their courtship.

When the king finally allowed questions to be asked, the first ones were directed at Janessa. Instinctively, Garrett took her hand in his, giving it a quick squeeze of encouragement even as he felt her tremble with nerves.

"Signorina Rogers, how does it feel to be marrying a prince?" the first reporter asked in Italian.

Janessa looked up at Garrett. "I am thrilled to be getting married, but I have to say, I am more interested in the man than the title." Surprise rippled through the crowd at her ability to speak Italian.

"How do you feel about leaving your country?"

Before Janessa could answer, Garrett edged forward. "Janessa has often said that Meridia is the most beautiful place on earth. I think she is excited that she won't need a painting on her wall to see this incredible scenery each day."

Janessa nodded in agreement.

The questions continued to flow, some to Janessa, others to Garrett and his family members. The answers became easier as the questions slowed down, no longer tumbling over one another. After thirty minutes, King Eduard closed the question-and-answer portion of the press conference. He then allowed the photographers an opportunity to take pictures of Janessa and Garrett, both with and without the other members of the royal family.

When at last King Eduard concluded the photo session, the family proceeded back inside to the parlor. A servant holding a pitcher of lemonade stood nearby. At Queen Marta's signal, she moved forward and began serving them as they all settled into their seats.

"You did very well," Queen Marta told Janessa, and then she included Garrett as well. "Both of you."

King Eduard nodded in agreement. "I didn't expect the press to warm up to you so quickly."

"I'm just glad that part is over," Janessa said.

"That makes two of us," Garrett agreed. He turned to his brother and grinned. "If it was this bad for me, I can't wait to see what happens when you get married."

"I'm going to elope."

"Even better," Garrett teased. "The press always loves a scandal, and the buzz about the heir to the throne eloping could last a year or more."

"I can see you won't be much help to me when the time comes." Stefano said wryly.

Queen Marta interrupted and asked Garrett, "When will you return to the chateau?"

"Wednesday," Garrett informed her. "Janessa is meeting with the caterers that afternoon, and the extra security we've requested will begin arriving Thursday morning."

Marta reached over and patted Janessa on the knee. "I wish I could be there to help with the details."

"I hope we can arrange that soon as well," Janessa agreed as a servant entered the room.

"Excuse me, Your Majesties." The servant dipped into a curtsey and addressed the queen. "Queen Marta, Signora Vorneaux has arrived."

"Thank you, Anna." Marta rose from her seat and turned to Janessa. "Signora Vorneaux has been designing gowns for me for years. I asked her to come help us fill out your wardrobe."

"Your Majesty, thank you, but it really isn't necessary."

"Oh, but it is. You will be attending social functions continually while you are here. Now that you are associated with the royal family, we must make sure your wardrobe is adequate."

Garrett nodded in agreement. "Janessa, please let Mother do this for you. Consider it a job requirement."

"If you insist." Janessa said politely and moved to the door where the queen was waiting for her.

* * *

Fifteen minutes later, Janessa found herself standing in the middle of her sitting room while Signora Vorneaux took measurements. She felt like a mannequin as the queen and Signora Vorneaux talked around her, discussing various styles and fabrics. When Queen Marta suggested a gown that would leave her shoulders bare, Janessa finally spoke up.

"I'm sorry, but I don't wear anything sleeveless," Janessa told them.

"But this gown would be perfect for the gala," Signora Vorneaux insisted.

"Yes, it is only for one night," Queen Marta agreed.

"Please understand that I am not trying to be difficult," Janessa began. "It's not just my style I am trying to preserve but also my religious beliefs."

"What religion are you?" Queen Marta asked, curiosity in her voice.

"I belong to The Church of Jesus Christ of Latter-day Saints," Janessa replied. "Many people refer to us as Mormons."

"Isn't that funny," Queen Marta commented. "Garrett's best friend from law school is Mormon."

"Really?" Janessa considered this new information, wondering how familiar Garrett was with her beliefs. "He never mentioned it."

"You'll meet him and his wife at the gala. They are making the trip from Washington a few days before the festivities begin."

"I look forward to meeting them," Janessa told her.

"Come sit down, and we'll decide what we should start with," Queen Marta instructed. "Signora Vorneaux can make whatever adjustments you require."

Janessa took a seat, grateful that the queen seemed willing to accommodate her clothing guidelines.

The queen motioned to the designer. "You brought your sketches."

"Of course."

Together they sat in the sitting room as the queen pored over sketches, discounting most of them because they were sleeveless. Others she set aside with suggestions that they be modified to accommodate Janessa's requests.

Janessa gave her input when needed, but mostly she just watched as the queen skillfully cajoled her favorite and now frustrated designer, ultimately cornering her into adapting her designs for Janessa. When

Janessa was finally left alone with Queen Marta, she shook her head in amazement. From what she could gather, the queen had ordered at least three dresses suitable for evening affairs as well as a gown for the gala. "Thank you for your generosity, but this really is too much."

Marta shook her head. "Not at all, but at least it will be enough to get you through the next week or two."

"I don't know how you do it all." Janessa settled back in her seat, studying the elegant woman across from her. "Your family spends so many hours each day seeing to the needs of others, and then you devote so many of your evenings to political and social events. It's a wonder you don't hide at the chateau for months at a time just so you can catch your breath."

Marta laughed. "Sometimes we do just that. When the boys were little, there were times when all I wanted was to be left alone to be a family. The chateau gives us that."

"It's a beautiful home." Janessa nodded.

"It will go to Garrett when he marries," Queen Marta said absently. "Not that it will change things much. He will always have a home here, just as he will continue to open the chateau to the family when it becomes his. Still, it's good for a man to have a place he can call his own."

Janessa considered her words, struck for the first time with a reality she had never before considered. What would the woman Garrett married be like? Would she appreciate the beauty of the land, the history of the chateau itself? Would she be Meridian and already understand and appreciate Garrett's role in this society? More importantly, would she recognize Garrett for the exceptional man he was, or would she only see the title?

The thought of him marrying someone other than herself made her feel unexpectedly jealous, and she looked down at the ring on her finger. Why was she reacting like this? She couldn't love him. She couldn't imagine anyone else loving him more.

Confused by her feelings, Janessa looked up and prayed that the queen wouldn't be able to sense the panic rushing through her.

chapter 15

Janessa stared down at the paper in her hand, sickened by the graphic images in front of her. The threats against the royal family continued to arrive with alarming regularity, usually through the mail system. Today's artwork showed an image of Garrett tied down to a set of railroad tracks with a train steaming toward him. Instead of an engineer, a photo of Janessa had been pasted in.

The words glued to the page spelled out the meaning: *The Americans will be the death of the royal family.*

Janessa picked up the telephone and called Levi to check on the current security levels at the chateau. He assured her that he would increase the number of guards patrolling the grounds until the enhanced security systems could be installed and activated.

After hanging up with Levi, Janessa put the latest threat into an envelope so that she wouldn't have to see it any longer. She then crossed to her window. She noted the peaceful scenery, but today it did nothing to ease the tension knotted in her stomach.

When a knock came at her door, she quickly scanned her room to make sure that nothing was out of place before calling out, "Come in."

Garrett stepped through the door, and for a moment Janessa just stared. She fought against her instinct to embrace him, to feel the reassurance that he was safe and whole. Unaware of her concern, he moved inside and closed the door behind him.

"I wanted to stop by and see how you're doing. I'm going to be in meetings the rest of the day and probably won't see you until dinner tonight." He moved farther into the room, looking at her with concern. "Are you okay?"

She nodded, more because it was expected than because it was true. "I was just talking to Levi about increasing the number of guards at the chateau until the new security measures are in place."

Garrett reached out and tipped her chin up so she was looking him in the eye. "Did something happen?"

"Another threat arrived a little while ago. You were going to be run over by a train." Her voice wavered. "And it was me driving it."

"I'm sure it's nothing to worry about. This happens all the time." Seeming to sense her needs, Garrett pulled her into his arms. His voice was soothing as he continued. "You can't take them too seriously."

"I don't know how you can live like this. Security is everywhere, and still these threats keep showing up. I'm good at my job, but it scares me that someone might manage to get through and harm you or your family."

He pulled back so that he could once again see her face. "With all of this extra security, I don't think that's possible."

"Garrett, anything is possible." Janessa took a deep breath. "We'll do everything we can to make it difficult for someone to get through, but no security is perfect."

"You've been working too hard." Garrett released her, brushing her hair back from her face. "Maybe you should take some time off, go for a swim in the pool."

Janessa shook her head, a tingle running down her spine at his touch. She took a step back in an effort to reestablish a professional distance between them. "We both know I don't have time for that."

Garrett started to disagree when he noticed a neat stack of papers on the end table. He picked it up and flipped over the top page. "What's this?"

"Nothing." Janessa reached out to take it from him, but he stepped back and held it out of her reach. She sighed with frustration. "Garrett, please give it back."

He ignored her, skimming over the first few pages. His tone changed from comforting to accusing. "Why are you involved with the new naval base for your country? I thought you came here to help us with security for the gala."

"I did. I just thought that my government might not have considered all of its options when deciding on a location for their base."

He flipped another page over, and his eyes narrowed. "Where did your information come from?"

"I haven't been spying on you, if that's what you're asking." She folded her arms across her chest and let out another sigh. "I believe this plan can help my country accomplish its goals without Meridia having to give up any more coastline to development."

Garrett flipped over another page and read some more before he looked back at her, his face more relaxed. "I didn't mean to accuse you. I just didn't realize you were working on this." His eyes were focused on hers as he quietly added, "Sometimes I forget what you are and why you're really here."

Janessa blinked and reminded *herself* of her reasons for being here as she held her hand out once again, relieved when he gave her back the proposal. "My director only presented it to our navy a couple of days ago. I haven't been authorized to discuss this with your family yet."

"It's not like you're revealing anything we don't already know," Garrett pointed out. He glanced at his watch. "I'd better get going. I'll see you at dinner."

Janessa nodded and watched him go.

* * *

The library in the palace was spacious, located in the same wing that housed the offices of the royal family. Lining the room were bookshelves that contained centuries of history and knowledge. Janessa sat at a large conference table situated in the heart of the room, wishing she could just grab a couple of books and go back to her room. Sadly, that wasn't an option. Currently, she was surrounded by an assortment of US officials who ate, drank, and breathed politics. The proposal she had sent to Director Palmer had been rewritten by someone with the State Department and then revised and polished. Each member of the group seated around her now had a copy in hand.

If today's meeting went well, similar meetings would eventually take place in Washington and at the embassy here in Meridia. For now, representatives from different organizations within the US government would determine the feasibility of the proposal that had evolved from Janessa's original idea.

Janessa was well aware of the US Navy's tactics to ignore the proposal, and their sending a mere lieutenant to represent the Navy at this meeting served to further cement her opinion. The State Department representative's presentation of the concept took only fifteen minutes. The discussion that ensued, however, lasted two grueling hours, during which many points were repeated more than once.

The Navy lieutenant directed a comment at Janessa, taking a superior tone. "I appreciate your eagerness to help us solve our problem, but I seriously doubt that the base you speak of could possibly serve our needs."

"On the contrary." Janessa spoke in a tone that was firm but not confrontational. "If you look on page four of your report, you will see the original specs for the base requirements. Based on the current information, the available space both on land and along the coast—even if we share this base—will exceed our needs."

Throughout the meeting, Janessa had been carefully noting the expressions of the attendees as well as their verbal responses. She believed that most were truly supportive of her idea. In addition to the representative from the State Department, both the members of the intelligence community and the attorneys in attendance believed the idea was worth pursuing. The Marine colonel had expressed a few strategic concerns, but thus far he had not opposed the proposal. The only dissenting voice was from the Navy, the organization they were trying to help.

Well aware that no more could be accomplished today, the State Department representative turned to Janessa. "Thank you for making time to meet with us today."

He shuffled his papers into his portfolio and spoke to the rest of the attendees. "I will forward your concerns to the secretary of state."

The room cleared quickly. Janessa spent a moment with the State Department representative as they reviewed further changes that might need to be made to the proposal. After everyone left, Janessa dropped back into her chair.

Believing herself to be alone, she leaned her elbows on the table and dropped her head into her hands. A sound at the doorway had her jumping to her feet.

Stefano stepped through the doorway, briefcase in hand. "I didn't mean to disturb you."

"That's okay." Janessa turned back to her notes on the table. "I'll get out of your way."

"Please sit for a moment." Stefano motioned her back to her seat and pulled out the chair across from her. "You're trying to help your country acquire a naval base here?"

Janessa nodded, wondering how much Garrett had shared with his brother. "My government hopes to have a proposal ready to present to your father within the next few weeks."

"Tell me about it." Stefano leaned back in his seat, keeping his eyes on hers.

"I haven't been authorized to discuss this proposal with your family yet," Janessa told him diplomatically. "I'm sure you understand that many changes will be made before it's considered complete."

"Please," Stefano insisted. "I am interested in the idea. Surely it won't hurt negotiations to have me behind you on this ahead of time. At this time, several members of the ruling council are adamantly against your Navy's presence in our waters."

"I'm sorry to hear that." Janessa felt the weight of disappointment fall straight to her stomach. She studied Stefano for a moment, recognizing the truth of his words. Showing him the proposal could hardly cause any negative ramifications, especially since Garrett had already read through most of it. She picked through her notes until she located her copy.

Stefano took it from her and flipped through the pages, scanning the needs of the US Navy as well as Janessa's assessment of Meridia's naval facility in Bellamo. Minutes stretched out in silence until Stefano once again looked up, his expression unreadable. "Where did you receive your intelligence about our naval base?"

"It's primarily guesswork." Janessa shrugged her shoulders. "I've ridden down there several times during my stay, and of course I can see the types of vessels it services by looking out my window."

"You guess very well." Stefano stood, the report still in his hand. "I'd like to keep this."

Reluctantly, Janessa nodded. She knew it wasn't protocol, but she also knew that getting Stefano on her side before the proposal was formally introduced could help things go more smoothly. "I suppose that would be okay."

With a curt nod, Stefano stepped back from the table and headed for the door.

Janessa watched him go, wondering what his impressions of the proposal were. Dismissing work for a moment, she gathered her things and made her way to the door. She stepped into the hall, nearly colliding with Garrett.

Garrett reached out and cupped her elbow in his hand to prevent her from tumbling backward. "Janessa." His eyes swept down, taking in the dark business suit she wore.

Disconcerted by the warmth of his fingers on her skin, she took a moment to steady herself before speaking. "I'm sorry. I didn't see you."

"Were you using the library?" Garrett asked.

"Yes, actually." Janessa let out a little sigh as he released her and dropped his hand back to his side. "I had a meeting regarding my naval proposal, and your father was kind enough to arrange for me to have it here."

"How did it go?"

"I think it could best be described as political." Janessa shook her head and let out a short laugh. "It's never easy trying to please everyone."

Garrett smiled and nodded in understanding.

Janessa motioned down the hall. "I should go write my report while it's still fresh in my mind."

"I thought you had a fitting with my mother's designer this afternoon."

"Are you sure?" Janessa asked, unable to recall scheduling such a thing. She certainly didn't wish to be tortured with actual dressmakers' pins after sitting on virtual pins and needles for the last two hours. Before Garrett could answer, his mother approached.

"There you are." Queen Marta motioned to the hallway behind her. "Signora Vorneaux is waiting."

"Forgive me, Your Majesty, but I don't recall having an appointment with her today."

"Of course not." Marta gave her a knowing smile. "If I had told you about it, you would have found a reason why you couldn't make it."

Janessa opened her mouth to deny it but promptly decided that any reply she could formulate would be inadequate, since the queen's assumption was correct, and they both knew it. She glanced over at Garrett and noticed him grinning.

"You try standing around for an hour waiting for someone to stick a pin in you," Janessa muttered.

Garrett just chuckled. "Enjoy your afternoon, darling."

chapter 16

Garrett stood in front of the framed mirror in his sitting room, adjusting the jacket on his dress uniform. The dinner party this evening had been a surprise to him, and he was already regretting not escaping the palace while he still had the chance. Had it not been for his mother's insistence that she needed Janessa for her final fitting Wednesday morning, he would have made excuses for both of them to leave for the chateau hours earlier.

Since announcing their engagement, Garrett felt like he had hardly seen Janessa except at social functions. Her days were filled with meetings with his mother, fittings, and conference calls with government officials from her country. Of course, he was so busy himself that he probably wouldn't have even realized how busy she was had he not sought her out each day in his spare moments.

His own days had been spent in meetings, among them a briefing given to him and Stefano by the security staff about the embassy bombing investigation. The findings that no known terrorist group had been responsible for the bombing had created a whole new set of problems. Fighting a known quantity was so much easier than analyzing the unknown.

A knock came at the door, and Garrett called out, "Come in."

Stefano stepped through the door, closing it behind him.

Garrett glanced his brother and shook his head. "If I had known Lady Renault was among the invited guests tonight, I would have left for the chateau this afternoon instead of waiting until tomorrow."

"I don't know what you're complaining about." Stefano leaned against an armchair, watching his brother's reflection in the mirror. "Cynthia Renault is young, beautiful—"

"Lying, deceitful," Garrett continued for him. "All she cares about is how she can improve her social standing."

"Now, is that any way to talk about a lady?"

The corner of Garrett's mouth quirked up. "I've always found her title somewhat ironic."

"Well, you shouldn't have to worry about her tonight, in any case." Stefano shrugged. "Now that you've found the woman you're going to marry."

"Let's hope Cynthia believes the engagement is real." Garrett had dated the woman only twice. Those two dates had been just enough for Cynthia to set her sights on becoming a princess and make Garrett want to run in the opposite direction every time she was near.

Stefano chuckled. "If this engagement were any more real, you and Janessa would already be on your honeymoon."

Garrett's heartbeat accelerated as he turned to face Stefano. "What are you talking about?"

"I'm talking about the fact that you've fallen in love with our American spy."

Garrett opened his mouth to refute his brother's observation but couldn't form any words. Reality seeped through him along with a sense of awe at how quickly he had come to love Janessa. Not wanting to lie to his brother, and certain that Stefano wouldn't believe him anyway, Garrett said nothing.

With a smile, Stefano continued. "I have to say that I was a little worried at first, but now that I've spent some time around her, I think she's a fine choice."

"Well, I'm so pleased to know you approve." Sarcasm coated Garrett's voice, nearly disguising his emotions. "And what do Mother and Father think?"

"You don't really think that Mother would personally oversee Janessa's wardrobe if she didn't like her, do you?"

The tension eased out of Garrett as he laughed at the truth of his brother's statement. "Mother doesn't like fittings any more than Janessa does."

Stefano stood and motioned to the door. "Come on. Let's go escort your fiancée to dinner, and we'll see how she handles the competition."

* * *

Lady Cynthia Renault stood in the center of the parlor, her sable hair flowing freely past her shoulders. Her siren—red dress dipped dangerously low in the front, held up by two thin straps. Beside her, Councilman Hennero laughed at something she said.

Standing between Garrett and Stefano, Janessa took one look at Cynthia and wondered just how long Garrett had dated the woman. She was definitely a head turner. And everything about her dress and her posture screamed that she wasn't about to watch Garrett marry someone else.

For about two seconds, Janessa was able to convince herself that it didn't matter who this woman was. Stepping closer to Garrett, she asked, "Did you date her long?"

Surprise flickered over Garrett's face as Stefano's laughter rang out.

"We went out twice years ago." Garrett tucked Janessa's hand through the crook of his arm and leaned closer. "And I have regretted it ever since."

"Ah." Janessa smoothed the skirt of her gown of shimmering gold, the first of Signora Vorneaux's finished products.

Garrett leaned down and kissed her cheek. "Trust me, darling. You are the only one for me." With that he moved forward to greet their guests.

Janessa let herself be led into the parlor and felt the attention shift toward them. The woman in the red dress studied her openly, and Janessa deliberately straightened her shoulders, fighting against her insecurities. She let Garrett's words replay in her mind. He couldn't mean it, of course, that she was really the one for him. For tonight, though, she decided she would let herself pretend she belonged at his side.

Music played softly in the background, and the scents of varying perfumes mixed into a completely unique smell. Garrett worked his way through the crowd with ease. He laughed at the right times, charmed the women, and answered questions diplomatically. Janessa tried to follow his lead, reminding herself to relax.

Janessa had already met a few of the guests in attendance, though many faces were new. Even a few dignitaries from the US Embassy were present. When she and Garrett finally circled to the woman in the red dress, she could feel Garrett tense.

"Your Highness." The woman curtsied and offered Garrett a sultry smile. "I was hoping you would be here tonight."

"Lady Cynthia Renault, may I present my fiancée, Janessa Rogers."

"Oh, of course." Cynthia laughed, her voice sharp. "The American."

"So pleased to meet you." Janessa smiled, ignoring the implied insult.

Cynthia's eyebrows rose, revealing her surprise that Janessa spoke Italian. Now she focused her attention on Janessa. "Garrett and I are old friends. You don't mind if I steal him for a minute, do you? I really need to speak with him in private."

"I'm sorry, but we are overdue in greeting his parents," Janessa declined without missing a beat. "I'm sure you understand."

Garrett followed her lead, stepping away from Cynthia. "Enjoy your evening."

Janessa lowered her voice as they were swallowed up by the crowd. "Where are your parents?"

"Here comes Mother now." Garrett slowed as his mother approached. He leaned down and kissed his mother's cheek, smiling as he watched her greet Janessa warmly.

"My dear, you look stunning." Queen Marta took both of Janessa's hands in hers.

"Thank you. So do you."

"Garrett, it's rather warm in here. Why don't you take Janessa for a walk in the gardens?"

"Mother, that's a splendid idea." Garrett motioned to the terrace doors. "I don't believe you've seen the gardens at night yet."

Janessa let herself be led along, stopping briefly to exchange greetings with Garrett's father. Several guests were also enjoying the night air. Garrett continued down the wide steps and crossed under an ivy-covered trellis into the garden.

"I suppose I should apologize for shutting down Lady Renault in there," Janessa began.

Garrett smiled in response. "Or I could thank you for sparing me from inventing an excuse."

Janessa shrugged. "I didn't think it would look right if she managed to find time alone with you."

"So you were just worried about appearances?"

"In your world, appearances often matter more than reality."

"And in yours," Garrett conceded, continuing farther into the gardens. "It seems like I've hardly seen you the past couple of days."

"We've both been busy."

Garrett stopped and turned toward her. "I've missed you."

"I—" Janessa stopped herself, appalled that she had nearly admitted to missing him as well. "I don't understand you."

"I think you're afraid to understand me," Garrett corrected. "Is it so hard to believe that I have feelings for you?"

"Garrett." Janessa put her hand on his chest as he edged closer. She searched his face, for the first time allowing herself to accept the sincerity she saw there. She fought against her own feelings and tried to make a stand. "Don't you understand? You've got to stop this. I can't do my job like this."

"I care about you, Janessa, and I believe you care about me. I've thought about this a lot, and I don't think we will endanger anyone's security by acknowledging our feelings for each other." Garrett toyed with a curl that had fallen onto her cheek. His voice lowered as he added, "Please give us a chance."

Garrett leaned down to kiss her, but before his lips touched hers, the ground rocked beneath them, and fire shot up into the sky from the village below.

"What was that?" Garrett turned, seeing the flames near the coastline.

"Make sure your family is okay," Janessa said as she moved with him to the front of the palace.

"Where are you going?" Garrett grabbed her arm as she turned toward the garage.

"To the village." Janessa managed two steps before Garrett stopped her.

"You aren't going down there by yourself." Garrett motioned to one of the valets, instructing him to retrieve a car from the garage. "I'm coming with you."

"Garrett, you need to stay here until the area is secured," Janessa insisted.

"The prince's fiancée wouldn't run down to the village by herself to see a fire."

Janessa recognized the logic in his argument. After a brief internal debate, she motioned to his bodyguard to follow as they dashed off to the village together.

chapter 17

Thick smoke hung in the village, making navigating the roads difficult. Another explosion rocked the ground as they made their way toward the market district along the seashore.

By the time they arrived, three fire trucks were already on the scene attempting to control the blaze. A two-story building was engulfed in flames, and the firefighters were able to do little more than try to contain the fire.

"Do you know what was in this building?" Janessa pointed at the fiery structure as Garrett parked at the edge of the crowd that had formed.

"It was a gas station for boats, if I'm not mistaken." Garrett climbed out of the car, noticing his bodyguards quickly approaching.

"You should wait here until the area is secured," Janessa said as she scrambled out of the car behind him.

Silently he shook his head and waded through the onlookers and thick smoke toward the barrier several policemen had established. The heat grew more intense with each step, as did the noise from the fire and the crowd.

One of the policemen saw Garrett approach and bowed before moving to intercept him. "I'm sorry, Your Highness, but you need to stay back. It's not safe yet."

"Was anyone inside?"

"We think the owner was. That's his wife over there." He pointed at an ambulance attendant trying to console a middle-aged woman nearby. Her face was stained with tears and soot.

"I want to talk to her." Garrett nodded toward the woman. "Do you know her name?"

"Signora Manero."

Janessa slipped her hand into Garrett's and gave it a comforting squeeze. "I'll come with you."

Garrett nodded. When the woman saw him approach, she blinked hard as though trying to ascertain if the prince really was coming toward her. Despite the tears streaming down her face, she dipped into a curtsey. "Your Highness."

"Signora Manero, I am so sorry for your loss." Garrett pulled a handkerchief from his pocket and passed it to her. He led her to the back of the ambulance, then sat next to her and held her hand as she continued to weep.

When at last the woman's tears slowed, Garrett asked quietly, "Can you tell me what happened?"

"I went to my sister's. I go to her house for dinner when my husband has business meetings." She wiped her eyes and took a deep breath before continuing. "We heard an explosion, and when we got here, everything was burning."

"Did he often have meetings at night?" Janessa asked, stepping out of the background for the first time.

"Once a month. Always the first Tuesday."

Garrett glanced down at Janessa, cueing in to her suspicions. "Do you know who he met with?"

"He said he was meeting with his suppliers." The woman paused, her eyes lighting with sudden clarity. "The strange thing is, they didn't look like they worked in the gas industry. Last month I forgot my purse at the station, and when I returned for it, my husband was talking to two men and a woman. Both of the men were wearing expensive suits, and I remember thinking how young the woman was to be at the meeting." The tears started flowing again. "Alberto was upset that I had interrupted."

"Don't think about that now," Janessa said, her voice soothing. "Is your sister here?"

The ambulance attendant stepped forward. "She is calling Signora Manero's children."

Garrett spoke to the ambulance attendant now. "You will see to her needs?"

"Yes, Your Highness."

Garrett conveyed his condolences once more before leading Janessa back to where he had left the car. He vaguely noticed his security men standing a short distance away. "I want to go down to the beach. We might be able to see more from there."

Janessa nodded, shifting around the barricade. They made their way between a clothing store and a restaurant down to the seawall. The flames were no longer visible, now smoldering beneath the constant spray of water. For the first time, they were able to see two boats that were also on fire and a fireboat that was moving in to contend with the smaller blaze.

"Do you think it was an accident?" Garrett asked, his eyes burning from the smoke.

"It's too soon to tell." Janessa shrugged. "The explosions could have been caused by something igniting the gasoline."

"Or someone could have detonated the gasoline."

"No one will be able to determine anything until morning," Janessa said. "We just need to make sure the area is secure, in case there's any evidence to find."

"The police will see to it," Garrett agreed.

"I know it's a difficult time for Signora Manero, but we also need the descriptions of the people who were meeting with Signore Manero."

Garrett nodded in agreement. "It looks like the police are working on that right now. I should get you back to the palace."

Janessa started to protest, then seemed to think better of it and sighed. "Do you think it would be okay if we came back in the morning before we left for the chateau?"

"I'll check with the fire chief before we leave." Garrett took her hand to lead her back to the car.

He opened her car door, helping her inside before moving to speak with the fire chief. A moment later he returned and climbed in behind the wheel. "The fire chief said we can come back tomorrow. They will start their investigation as soon as they have enough light."

"I hope they'll be able to find some answers," Janessa said, glancing back at the smoldering fire.

"Me too," Garrett agreed before lapsing into silence for the rest of the drive.

As he finished parking next to the garage, Janessa reached over and laid a hand on his.

"Are you okay?" Concern filled her voice.

Garrett looked down at her hand covering his. It was a simple gesture and surprisingly soothing. "Not really, but I think you understand." He climbed from the car and went around to open her door. "When something like this happens, I feel so helpless."

"It's difficult, isn't it? Having the responsibility for so many people and knowing that there are times when nothing you do will protect them." Janessa stepped out of the car, and the two of them started toward the house.

"I should have been able to do something."

"You comforted a widow when she needed comfort the most." Janessa took his hand and squeezed it. "There was nothing more you could do."

"We have to find out who did this," Garrett insisted.

"We will." Janessa nodded. "When the smoke settles, we'll find out exactly what happened."

* * *

Janessa packed the last of her things and zipped her suitcase shut. She had hardly slept due to the events of the previous evening tumbling through her head. The gas station fire should be a routine matter for the local authorities to handle, but the possibility of its being connected with the embassy bombing nagged at her. She was certain Garrett felt it too.

She tried to concentrate on what needed to be done and how her government might be able to help. It was easier than thinking about what had happened right before the fire.

Dropping onto the window seat, she stared out at the cloudy day. Garrett's words kept replaying in her mind. Each time she wondered if she was just reading too much into them. He'd said he had feelings for her, but she still wondered exactly what that meant. Could it be possible, she asked herself, for Garrett to fall in love with her? Or had he said the same thing to the dozens of other women he had been photographed with over the years? He seemed so sincere that she was beginning to believe that his feelings for her might actually be genuine.

Wearily, she leaned her head against the window. The real question was, what was she going to do about her own feelings? Everything in her demanded that she settle for nothing less than a temple marriage. Her heart simply wasn't listening.

A knock on the door sent her heart racing. Expecting to see Garrett on the other side, she pulled the door open to find the queen there instead.

"Are you all packed?" Queen Marta asked as she entered the room.

"Yes. I was going to stop in the village this morning before we leave to see if there have been any new developments."

"Garrett already left with Frederick Donovan, our country's director of security." Marta took a seat and motioned for Janessa to do the same. "Since Garrett has already met the widow, he wanted to stay for a day or two until everything settles."

Annoyance and frustration shot through Janessa. Garrett had left without her. "Perhaps I should postpone my appointment with the caterers," she suggested.

"No." Queen Marta shook her head. "I know you want to be part of the investigation, but we need you at the chateau. I'm not happy that Garrett is insisting on working with Frederick on this, and I certainly don't want the press to see both of you involved. Remember, if the public sees you going about your duties as hostess, no one will suspect that you are anything but what you appear to be."

Janessa closed her eyes a moment before nodding in agreement.

"Good," Marta said as a knock came at the door. "Now that we have that settled, let's get through this fitting so you can be on your way."

Janessa sighed. "I'd rather dig through ashes."

"So would I."

* * *

Janessa moved up the steps of the chateau as Martino opened the front door. As always, his tone was formal and aloof when he spoke to her. "Welcome back."

"Thank you, Martino." Janessa walked into the parlor, for once relieved to know that the staff would see to her bags. "Have the caterers arrived yet?"

"They are in the dining room," he told her. "Today you will finalize the menu, so they brought samples."

Wearily, she leaned against the arm of a sofa. "Could you please ask Patrice to join me? I have the queen's notes, but I'd like to have Patrice's opinion as well."

"Of course." Martino took a step toward the door before turning back to her. Surprisingly, his tone softened fractionally as he asked, "Are you all right?"

Janessa nodded and gave him a weary smile. "I'm just tired."

Five minutes later, she no longer had time to be tired. The caterers bustled around, offering her tastes of various items, noting how much should be prepared, and determining how and when each item would be served. Patrice, who thankfully was well experienced in both protocol and menu selection, was a tremendous help.

Two hours later, when the caterers left, Janessa turned to Patrice. "Thank you so much for your help. I never could have done it without you. I guess making these decisions is just business as usual for you."

"This is the first time, actually," Patrice told her with a smile. "Never before have I been consulted on the menu."

Janessa looked at her, surprised. "I suppose the queen didn't want to pull you away from your other duties. As long as you're willing, I have every intention of relying on your expertise."

"It's my pleasure." Patrice moved to the door. "Do you want me to fix you some lunch?"

"I don't think I could eat another bite," Janessa said, laying a hand on her stomach. She lowered her voice and peeked through the door to make sure the caterers were indeed gone. "By the way, I much prefer your quiche Florentine."

Patrice laughed. "So do I."

chapter 18

Rain drizzled down onto the blackened earth by the seashore. Garrett stood beneath an umbrella, listening to the fire investigator's initial report. Arson was not a common crime in Meridia, but the investigator's findings left little doubt. He was certain that the fire had been deliberate.

The positive press from the day before about his engagement to Janessa had taken a back seat to last night's tragedy. Today's headlines were filled with news of the gas station fire as well as reminders of the embassy bombing two weeks before. With the gala less than a month away, security concerns were once again increasing.

The fire the night before had originated at one of the gasoline holding tanks. Records indicated that Alberto Manero had passed a safety inspection six weeks earlier. The possibility of an accidental fire starting there was basically nonexistent.

A visit to Manero's widow had revealed minimal information about the people Manero had met with. His wife had described the woman as young and beautiful with dark hair. The men had worn expensive suits, and one was middle-aged while the other she guessed to be a bit younger. Beyond that she could remember little except that they had been meeting on the first Tuesday of each month for the past several years.

Neighboring shopkeepers had not noticed anyone near the gas station the night before, and only one body had been recovered from the fire. Some subtle probing into Manero's bank accounts revealed nothing unusual. By the same token, no record of any consistent business dealings existed either. His supplier had been the same since before he had taken over the business from his father. His clients were simply the residents and tourists in the village. The people he had been meeting with each month were a complete mystery.

After the investigator finished briefing Garrett and Frederick Donovan, Meridia's director of security, Garrett instructed his driver to take him to the American Embassy, where he asked to meet with Tony Coletto. According to Frederick, Coletto was the man the Americans had sent to investigate the bombings. Their sources revealed that Coletto had been with the CIA for the majority of his working career, specializing in terrorist activity.

As soon as Garrett was shown into Coletto's office, he got straight to the point. "I hope your government can help us with a small matter in the embassy bombing investigation."

"What do you need?" Coletto asked, leaning forward in his seat, looking puzzled.

"I want you to see if you can find any offshore bank accounts for Alberto Manero."

"Forgive me, but I wasn't aware that you were involved in the embassy bombing investigation. I have been dealing with your director of security up until now," Coletto said.

"I realize that. In fact, I met with Frederick this morning regarding the fire last night. He agrees that this information may be crucial to the investigation," Garrett told him.

"You can't possibly think that a gas station fire has anything to do with the embassy bombing."

"I don't know." Garrett shrugged. "I just know that this village hasn't had a fire in nearly ten years. Now we've had two in less than a month."

"Do you know how the fire started?"

"It started at one of the holding tanks." Garrett tapped a finger on the arm of his chair, studying Coletto. "I looked over the reports on Manero's bank account records. Something doesn't add up, particularly the reason behind a so-called business meeting he had each month. I can only assume that he was involved in something besides selling gasoline."

"I'll send this request to the CIA. It may take some time, but we'll do what we can."

"Thank you." Garrett nodded. "Have you had any new developments on the bombing?"

Coletto shook his head. "Logically, a terrorist group should be responsible. Unfortunately, we can't find any evidence to substantiate that theory. In fact, each day we seem to uncover more evidence against the possibility."

"Who would gain from the mere appearance of a terrorist attack?" Garrett wondered.

"If you figure that out, let me know."

* * *

"Who authorized you to discuss our naval base with the royal family?" The US ambassador's voice boomed over the phone line, and Janessa held the phone an inch from her ear to protect her hearing. She'd been doing so well managing to stay out of trouble since arriving in Meridia. That was before Stefano had decided to have a chat with Aaron Mitchell, the US ambassador in Meridia.

"Sir, I did not engage in any negotiations nor official discussions with the royal family," Janessa said, trying to keep her voice calm. "It was an unplanned disclosure but truly seemed to be in our country's best interest."

"It's not your place to judge that. You were out of line, Rogers. I might even go so far as to say it was a complete breach of security. If I have my way, you will be on your way home before the day is over."

"Surely you don't think that's wise," Janessa managed, trying to ignore the panic rising in her stomach. "My position is far too public for me to leave, and I believe the royal family wishes for me to complete my duties here."

"No one is irreplaceable," Ambassador Mitchell insisted loudly right before hanging up the phone.

Wearily, Janessa set down the phone and rubbed her fingers against the throbbing at her temples. She knew she should go talk to Levi about a backup plan in case the ambassador was successful in sending her home, but she couldn't bring herself to face the possibility quite yet.

She considered wryly what Garrett would think if she were sent home. This would be the second time since she met him. She hoped he would understand that, once again, her actions didn't warrant such extreme punishment. She was still annoyed that he had gone to meet with the fire inspector without her, but she pushed that aside and picked up the phone. Though Garrett had given her his phone numbers before she arrived in Meridia, she had never before considered using them.

The phone rang several times before Garrett answered with a breathless hello.

"Garrett? It's Janessa," she started, annoyed when her voice wavered. She took a deep breath and forced the words out. "I was hoping you could help me with something."

"Is everything okay?"

"Not exactly." She took another deep breath. "The US ambassador here wants to send me home." Before he could ask any questions, she rushed on. "Apparently your brother commented on my naval proposal, and the ambassador believes that I have breached security."

"That's ridiculous!" Garrett insisted. "My family has already been briefed several times regarding the US naval base."

"I know." Janessa made a frustrated gesture with her free hand. "Garrett, I'm not sure what to do. I don't know how someone else could replace me at this point."

"Janessa, no one is going to replace you," Garrett assured her. "I'll take care of it."

"Thank you." Janessa let herself slide down onto the sofa as she cradled the phone between her shoulder and her ear. "I'm sorry I had to bother you with this."

"It's not a bother. I was going to call you anyway to let you know I got the fire chief's report today," he told her. "The evidence suggests that it was arson."

"You already suspected as much," Janessa commented, fighting back the frustration that she wasn't able to be more involved. "Are there any leads as to who is responsible?"

"Not yet. We have a couple of suspicions we're looking into," Garrett said. "I'll give you the details when I see you."

"Do you know when you're coming back yet?"

"Tomorrow, I hope," he replied. A bit of mischief laced his voice when he added, "By the way, my mother offered to send her designer out to the chateau. She thought you should probably have another fitting or two for your ball gown."

"Maybe I should let the ambassador send me home after all."

Garrett's laughter rang through the line. "If something comes up, I'll give you a call. Otherwise, I'll see you tomorrow."

"Alright, I'll see you then."

* * *

The instant Garrett hung up the phone, it rang again. "Hello?"

"I can't believe you're finally home." Tim's voice came over the line. "I've been trying to get a hold of you for days."

"Things have been pretty hectic around here." Garrett settled back into his favorite chair. He ran through his schedule in his head and decided he could spare a few minutes.

"I know. I've been reading all about it," Tim began. "Are you really engaged? You never even mentioned this girl before."

"I ran into her in Caracas." Garrett chose his words carefully. He hated to mislead his friend, but he couldn't risk breaching security, especially over the phone. "We hadn't seen each other for some time."

"I can't believe you're getting married," Tim said and then hesitated. "How does she feel about you getting baptized?"

"I haven't talked to her about it yet."

"What?" Tim interrupted. "Have you changed your mind?"

"No, nothing like that." Garrett laughed at the sudden concern in his friend's voice. "I promise she'll support my decision. She's Mormon."

"Garrett, that's great!" Tim's tone changed instantly. "Have you decided on a date yet?"

"We haven't gotten that far," Garrett told him evasively. Desperate to change the subject, he asked, "What ever happened with the FBI? Did you get the job?"

"I start training in two months," Tim told him cheerfully. "I was hoping to start bringing in a paycheck earlier, but at least this way we'll have time to come to Meridia the week before the gala and do some sightseeing."

"That's great." Garrett stood up as a knock sounded at the door. "I've got to get going, but I'll give you a call when I have a little more time."

"In other words, I'll talk to you when I get there in a couple weeks." Tim laughed. "Take care of yourself."

"You too." Garrett disconnected the phone and opened the door to find his brother on the other side.

"I thought you'd want to see this." Stefano handed him a thin file. His face was serious. "It just arrived today."

Flipping it open, Garrett drew a quick breath, and his vision blurred with fury and terror. His eyes darted up to his brother, who was still standing in the doorway. "I can't let this happen."

"You know the family will support whatever you decide," Stefano said soberly.

Garrett just nodded as his brother turned to walk away, leaving him with the terrifying images and the fears they invoked.

chapter 19

Janessa stepped outside, relieved to escape the chateau. She had met with the florists that morning, and it had taken three phone calls to the queen to settle everything for the gala. Thank goodness Queen Marta was so patient with the details. She smiled as she thought of the way Marta could shift from being a queen to a mother in an instant. In business matters, Marta was like a general ordering troops into action. When speaking of her family, however, her voice turned soft, and Janessa suspected that her happiness was deeply entrenched in the well-being of her husband and sons.

Janessa took a deep breath of fresh air and considered her next task. The extra security measures were in place, but she needed to double check all of them. A smile lit her face when she saw a van pulling into the drive. Alan Neisler waved from the driver's side window as he pulled to a stop.

"I was wondering when you were going to show up."

"Did you miss me?" Alan laughed as he stepped out of the car. He took a look at the chateau and let out a low whistle. "Pretty fancy."

Janessa laughed. "Wait until you taste the food."

"I love it here already," Alan replied. He lowered his voice and added, "I even remembered my autograph book."

Janessa narrowed her eyes. "Don't you dare ask Garrett for an autograph."

"Garrett, is it?" One eyebrow lifted. "You're on a first name basis, I see."

"Don't start with me." Janessa sighed, wishing she had more time to talk to her friend. "I hate to put you straight to work, but I'd like you to do an initial sweep of the chateau. I'm going to go out for a ride to see if the new motion detectors can track me."

Alan nodded as he led the way to the back of the van. He opened the back to reveal his partner, Max, a four-year-old German shepherd. "Let me give Max a few minutes to stretch his legs, and then we'll get started."

"Sounds good," Janessa agreed as Martino walked up beside them. She turned to address him. "Martino, this is Alan Neisler. Can you please show him to his quarters?"

"Of course, signorina."

"I'll see you both later." She headed for the stables and found Paolo inside brushing down one of the horses.

"I was wondering if you would find time to come to the stables today." Paolo motioned for her to follow him and led her deeper inside. He stopped and motioned to the tall, white Arabian that was favored by Prince Stefano. "This gentleman needs some time out in the open. Prince Stefano calls him 'Lightning.'"

"He's a beauty." Janessa took the lead rope from the hook just outside of the stall and pulled open the stall door. With calm efficiency she clipped the rope to the horse's halter and led him to the tack room so she could saddle him.

"Keep your wits about you with this one," Paolo warned her. "He likes to have his own way."

"So do I." Janessa laughed. "I'm sure we'll get along fine."

Janessa retrieved the saddle that Paolo now kept reserved for her. Out of habit, she checked the length of the stirrups. After sharing equipment with five siblings growing up, she was still surprised to find anything the way she left it. After slipping the bridle on, she led the horse outside to mount.

Lightning pranced from side to side under the weight of his rider for a moment before settling down. Janessa patted him on the neck and urged him toward the hills. Moving as one, horse and rider climbed up a rise and disappeared among the trees.

* * *

Garrett entered the chateau through the private entrance and headed straight to Janessa's room. The threats against his family, which continued to arrive at the palace daily, now had a new twist. Janessa was among those being threatened. His stomach sickened as he thought of the latest threat against her, and he knew he wouldn't rest until she was safely home in her own country.

The demand was simple enough: don't grant the United States access to Meridian waters—or Janessa would be killed. Who would benefit from such a demand was still a mystery, but Garrett didn't think about that now. All he could think about was how to get Janessa to leave Meridia.

He knocked on the door and waited impatiently before he pounded his fist against the door in three quick raps. Frustrated that she wasn't there, he turned and stalked down the hall, his irritation compounded by stress and lack of sleep. The last two days had been grueling as he continued to face his country's vulnerability. Despite a strong Navy, a well-trained police force, and efficient emergency personnel, someone was causing destruction in Meridia, and no one knew why.

With his thoughts still on Janessa, Garrett made his way down to the parlor, where he found Martino instructing one of the maids.

"Where is she?" Garrett demanded, his tone sharper than he had intended.

Martino's eyebrows rose, but his tone was businesslike when he spoke. "Signorina Rogers left the chateau over an hour ago. She said something about taking one of the horses out for a ride." He motioned down the hall. "The new sensors are in place. I believe the security guards are tracking her movements."

"Well, let's see if they know where she is then." Garrett followed Martino to the security office. When he stepped inside, he noticed the extra panel of sensors in addition to the monitors feeding visual images to the security office.

"Good afternoon, Your Highness," the guard greeted him. Beside the guard, Levi Marin was fiddling with some controls.

"Do you know where Signorina Rogers is?" Garrett asked, trying to control his impatience.

Levi glanced up at him as he answered. "The last time she triggered a sensor, she was headed east toward the naval base."

"How long ago was that?"

"About twenty minutes ago." Levi looked at him apologetically. "I've already sent two guards out to look for her."

Garrett sensed the concern in Levi's voice and was afraid to ask whether he was worried about Janessa or a faulty security system. "She's alone?"

"Yes, Your Highness."

The muscle in Garrett's jaw tensed, but he said nothing as he nodded and headed back down the hall. He could already be too late. For all he knew, someone had gotten to her before he arrived.

His eyes were burning and dry as he pushed open the front door. He squinted beneath the noonday sun at a horse and rider galloping on the beach. As they moved closer, he realized the horse was one of their own, the stallion his brother had acquired several years before.

His relief was instant when he saw the red hair. He took a moment and just watched as Janessa continued past the chateau and headed into the trees near the stables. Several minutes later, Garrett found Janessa still astride his brother's horse. Swamped with relief and concern, he struggled to control his emotions. "Janessa."

The horse sidestepped, forcing Janessa to keep her attention on her mount rather than on Garrett.

Paolo moved forward to take the reins while Janessa dismounted. He looked from Janessa to the prince, bowing slightly. "I'll cool down the horse, signorina."

"Thank you, Paolo." Janessa nodded. She ran her fingers through her hair and turned toward Garrett. Her eyes widened when he closed the distance between them in two long strides and pulled her into his arms.

Her arms came around him instinctively as she looked up at him, concerned. "Is everything okay? Your family?"

"Everyone's fine. I need to talk to you." He skimmed a knuckle down her cheek, just staring for a moment before he took her hand and led her down the path.

When they reached the gardens, Garrett slowed and turned her to face him. A million thoughts raced through his mind, but overshadowing them all was his concern for her safety. "Janessa, I'm sending you back to the United States."

Her face went white. She looked as though he had slapped her. She pulled her hand from his and took a step back. "I beg your pardon?"

"You fly out first thing tomorrow morning."

She took another step back and created more than just physical distance between them. Her tone was cool when she spoke. "May I ask why? I thought you wanted me to stay. You said I could finish my job here."

"This has nothing to do with your job and everything to do with you." Garrett's voice sharpened, and he ran a hand through his thick, black hair. "We have received more threats against my family. You have also been threatened."

"I see." Janessa tilted her head, her eyes narrowing. "Will you be leaving as well?"

"Of course not."

"And your family?"

"We live here."

"For now, I live here too." Janessa turned to walk away, only to be whirled back around when Garrett grabbed her arm.

"Don't you understand? You have to go!"

"I won't go." Janessa's voice was calm, but fury vibrated through each word. "I won't be chased away any more than you will."

Garrett clenched his teeth. He watched her storm away before turning to look out over the Mediterranean. Waves of emotions rolled over him—annoyance, frustration, and the underlying fear that she would fall victim to the violence threatening his family.

He should have known she wouldn't leave. Her sense of duty was every bit as strong as his own, and he knew he couldn't leave Meridia right now regardless of the threats, not even for Janessa. He spotted one of his bodyguards nearby, and an idea began to form. If Janessa refused to leave, he would do everything in his power to make sure she was protected.

* * *

Janessa stopped outside of the security office and took a deep breath. She wouldn't be able to do anyone any good if she let her anger get in the way. Pushing the door open, she saw the surprise on the security guard's face and the frustration on Levi's.

"If you're surprised to see me, this isn't good news."

Levi nodded to the guard. "Why don't you take a break and let everyone know we found her. I'll run the activity report for the past two hours, and when you get back, we'll see if we can fix the problem."

"Thanks." The guard nodded and exited the room.

As soon as the guard was gone, Levi punched a button and paper started feeding through the printer. He turned to Janessa. "The last time you set off a sensor was half an hour ago. We've got a big gap somewhere."

"That would have been about the time I got down to the beach." Janessa nodded. "We should probably post guards down there until we figure out how to compensate."

Levi nodded in agreement. "I'll print out an extra copy of the activity report so you can take one with you."

"Thanks," Janessa said as she noticed Garrett on the monitor displaying the garden entrance. He looked so serious as he stared out over the water. The armor was back, she realized—the same impenetrable shield he'd carried with him when she had first met him.

Slowly, her fury went from full boil to simmer as she watched him. She was surprised that, despite her annoyance, she wanted to comfort him and help soothe away the worry. At the moment, however, she doubted he would let her. He looked so unapproachable standing there, so royal, so alone.

"Here you are." Levi handed the report to Janessa, snapping her back to the present.

"Thanks. I'll touch base with you in the morning." Janessa took the printout and headed for her quarters.

Once inside her sitting room, she dropped down onto the sofa and scanned the report. She shook her head in frustration as she flipped through the pages. She could track exactly where she had ridden that afternoon, right up until she disappeared from the sensors and penetrated the chateau's security. No one had even known where she was until Garrett had seen her. At night, she could have slipped into the chateau completely undetected.

She moved to the desk and retrieved an overhead photo of the chateau that Martino had given her. With a sigh, she pushed Garrett from her mind and got back to work.

chapter 20

Garrett knocked on Janessa's door twice that evening before she finally answered it. Her hair was still damp from a recent shower, and her feet were bare. Her blue jeans were comfortably faded, and the sleeves of her button-up shirt were rolled past the elbows. Despite her casual attire, her voice was formally aloof when she asked, "May I help you?"

"I came to escort you to dinner."

Confusion flickered over her face. "I wasn't aware we had dinner plans."

"You were working, and I didn't want to disturb you." Garrett held out his hand. "You need to eat something."

Janessa glanced down at her clothes. "I need to change."

"There's no need," Garrett insisted.

She gave a little sigh and slipped on her sandals by the door. Reluctantly, she followed him down the hall. He pushed his door open to reveal a table set for two. A bud vase held a single red rose, and two slim candles were waiting to be lit.

When Garrett and Janessa entered the room, a member of the kitchen staff lit the candles and set appetizers on the table.

Garrett pulled out a chair for Janessa, pleased that she sat without argument, even if she did look disgruntled. Once he was seated across from her, he nodded to the servant. "That will be all for now, Brenna."

As soon as they were alone, Janessa spoke. "Okay, Garrett. What's your agenda here?"

"I'm not intending to seduce you, if that's what you mean," he said teasingly before taking a more serious tone. "I just wanted to spend some time with you. Do you mind?"

Her shoulders lifted as she considered his question. "Perhaps I do."

"You're still angry."

"I'm trying hard not to be." Janessa reached for her glass of water, her fingers fiddling with the stem of the goblet rather than picking it up. She let out a little sigh and lifted her eyes to meet his. "I realize you're used to people obeying your commands, but, as I've told you before, I'm not one of your subjects, and I don't appreciate being treated like one."

"I'm worried," Garrett said. "I couldn't bear it if something happened to you."

"How do you think I feel?" Janessa blinked against tears that suddenly threatened. "Every day I know that if I don't do my job, I could lose you or someone close to you. And even if I do everything I can think of, that possibility still exists."

Garrett considered her wording. Was it possible that her feelings mirrored his own? He glanced toward his room and thought of the Book of Mormon hidden in the drawer of his nightstand. Looking back at her, he chose his words carefully. "Things are going to be difficult for the next few weeks. I guess we both need to have faith that the Lord will help us through it."

"Believe me, I pray for His help night and day."

"So do I." His voice was barely more than a whisper. He cleared his throat against the emotions welling up inside him, both his growing love for Janessa and the fear that went with it. As much as he understood her desire to keep a professional distance between them, he knew he had already lost the battle. A little hesitantly, he reached for her hand. "We pray to the same God, you and I."

"What do you mean?" Her eyes had dropped to their joined hands, and she gently pulled her hand away.

"I've read the Book of Mormon. I know it's true." Garrett took a deep breath and continued. "I investigated the Church when I was in the States. I had hoped to talk to my family about my desire to get baptized when I returned home, but then your embassy was bombed . . ." His voice trailed off.

It appeared that Janessa was barely managing to keep her jaw from dropping open at his disclosure, and now she struggled to form a sentence. "You . . . want to get baptized?"

He nodded, studying her as she absorbed this new information. He could almost see the wheels turning in her head, the rapid readjustment between who she thought he was and the man he intended to become. Confusion, pleasure, and concern crossed her face before she managed to ask, "Why didn't you tell me this before?"

"We've both had a lot on our minds lately." Garrett tilted his head as he studied her. "With my position, I've been reluctant to tell anyone before I discuss this with my family. You are one of only three people who know of my plans."

"Who are the other two?"

"My best friend from law school and his wife."

Janessa shook her head and let out a little laugh. "I can't believe you're planning on getting baptized. Royalty isn't exactly common in the Church."

"You can understand why I've been hesitant to talk about it."

"How did this happen?" Janessa asked now. "I mean, how did you learn about the gospel, especially without the press getting wind of it?"

"You have to understand that I've only been to church a handful of times because of the press," Garrett began. "As for my conversion, it happened pretty gradually. I had started reading the Book of Mormon, mostly out of curiosity, and then my friend Tim got married at the end of our first year of law school. I was told I couldn't go to the ceremony because it was in the temple."

"You definitely wouldn't be used to that." Janessa bit back a smile.

Garrett's eyebrows lifted, and then he shook his head and smiled. "I stewed about it all summer, that someone would deny me access to my best friend's wedding. For whatever reason, I kept reading the Book of Mormon, though. It probably took me another year before I prayed about whether the book was true or not."

"Did you get an answer?"

"In a strange sort of way." Garrett smiled. "It was more like the impression of *Why are you asking this question? You already know the answer.*"

"Everyone gets answers in different ways." She nodded in understanding. "Tell me, what led you to investigate the Church?"

"I guess you could say I had been feeling unsettled."

"What do you mean?"

Garrett shrugged. "As far as material things, I had everything I wanted, but friends weren't easy to come by. Stefano and I were very sheltered growing up, and our social calendars were carefully planned. I tended to be rebellious, always testing the limits."

"Oh really?" Amusement filled her voice.

"I was a royal pain—pun intended," he said wryly. "I've done a lot of things I'm not proud of . . ."

"That's the beauty of baptism. All of our past sins are forgiven in that moment," Janessa said sincerely.

"I want to believe that." He took a deep breath. "So anyway, when I went to the US, I got a taste of the real world. It was the first time I was able to make friends outside of the royals and high society in Europe. I really needed that. In fact, sometimes I think the main reason I started reading the Book of Mormon was because I knew it would drive my father crazy if he thought I was going to leave the Meridian Church. I never realized that I would gain a testimony while I was trying to find my independence."

Her eyebrows lifted. "Are you sure you aren't still trying to rebel against your father?"

"I'm through rebelling. After being away from Meridia for so long, I finally realized how much I want to play an active part in my family again. Now I pray that they will support my decision to get baptized."

"Perhaps you should try to schedule your baptism sooner rather than later," she suggested. "With everything that's happening, you could really benefit from having the gift of the Holy Ghost. Besides, the press might not exploit the event the way they would if they didn't have anything else to report."

Garrett's voice became serious. "I prefer to keep the event private, if at all possible."

Janessa nodded with understanding. "I think it's possible."

"I hope so. By the way, a member of the First Presidency will be dedicating the site for the new temple on Tuesday. I'll be representing the royal family at the dedication and the groundbreaking ceremony. I'd like for you to come with me."

"I'd love to come," Janessa agreed. "Do you have any idea how long it will take for the temple to be built?"

"My father has been pretty cooperative with the Church so far, and there aren't any shortages of materials or workers right now, which is in our favor. I heard they expect to dedicate it in about a year."

"That's quick."

Garrett nodded and watched her for a moment in the flickering candlelight before taking her hand and brushing his lips across her knuckles. This time she didn't pull her hand away. "I know you think you can't do your job and be involved with me at the same time, but—"

A heavy-handed knock at the door sounded just as shouts erupted outside. Garrett was halfway to the door when two gunshots sounded outside the chateau.

"Get down!" Janessa shouted as the door burst open and Levi surged through. He knocked Garrett to the ground before Janessa could react.

"What's going on?" Janessa demanded, now crawling across the floor to the two men sprawled near the door.

"The guards on the beach saw someone near the stables," Levi told her. "I'm clearing the chateau until we can sweep for explosives."

Another shot sounded. Janessa pulled her cell phone out of her back pocket and started dialing. "Don't send anyone outside yet. First have the dog check the garage."

"You think someone is trying to get us to rush out without checking the cars?" Levi asked.

Janessa's shoulder lifted. "I don't know. The entrances to the chateau are well protected. It's a lot easier to bypass the security for the garage." When Martino came on the line, she told him to keep the servants in the kitchen until he heard from her while Levi made the call to have the garage checked out.

"Why the kitchen?" Garrett asked now, his head swimming as he watched Janessa transform into an intelligence officer before his eyes. He was finally beginning to reconcile who she was with what she was.

"It would be the hardest place to plant a bomb. Patrice rarely leaves the kitchen, and that area of the house has servants coming and going constantly," Janessa told him. "Do you want me to have your bodyguards stay with you here, or would you rather go downstairs with the servants?"

"I'm not going to hide in the kitchen while you go searching for bombs," Garrett said edgily.

"That's fine. You can stay here," Janessa said as though she had taken his words literally.

"Janessa, I'm coming with you," Garrett insisted, for the first time noticing one of his bodyguards standing in his doorway.

She laid a hand on his arm, her voice softening. "Please let me do my job. I'll be back in a couple of minutes."

Though everything in him demanded he protect her, Garrett said nothing as she stood and walked out the door.

chapter 21

Janessa rushed down the main stairwell with Levi on her heels. "We need to check out the chateau, starting with the rooms near the kitchen." Janessa turned to face him when she reached the landing. "As soon as the garage is cleared, we'll bring the dog in to help."

"I'll have security start a sweep," Levi agreed, pulling his phone out to issue the orders.

"I'm going out to the garage," Janessa told him, heading for the private entrance. Cautiously, she checked the heavy wooden door for booby traps before opening it. Once she was satisfied it was safe, she pushed it open and headed straight for the garage.

A guard standing near the garage entrance moved to intercept her. "Excuse me, signorina. You can't go in there."

"It's okay," Janessa started, searching for an explanation as she tried to step past him.

"No, you must wait until it is safe." The guard abruptly moved into her path, effectively cutting her off as another gunshot rang out.

Instantly the guard cried out, his body jerking as he stumbled to the ground.

Janessa leaned down to help as a second shot thudded into the side of the garage just above her.

"Get inside!" the guard urged, trying to scramble through the garage door despite his injury.

The moment they both cleared the door, Janessa shut it behind them as yet another gunshot sounded. "Where are you hit?"

"My leg." His face was already damp with perspiration, but he motioned to the row of cars. "Don't worry about me. We need to get you out of here."

Janessa turned then, and her heart nearly stopped beating. The dog was sitting at attention right beside the sports car Garrett favored. "Oh, no." The words breathed out of her as she let herself look beyond the dog to his handler. She had been friends with Alan long enough to know that the dog had discovered a problem.

Lying on the garage floor, Alan aimed a flashlight at the underside of the car. He looked over to Janessa and called out to her. "Come here. I need your help."

"Go ahead. I'll be okay," the injured guard told her, already pulling off his shirt and pressing it against the wound.

Cautiously, Janessa crossed to Alan, squatting down to see for herself what they were dealing with. "What do you need me to do?"

"I need you to hold these wires apart." He pointed at a series of loose wires hanging from the bomb casing. "I can't tell which one feeds to the detonator."

She swallowed the lump in her throat and lay down on the garage floor. She slid under the car far enough so that she could reach the explosive device. Following Alan's instructions precisely, she carefully separated the wires. She had learned about explosives in her training, but never before had she been faced with a live exercise.

"Can you disarm it?"

"I have good news, and I have bad news." Alan didn't bother to ask her which one she wanted to hear first. "We can disarm it, but we have to activate it first."

"What?" Janessa turned her head to look at him.

"There are too many wires. It's booby trapped so that if I try to disarm it, it will immediately explode." Alan pointed at the edge of the metal box that housed the bomb. "Once the bomb is armed, the booby trap will be bypassed and we can cut the wires. I'm going to need you to cut this red one when I tell you."

"Okay." Janessa nodded as Alan handed her a second pair of wire cutters.

He motioned to an LCD display taped to the base of the bomb. "As soon as the bomb activates, you'll see the countdown right here. Call it out to me." Alan settled himself beside her with his wire cutters in hand. He prepared to clip the first wire and turned to her. "Ready?"

"Yeah." Janessa fixed her eyes on the LCD screen. She didn't see how he activated the bomb, but her heart raced when she saw the display. "We only have five seconds!"

Alan clipped the first wire and then the second.

Janessa carefully held her wire cutters in place and waited, glancing back at the monitor as Alan clipped the blue wire and then the yellow one in succession. She looked back to the monitor as it illuminated one second.

"Now!"

She squeezed the wire cutters and then shut her eyes as she anticipated time running out. A second passed, and then two. Slowly, she let out the breath she was holding and looked over at Alan.

He lowered his head to the concrete floor and took two deep breaths. "That was close."

"You're telling me."

"No, Janessa, you don't understand." Alan slid out from under the car and rolled to a sitting position. "There was just enough time on this bomb to *almost* disarm it. If you hadn't been here, I wouldn't have made it. Whoever planted it wanted to make sure that if they didn't get the prince, someone died protecting him."

Janessa crawled out from under the car, her mind reeling. She glimpsed the injured man by the door and tried to push aside the terror surging through her. "The guard was shot. I need to get an ambulance up here."

She only managed three steps before Alan called out to her. "Janessa, make sure the prince understands how close this was."

Solemnly, she nodded.

* * *

Garrett paced across the room, his phone to his ear as Martino gave him another update. The ambulance was preparing to leave with the wounded guard, and the security sweep of the chateau was finally complete. The bomb that had been found in the garage had been removed and was even now being transported to the naval base for further analysis.

Unfortunately, whoever had infiltrated the chateau grounds was long gone. The motion sensors had helped track his movements through the woods behind the chateau as far as the road. It was presumed that a car had been waiting for him near where the trail went cold.

Garrett hung up the phone upon hearing that Janessa was on her way to see him. He crossed the room and opened the door, glancing into the hallway to see his bodyguards posted outside his door and Janessa and Levi heading toward his quarters. He met Janessa halfway, concerned at how pale she looked. Without a word, he gathered her into his arms, resting his head on top of hers.

They just stood there for a moment, and he could feel Janessa trembling. He pulled back to look down at her and saw her vivid green eyes blinking rapidly to fight the tears trying to form. "Come inside." Garrett released her, keeping one hand on her back to guide her into his quarters.

Levi followed them inside and closed the door himself. "Did Martino bring you up to date?"

"I just hung up with him." Garrett nodded. "How is the guard?"

"His prognosis is good," Levi told him and then glanced over at Janessa.

A silent message passed between them, causing Garrett to turn his attention back to Janessa. "Is there something I don't know about?"

Janessa took a deep breath. "If we had evacuated the chateau, which car would you have taken?"

"Mine," Garrett answered without hesitation and then elaborated. "The Porsche my father gave me when I joined the Navy."

"Why?" Janessa asked.

"I don't understand. What does it matter which car I would have taken?"

"It's important, Garrett," Janessa insisted. "Why are you so sure you would have taken the Porsche?"

"For one thing, I wouldn't want to use a driver, since Enrico would need to see to his own family." Garrett shrugged a shoulder. "And the Porsche is the only car I keep keys for."

"Who would know that?"

"I don't know. Some of the household staff would know, along with my family and a few close friends." He stepped closer and put both hands on her arms. "Tell me what's going on."

"Only one bomb was found. It was attached to the underside of your car." Janessa stared up at him, unable to control a shudder. "Whoever planted it knew that you would take your car."

Garrett stared at her as he absorbed the news.

"Whoever is threatening your family isn't just some lunatic off the street. It's someone who knows you—and knows you well."

Levi stepped forward. "Janessa, you'd better go call Director Palmer and let him know what's going on. I'll make sure the guard is doubled tonight. I'm sure the prince can help me get some extra personnel from the naval base to shore up our defenses for the next few days."

Janessa nodded and quietly crossed the room. With one last look at Garrett, she stepped out into the hall and closed the door behind her.

With some effort, Garrett turned his attention to Levi. "What kind of help do you need from the naval base?"

"Actually, I don't think we need any. I just wanted to speak to you privately."

Garrett sat down in a chair and motioned for Levi to sit as well. "Is there a problem?"

"I just finished debriefing the guard who was injured," Levi told him. "After speaking to him and Janessa, I believe that whoever shot your guard was aiming for Janessa."

Garrett's lips pressed together as he fought against his emotions. "Have you talked to her about this?"

Levi shook his head. "She already knows, but she doesn't want to admit it."

"I'll speak with your director and have him call her back to the United States."

"Your Highness, you probably already know that she's too stubborn to leave. Regardless, we need her here," Levi admitted. His eyes were somber as he added, "Whoever planted that bomb predicted how we would react. Janessa saved your life tonight."

Garrett stared at him a moment, the quiet words piercing through him. Wearily, he ran a hand over his face. "If I can't send her home, how do you suggest I keep her safe?"

"I know she's not going to like it, but I want to assign her a bodyguard."

"I'm one step ahead of you there. In fact, I already have someone in mind, but he doesn't arrive until next week. Can you make sure she is protected until then?"

"I'll talk to Alan. Between the two of us, we'll make sure she doesn't go anywhere on her own." Levi stood up and looked back at the prince. "Do you want to tell her she's getting a bodyguard, or shall I?"

"She doesn't need to know."

With a nod, Levi left the room.

chapter 22

Janessa allowed her emotions full rein when she reached her rooms. Tears flowing freely, she closed the door behind her, for the first time flipping the lock to ensure her privacy. She moved into the bedroom, escaping into the darkness. She threw open the window, and the curtain immediately billowed in the breeze. The scent of salt and sand mixed with the roses beneath her window, creating a combination she would always associate with this place.

She resented the person who had turned this peaceful setting into a nightmare, not only for invoking violence tonight but also for robbing all of the residents of their peace of mind. Even after so many improvements to the chateau's security systems, someone had still managed to breach it.

The knowledge that someone close to Garrett was involved weighed heavily on her. She still believed the servants to be trustworthy, especially since they could have planted a bomb at any time. And certainly his family wouldn't try to kill him. That left his friends, of whom she knew little.

Though she hated the idea of prying into Garrett's private life, Janessa knew that she had to take that necessary next step to prevent another incident like tonight. In the back of her mind, she knew she needed to concentrate on the old girlfriends. If someone was targeting her as well, she had to consider the possibility that an old girlfriend might be involved.

The phone rang, and Janessa straightened instinctively. She wiped her eyes with her sleeve and moved to answer the phone.

"Janessa? This is Director Palmer."

"Hello, sir." Knowing it was only midafternoon in DC, Janessa wasn't entirely surprised to hear from him. She sat on the side of her bed, sure that Levi had already contacted him regarding tonight's incident, and concerned that he felt her work here was inadequate.

"I have some information Prince Garrett asked us to look into," he told her. "We searched for offshore bank accounts for the gas station owner. Our finance department found three accounts totaling nearly five million dollars."

"They're sure?" Janessa asked, reaching for a pad of paper and a pen. "How could a gas station owner make that much money?"

"He couldn't. I'm sending the bank records in the next diplomatic pouch. Expect it to arrive tomorrow afternoon."

"Thank you, sir," Janessa said, suddenly wondering why she hadn't heard about Garrett's request for information. "Can I ask which of our personnel submitted the prince's request for information?"

"Tony Coletto, the agent we sent out to investigate the embassy bombing." Before Janessa could respond, Director Palmer asked, "How is the security coming there?"

"We had a close call tonight," Janessa admitted wearily, turning her thoughts back to the events of the evening. She hated to admit failure, but she would rather tell him herself than have him receive a diluted version from someone else. She went on to tell him about the events that had transpired, including Alan's assessment of the bomb.

"I know it's difficult, but do what you can to keep this out of the press," Director Palmer advised her. "Also, remember that our military is at your disposal. Let me know if you need anything beyond what Meridia can provide."

"I will. Thank you."

Janessa hung up, breathing a shaky sigh of relief. She had expected some kind of reprimand, but instead the director had offered her further resources. She moved to the window and looked out into the darkness. She could hear the waves crashing in the distance and could see a pair of guards on the beach helping bridge the gap in the sensors.

Tears started flowing once more as she thought of Garrett. Both of them had skirted death tonight, and the 'what ifs' terrified her. She wished she could tell him how she had felt when she'd clipped that red wire, when she thought she was too late. What would he think if he knew that his face had been the single image that flashed into her mind?

Absently she dried her cheeks on her sleeve. She looked down at the ring on her finger, reminding herself that it was just a prop and that it had to remain that way. She had almost lost him tonight. When he had demanded to come with her, for a brief moment she had wavered, wanting him close, where she could be sure he was safe. That kind of distraction could have cost both of them their lives. No matter how much she had come to love Garrett, their engagement would have to remain a charade.

Her heart ached as she contemplated Garrett's disclosure about his plans to be baptized. She was in love with a man who would soon be LDS and wanted to pursue a relationship with her—and she would have to continue to turn a cold shoulder toward him.

* * *

Janessa descended the stairs late Friday morning already dressed for the luncheon that would take place in less than an hour. Outwardly everything was business as usual at the chateau, but she could feel the underlying tension among the staff and security personnel.

She had spent much of the night reviewing the weaknesses in the current security. She was certain that the infiltrator from the night before had made it onto the grounds from the beach despite the guards that had been posted there. She couldn't be sure whether someone had swum ashore from a boat off of the coast or had managed to slip past the guards on the beach, but one way or another the weakness had been found and exploited. Now she hoped that they could fully secure the beach so she could turn her attention to the service personnel, the guest lists, and Garrett's friends.

She knew she wasn't the only one who hadn't gotten much sleep. She had seen Alan out with Max at the break of dawn checking the grounds. He had stopped long enough for breakfast and to give the dog a rest before running another sweep of the chateau's interior. She had also seen Levi several times throughout the morning as he continued to check in with her to give her updates.

Though Janessa would have preferred to cancel today's luncheon, Levi had reminded her that their best defense against terrorism was to proceed as though nothing had happened. This knowledge did little to calm the nerves in her stomach. She noted the fresh flowers spilling out of urns at the base of the stairs and tried to keep her mind on the upcoming event.

Among today's guests were the main contributors to the museum in Bellamo, as well as a few French dignitaries who had helped orchestrate the current exhibit on loan from the Louvre. Martino had informed her earlier that Garrett had left for meetings at the museum to prepare for the opening of the exhibit the next day. She had worried about him ever since.

Despite Levi's assurances that the number of Garrett's bodyguards had been doubled and that the security at the museum had been tightened, she couldn't stop seeing that bomb planted beneath his car. Weary from lack of sleep, she made her way to the kitchen. She pushed open the door to find Patrice mumbling to herself in French. For the first time all day she felt the corner of her lips quirk up.

"Rough day?" Janessa asked in French.

"Two girls are out sick, and lunch is supposed to be served in less than an hour. It seems unwise to call the catering service for temps, given the drama here last night." Patrice picked up a meat cleaver and neatly cut a club sandwich in half.

"You're absolutely right. What can I do to help?"

Patrice turned to Janessa, surprise flickering over her face. She started to refuse the help, but before she could speak one of the servants hurried through the door to tell Patrice that the first guests had arrived.

Janessa grabbed an apron off of the hook by the door and stepped to the sink to wash her hands. "Where do you want me to start?"

Patrice barked out orders, and Janessa followed the best she could, grateful to have something to distract her from thinking of the night before.

An hour later, Martino entered the kitchen. He looked from Patrice to Janessa and shook his head in disapproval. "Signorina, Prince Garrett has been expecting you at the luncheon."

Janessa turned to Patrice and asked, "Can you manage without me?"

She nodded. "Leave that and go to the party."

Janessa removed her apron and walked through the door Martino held open for her. She moved outside to the terrace where the tables were covered with pale blue tablecloths, and the guests could enjoy both the view of the Mediterranean and the gardens.

Isabel Dumond laughed at something Garrett said, and Janessa imagined that she had been by his side for the past hour. Janessa wondered which of Garrett's admirers she worried about more—Cynthia Renault, who had flaunted her movie star good looks when they had been in Calene, or Isabel Dumond, who followed Garrett around like a puppy dog every time she had the opportunity.

She supposed that Isabel's youth might account for her more subtle pursuit of Garrett, along with the fact that Garrett worked closely with her father at the museum. Isabel probably wasn't more than twenty-three or twenty-four, but Janessa suspected that she had been planning on being in Garrett's life for some time.

A photographer shifted to take a picture of Isabel and Garrett. Isabel smiled, clearly pleased with the media attention. Inwardly, Janessa knew that she would never be that at ease in front of cameras. The photographer took several pictures before noticing that Janessa had arrived. With a sigh, she moved forward to play her part.

"Isabel, thank you for keeping my fiancé company in my absence." Janessa smiled as though she hadn't a care in the world. She leaned over and kissed Garrett's cheek, linking her arm through his. "I'm sorry I'm late."

"I'm just glad you're here now." Garrett patted her hand and smiled. "Would you excuse us, Isabel? There are several people who have been waiting to meet Janessa."

Isabel nodded, her smile dimming considerably.

"Where have you been? I was worried," Garrett whispered as they moved away.

"I was helping in the kitchen. Two of the girls were out sick, and Patrice looked desperate."

Garrett looked down at her, surprised. "Next time have her call the caterers in Bellamo for help. They've always been willing to send a couple of their employees our way since we always use them to cater our large events."

"Patrice didn't want to risk it after last night," Janessa shrugged, forcing a smile as they approached several guests. "Exactly how many people do I have to meet today?" she whispered.

"Only about twenty."

"Wonderful."

* * *

As Garrett descended the main staircase, he was grateful that all of their luncheon guests had departed. He had changed into slacks and a polo shirt after one of their last guests had managed to spill her drink on him. Now he hoped to find some time to spend with Janessa.

He was glad she had been perfectly safe, but he wasn't happy that she had reduced herself to kitchen help and left him scrambling to make excuses as to why she wasn't present at the beginning of the luncheon. That fact aside, she hadn't been herself today. She had greeted their guests and asked the right questions, but he could feel her distancing herself from him, and he didn't think it was just concern about the night before.

When he turned the corner into the parlor, his eyes narrowed. A man in uniform sat next to Janessa on a sofa, and their heads were bent close as they spoke quietly. Garrett cleared his throat, causing both of them to look up. The officer immediately stood. His hair was short and blond, and Garrett recognized his uniform as that of a commander in the US Navy.

Janessa stood as well, straightening the papers she held in her hand. "Prince Garrett, this is Commander Dan Peters. He's here to help us with the security problems we encountered last night."

"I would be interested to hear about it." Garrett noticed a member of his staff down the hall. "Why don't we continue this discussion in the library?"

With a shrug, Janessa allowed Garrett to take her arm and escort her down the hall as the commander followed behind them.

As soon as they were inside, Garrett motioned for everyone to be seated and took his place beside Janessa. "Have you figured out where the breach occurred last night?"

Janessa nodded. "The motion detectors work beautifully along the hillside, but during low tide, we have a blind spot on the beach.

We're also vulnerable to someone coming ashore from a small vessel off of the coast."

Commander Peters nodded in agreement. "We have a different type of sensor we use on the ocean floor, a type of sonar, that we think will bridge the gap."

"How long will it take to install?"

"The equipment won't arrive until next Wednesday. Until then, that area remains vulnerable," Commander Peters said, the easygoing cadence in his voice identifying him as a Californian.

"We will have to keep guards posted on the beach until your equipment can be installed," Garrett stated. He looked from the commander to Janessa. "Is that the only pressing security problem?"

"For now." Janessa nodded. "I do have other information I need to discuss with you though."

Commander Peters stood to leave. "I can show myself out."

"Thank you for your assistance." Garrett stood as well, reaching out to shake his hand. "If there is anything you need from my government, please let me or Miss Rogers know."

"I'll see you next week." He nodded, closing the door behind him as he left.

Garrett sat back down as Janessa pulled several sheets of paper out of the diplomatic pouch she held. She handed them to Garrett as she spoke. "My agency found what you were looking for. Alberto Manero did have several offshore accounts totaling over five million dollars."

"Five million?" Garrett repeated, his eyes widening.

"My director feels Manero must have been involved in something illegal, but we don't have a clue as to what. Without knowing any of his business associates, it makes it difficult to narrow down the possibilities."

"Not that difficult." Garrett leaned back, scanning the bank records. The deposits varied in amount and frequency, ranging from fifteen thousand dollars to half a million. "The port in Calene is busy, and we often have tourists come in on leisure vessels. Smuggling has been a concern for as long as I can remember."

"You think he was involved in smuggling?"

"It's highly likely." Garrett nodded. "He had access to every small vessel in the area. All someone would have to do was go gas up their boat, and Manero could easily distribute whatever contraband he wanted to through them without raising suspicions. Besides providing gas, Manero also ran a small store. To everyone in sight, it would look like someone was buying supplies."

"If your father allowed the United States access to your waters, what would that do to a smuggling ring like this?"

Garrett let out a long breath. "Twice as many naval vessels would mean twice as many chances of getting noticed. Even more of a concern would be the unpredictability of the US Navy, particularly during the first year or two."

"Then we may have been looking in the wrong direction this whole time. The embassy bombing may have just been set up to look like a terrorist attack, when it was simply a matter of someone trying to protect their business interests."

"It's possible. Manero and his associates may have bombed your embassy to create tension between our countries in an attempt to keep your Navy from building a base here."

Janessa's mind whirled. "And the gas station fire could have been the result of some internal strife within the smuggling ring."

"I need to call our director of security and let him know about this." Garrett picked up the phone in the library.

"And I'll call Director Palmer." Janessa stood and moved toward the door. "Maybe our finance staff can trace where those deposits came from."

"Tell him thank you for the information."

Janessa nodded, then hesitated when she reached the door. "Can I ask you something?" When he nodded, she continued. "Why didn't you ask me to get this information for you?"

"I don't know. I guess I didn't think about it."

"I see." Janessa stiffened. "In the future, I would appreciate it if you would send your requests through me."

"What does it matter?"

"I can't do my job well if I don't know everything. Part of my role as this team's leader is to coordinate all of the intelligence we collect."

"Janessa, I didn't mean to upset you," Garrett told her, somewhat surprised to hear his own apologetic tone. "You had already returned to the chateau when our director of security and I thought to ask for the information. Coletto was there in Calene, so I went to him."

Her shoulders relaxed fractionally, and she gave him a brief nod as she left the room.

Garrett watched her go, surprised by the barriers she seemed to have put up between them. He had thought that after he told her of his desire to be baptized they would grow closer. Somehow, the opposite had happened.

chapter 23

Janessa sat at her desk with her back to the window. The final security sweep of the chateau had been completed nearly an hour before; two sets of guards were in position on the beach, and analysts at the CIA were working on tracing the deposits into Alberto Manero's accounts.

Her e-mail account had received 162 messages since she had left the US, most of them since the newspapers had reported her engagement to Garrett. Unwilling to lie directly to her friends and family, she ignored all of them and wondered idly what the record was for unread e-mails.

She had sent her sister, Mary, a letter the day before, but so far that was the only communication she had allowed herself with her family. For now, she had to rely on her sister to pass along what little information she could provide.

After storing her laptop, she secured her documents in her briefcase and then placed the briefcase in the wall safe Martino had revealed to her just the day before. Since the incident with the bomb, Martino had warmed up slightly. He was still formal and aloof, but he didn't seem to resent her quite as much as he had when she first arrived.

With her work done for the moment, Janessa went out onto the balcony and looked out into the darkness. The stars shone brightly above her, competing only with the lights from the chateau and the full moon. A mile down the beach, she could see one of the guards manning his station.

Restless, she turned and slipped on her sandals as she left her room and made her way outside onto the terrace. She walked by the swimming pool, pausing for a moment as she leaned on the wrought iron fence and looked out into the darkness.

The waves crashed on the beach below in the timeless battle between land and sea, the crests of the waves visible in the light of the moon. She would miss this place when it came time to go, more than any other, and nearly as much as she would miss Garrett. The overwhelming fear for his safety had settled deep inside her, along with an emptiness she had never before experienced.

Footsteps sounded behind her, and Janessa whirled around. She lifted a hand to her pounding heart, not sure if she was relieved to see Garrett approaching. "You startled me."

"I'm sorry." Garrett leaned on the rail next to her. "I saw you from my window, and I wanted to make sure you were okay."

"I was just thinking," Janessa said wistfully, turning back to look over the water once more. "It will be hard to leave here when the time comes."

"So don't leave."

"Just yesterday you were trying to get me to leave," she reminded him. "Besides, this is your home, not mine." She didn't quite manage to keep the regret from her voice. "Even if I were assigned to the embassy here, it would only be for a year or two."

"I don't want you to go." Garrett took her hand in his and moved closer as she turned to face him. "Even after the gala is over, I want you to stay. I want you to give our relationship a chance."

She desperately wanted to comply but forced herself to remember the reason she was here, the reason she couldn't afford to love him. "I almost lost you last night." Janessa's voice was soft. She lifted her hand, measuring her thumb and finger a centimeter apart. "I came this close to not doing my job well enough to protect you. Neither one of us can afford for me to be distracted by my feelings for you."

"What are your feelings for me?" Hope shone in his eyes.

"Don't you understand?" Her voice rose fractionally. "I don't want to have feelings for you."

"But you do," Garrett insisted.

"Do you realize how close we both came to dying last night?" Janessa's voice caught. She took a steadying breath before continuing. "The bomb on your car had just enough time on it so that someone could *almost* disarm it. Even with two of us, I didn't think we were going to make it. Whoever planted it wanted to make sure someone died last night."

Garrett's hand squeezed hers as the muscle in his jaw twitched.

Janessa watched a wave of frustration surge through him before he controlled it. She hadn't wanted to tell him about the bomb, but she had to make him understand. "Already you're having trouble letting me do my job. I can't have a personal life right now. It will only get in the way."

"Watching you walk out of my room last night, seeing you leave so you could protect me, was the hardest thing I've ever done in my life," Garrett admitted. "If I had lost you last night, do you think it would have hurt any less, knowing that the ring you wear doesn't hold any promises?" He took a deep breath before continuing. "I understand your responsibilities here. That doesn't change the fact that I'm going to do everything I can to make sure you're safe, too. I love you too much to lose you."

Her eyes darted up to his, her mind whirling as she replayed his words in her mind. Could he really love her as much as she loved him? She had spent so much time convincing herself that his feelings for her would never go beyond her brief assignment in Meridia. Now she stared at him, amazed and confused.

Garrett reached for her left hand, holding it up so that the ring sparkled in the moonlight. "I do love you. I want you to marry me so that we can spend the rest of our lives together—the rest of eternity together." He linked his fingers with hers, and she felt tears threaten. "The real question is, what are your feelings for me?"

Janessa was unsure how to respond. She knew she did love Garrett, and here he was actually proposing to her. "I didn't want to love you." Janessa's resolve to keep a professional distance crumbled as a tear spilled over. "I just couldn't stop it."

Garrett slid his arms around her, pulled her close, and held on. They stood there for a moment, the only sound coming from the waves crashing on the beach. Garrett finally leaned back so he could see her face. "I know you worry that our feelings will keep you from doing your job, but I think trying to ignore these feelings is going to cause us more trouble than if we just face them." His eyes searched hers, and he trailed a finger down her cheek. "Please say you'll marry me."

Janessa studied his face in the shadows. More than anything, she wanted to share a life with Garrett. If only their backgrounds weren't so different. "Garrett, we both know that I could never live in your world."

"You already do," he said softly. He lifted a hand and motioned to the chateau. "I'm the second son. My role won't always be in the spotlight. You can work with me in overseeing our military operations or going on diplomatic missions. Being royalty isn't simply dining at the palace." He leaned closer and briefly touched his lips to hers. "Please marry me."

He was offering her everything she had ever dared to hope for, and as warmth spread through her heart, she knew what her answer was. She laid her hand on his cheek, and a smile bloomed on her face. "Yes, I'll marry you."

His smile was immediate, making her forget everything and everyone else. He lifted her off the ground, spinning her in a complete circle as her laughter rang out.

Her feet had barely touched the ground when a sobering thought crossed her mind. "What are your parents going to think?"

Garrett's smile didn't dim in the slightest. "They already know about everything except about me getting baptized."

"You already told them that we're really getting married?"

"I think it would be more accurate to say that they told me." Garrett laughed. "I believe my brother put it best when he said that if we were any more engaged, we would be on our honeymoon."

Janessa's jaw dropped. "How do you manage to keep anything from your family? They see everything!"

"You're going to fit right in," Garrett agreed with a grin.

* * *

"Are you sure you don't want me to drive you, Your Highness?" Enrico asked Sunday morning when Garrett headed for his car. All of the cars had already been checked for explosives and any other tampering earlier that morning, but tensions among the staff were still high.

"It's Sunday, Enrico," Garrett pointed out. "Go enjoy a day off with your family."

Enrico's eyebrows went up, but he smiled as he gave a small bow. "Yes, sir." He then turned and went back inside.

"Do you think he'll know what to do with a day off?"

"Knowing Enrico, he'll go spend some time with his father. Paolo and Enrico have been playing the same game of chess for more than a year."

"The same game?" Janessa asked, humor and disbelief filling her voice.

"That's what happens when you don't have a time limit on the moves." Garrett grinned at her. "I think the game is just an excuse they use to sit and talk."

"You're probably right," Janessa commented as she slid into the passenger seat. She had promised herself she wasn't going to think about the bomb Alan had removed from this very car several days before. At least she'd promised to try. "I hope you're good with directions."

"I already know where the church is," Garrett told her as he started the car and pulled out onto the road. He glanced into the rearview mirror and saw his security detail pulling out behind him. Turning his attention back to Janessa, he added, "I've just never had the opportunity to go before."

"So now I'm your excuse?" Janessa's eyebrows lifted.

"There's no way I can answer that without getting into trouble," Garrett said with a wry smile. "I do need your help in setting up my baptism though."

"You can probably have an interview with the branch president today," Janessa suggested. "Is there anyone in particular you would like to have baptize you?"

"My friend Tim O'Donnell will be arriving Tuesday. He's the one who gave me the Book of Mormon," Garrett told her. "If possible, I would like to be baptized sometime this week."

"I thought you would want to wait until after the gala."

Garrett glanced over at her. "It's my understanding that I can't go to the temple until I've been a member for a year."

She nodded, still trying to adjust to the new reality that they would soon be planning a real wedding and a life together. "That's right."

"Then each week I wait to get baptized means another week before we can go to the temple together."

"You have a point," Janessa agreed with a smile.

Garrett reached over and gave her hand a squeeze before settling back in his seat for the long drive.

* * *

Several miles later, Garrett pulled around the corner to the church. "There aren't very many people here," he commented when he pulled into the parking lot.

"This is just a branch. It only has about forty or fifty members," Janessa told him. "From what I understand, most of the members in Meridia live in and around Calene."

"That makes sense." Garrett nodded. "The new temple is being built about twenty miles this side of Calene."

"Wouldn't it be amazing if the temple were done before we get married?" Janessa commented as Garrett took her hand and started toward the entrance.

"I'm not sure how I feel about such a long engagement, but we can talk about it once the gala is over," Garrett said as he ushered her inside.

Before she had a chance to respond, the missionaries approached them.

Garrett introduced himself simply as Garrett Fortier and was amused when he didn't notice any glimmer of recognition from either of the elders, neither of whom appeared to be natives of Meridia. He led Janessa to a seat in the back and was surprised when she didn't sit down.

"I have to play the piano," she told him with an apologetic smile. "At least I have to try. I'll come down and sit with you after the sacrament hymn."

With that she continued down the aisle and took her seat on the piano bench. A moment later the branch president stood to welcome the congregation and begin the meeting. His eyes scanned the small congregation, pausing as he noticed Garrett sitting in the back. He did a double take before announcing the opening hymn. Garrett noticed a few curious glances cast his way during the opening song, and the young deacon that came to offer him the sacrament goggled when he recognized who he was serving.

Garrett watched as a combination of men and boys continued to pass the sacrament. He considered how different this branch was in comparison to the ward he had attended with Tim. At the same time, everything was so much the same.

As the meeting progressed, he imagined he could be sitting anywhere in the world listening to testimonies similar to those being given here today. At the conclusion of the meeting, Janessa once again moved to the piano at the front of the chapel. After the prayer she stopped and spoke with the branch president before returning to his side.

"We stay here for Sunday School," Janessa told him as she reclaimed her seat. "Also, the branch president said he can meet with you right after church."

Garrett nodded, settling in for the next meeting. Janessa slipped her hand into his, and in that moment he knew everything in his life was exactly the way it was supposed to be.

chapter 24

Queen Marta moved down the hall to her husband's office on Monday night. She had already put in a sixteen-hour day, many of those hours spent dealing with correspondence and various charities she was involved in. But for now, she wasn't thinking about her own busy schedule but rather her husband's overburdened workload.

She knocked on his door once before pushing it open and was not surprised to find her husband and eldest son still hard at work. They sat elbow to elbow at the worktable in the corner of the room poring over the latest intelligence reports.

She laid a hand on Stefano's shoulder and looked at her husband. "You both need to get some rest."

"We're almost finished," Eduard told her, tapping a finger on the report in front of him. He looked up at Stefano and nodded. "I think Garrett and Janessa are onto something here. If the CIA can trace those deposits, security might be able to solve this whole problem before the gala."

"We only have three more weeks," Marta reminded her husband. "Do you think they can figure it out by then?"

"I hope so," Eduard told her.

Another knock came at the door. This time Garrett stepped through, leading Janessa. "I thought I would find you here."

"What are you doing here?" Marta asked, moving to embrace her youngest son. She looked closer, noting the combination of excitement and concern in his eyes. "I thought you were staying at the chateau through next weekend."

"I have a groundbreaking ceremony tomorrow morning," Garrett told her. "Besides, I wanted to talk to you both."

"Has the CIA traced the money?" Eduard asked.

"No." Garrett shook his head, reaching for Janessa's hand. "Actually, this is personal."

Marta noticed Janessa give Garrett's hand an encouraging squeeze and fought back a smile. It seemed the engagement really had gone beyond a publicity stunt. Prepared to act adequately surprised at the announcement, she shifted to her husband's side and waited for him to continue.

"I wondered if you all could clear your schedules tomorrow afternoon," Garrett began, glancing down at Janessa for a moment before continuing. "I would like you to attend my baptism into the Mormon Church."

"What?" King Eduard's voice boomed as he stood.

Stefano stood as well and gaped at Garrett. Marta struggled to keep her jaw from dropping.

"I know this comes as a shock, but I've been thinking about this for some time," Garrett continued before his father could cut him off.

"You are a Fortier. Joining another church is not an option. You can't throw out centuries of tradition."

Still stunned, Marta laid a hand on Eduard's arm. "Let him speak."

Garrett took a deep breath. "Mother, you mentioned something when I first returned home from the United States. You said you hadn't ever seen me more content." He looked from his mother to his father and continued. "This church gave me that. I found a truth I had been searching for without even knowing it."

"Never since the Church of Meridia was founded has a Fortier belonged to another," Eduard stated.

"I realize I am the first, and I feel the burden of that decision." Garrett nodded solemnly. "But my religious choices have nothing to do with my duty to this country or this family. I can have both if you will let me. I'm only asking for the same religious freedom you give the rest of our citizens."

Marta considered the historic implications her son's actions could cause for this family and their country. Undermining her resolve against his request was her desire for him to find happiness. "Why must you be baptized? Surely you can attend this church on occasion without going to such extremes."

Janessa spoke now, her voice calm. "Without baptism, Garrett would not be able to receive the fullness of the blessings offered by our church—"

Before she could continue, Eduard interrupted. "This is your doing. He never mentioned this church before you arrived."

"Father," Garrett started before Janessa could defend herself. "I made this decision long before I met Janessa. Knowing her just gave me the courage to act on my decision."

Stefano interrupted his father's tirade as he muttered, "The press is going to have a field day with this."

"This is a private matter. I have no intention of informing the press."

"How can you avoid it?" Eduard asked, his voice still several decibels above normal.

"Janessa and I are attending the groundbreaking ceremony for the new Mormon temple tomorrow morning. Afterward, there is a luncheon at a local meetinghouse. Since I have every reason to be there, the press won't suspect that I am also getting baptized." Garrett handed a paper to his mother. "The baptism is at three o'clock. Here are the directions."

Janessa looked at King Eduard and spoke directly to him. "Your Majesty, this is an important day for your son, one he has looked forward to for some time. It would mean a lot if you could be present."

"Even if we could get to the church without the press noticing, your association with the church will eventually get out," Queen Marta said even as her fingers closed around the paper her son had handed her.

"That's true," Garrett agreed. "But right now the press has enough stories to keep them busy. With the fire and our engagement, I should be able to keep this private for a while. If I'm lucky, this story will be old news by the time it leaks out."

"I can't condone this." King Eduard spoke now, his face stern. "You are second in line for the throne. What if you were to someday ascend to the throne? How could you possibly oversee church affairs while belonging to another?"

"Church and state have been separate for generations." Garrett struggled to keep his voice even. "Besides, whether I get baptized or not, I will always be Mormon in my heart."

Aware that her husband had already dug his heels in, Queen Marta turned to her youngest son. "Garrett, why don't you and Janessa go get some sleep. We'll talk in the morning." She turned to Stefano.

"I think I'll turn in also." Stefano stood and moved to the door. "Good night."

As soon as the room cleared, Marta took the seat Stefano had vacated. "Well?"

"Well, what?" Eduard leaned back in his chair. "I can't approve of this."

"I don't think he expects you to."

"That American spy is creating havoc in our family."

"That American spy is going to be your daughter-in-law," Marta pointed out. "Are you really prepared to disown Garrett over this?"

Eduard opened his mouth and then quickly shut it again. He rubbed a hand over his face before looking at her once more. "Daughter-in-law? It was supposed to be a fictional engagement. I don't know what Garrett is thinking—joining another church, falling for an American spy. He has lost all touch with reality." Eduard shook his head in frustration. "Do you realize that this will change the very fabric of the royal family?"

"I know." Marta reached for his hand and continued. "I'm not any happier about this than you are, but I don't think he's going to change his mind. With or without our approval, he's going to be Mormon tomorrow afternoon."

Eduard pushed out of his chair and stalked to the window. He stared blankly into the darkness before turning back to his wife. "You really think he would choose this church over his own family?"

"He doesn't want to make that choice, but yes, I think he would." Marta sighed. "Especially now that Janessa is tied to his decision."

"How long do you think Janessa will stick around if we cut him off?" Eduard considered. "Once she sees Garrett lose his wealth and position, surely her interest will fade. Perhaps that's what Garrett needs to make him come to his senses."

"Eduard, we both know better." Marta stood and closed the distance between them. "Even with her foreign upbringing, I thoroughly approve of her for our son. I've taken note of her tastes and her personality, and I believe she is just the sort of woman Garrett needs, the perfect princess.

She's not the sort to be interested in him for his money or his title. If she were, she would never encourage him in this."

His eyes narrowed. "Maybe it's time we find out for sure."

* * *

King Eduard didn't believe in wasting time. He was also accustomed to getting what he wanted. Though it was barely seven o'clock in the morning, he instructed his secretary to send for Janessa. He settled into his chair and glanced at his schedule. As usual, it was full from eight in the morning until well past business hours.

Expecting that Janessa would take her time in answering such an early morning summons, he flipped open the file containing her most recent security reports. He had already read the report about the bomb that had been intended for his son, and he was fully aware that Janessa had nearly died helping disarm it. That last tidbit of information had not come from Janessa's report but rather from the injured security guard.

The knock at the door surprised him. He glanced at his watch to see that less than five minutes had passed since his secretary had called Janessa. "Come in."

She pushed the door open and stepped inside. "Good morning, Your Majesty." Janessa dipped into a curtsey before continuing. "You asked to see me?"

"Yes." Eduard motioned for her to sit down as he studied the petite woman in front of him. This woman had saved his son's life, but now her mere presence threatened to unravel generations of tradition and heritage. "I wanted to speak to you privately before I discuss my decision with my son."

Janessa took the seat he indicated and fiddled with a ring on her right pinkie. "With all due respect, Your Majesty, I have nothing to do with Garrett's baptism."

"I disagree." Eduard kept his voice mild, his expression bland. "He said himself that your presence gave him the courage to go through with this baptism."

Janessa's chin tilted up a fraction. "And he told me that he was planning on discussing this decision with you the day of the embassy bombing."

Eduard considered her answer and decided to push a different button. "I have it from reputable sources that you and he are pursuing a relationship beyond the requirements of your assignment."

Heat stung Janessa's cheeks. "My relationship with Garrett has nothing to do with his decision."

"You have been here long enough to appreciate the lifestyle my son has been born into." He waved his hand to encompass the palace. "I can't believe he won't at some point regret his decision and resent your part in it. And if I disown him today—strip him of his wealth and title—what will be your response?" Eduard pushed on.

Janessa took a sharp intake of breath and remained speechless for several moments. Then she cleared her throat and spoke calmly and professionally, surprising them both. "First, I would urge you to provide him with adequate security to ensure his protection if he is not permitted to stay at the chateau until the gala. Second, I would ask that you allow me to complete my assignment here. I have no interest in seeing any of you hurt, regardless of any decision you make."

Eduard considered her words, tapping his fingers on the report in front of him. "You surprise me."

"You may not know me well or feel particularly fond of me right now, but I hope you love Garrett enough to make sure he is safe regardless of whatever decision you make. He wants to remain an active member of this family, but if you force him to choose, ultimately the choice is his and his alone." Janessa stood. "Now, if you will excuse me, I have some work to attend to."

Eduard nodded his assent and watched her leave the room. His wife had been right, as usual. Not only was this woman in love with his son, but she would be a wonderful addition to the royal family—if only he could ignore the issue of religion. With a sigh, he picked up his phone and dialed the number for his private quarters. He and his wife had some major decisions to make.

chapter 25

Janessa sat beside Garrett in the back seat of the limousine as they headed for the groundbreaking. Garrett's parents had yet to speak to him today, and Janessa's heart ached as she thought of her conversation with his father that morning, a conversation Garrett still knew nothing about.

"You're awfully quiet this morning." Garrett pressed the button to raise the window between them and the driver. As it slid into place, he asked, "Is everything okay?"

Janessa let out a sigh. She couldn't keep this from him. After all, he had a right to know where his father stood before it was too late. "I spoke with your father."

"What?" Garrett shifted so he could see her more clearly. "When?"

"He sent for me first thing this morning." Janessa laid her hand on his. "Garrett, he asked what I would do if he disowned you."

"What?" Garrett's hand fisted beneath hers, and his eyes darkened.

"He basically wanted to know if I would stick around if you lost your money and your title."

Garrett let out a sigh of frustration, but his eyes stayed locked on hers. "What did you say?"

"I told him that my biggest concern is for your safety and the safety of your family." Janessa's voice softened as she added, "I'll understand if you want to put off your decision. You don't have to get baptized today."

Garrett drew his hand away. "Is that what you think I should do?"

"Garrett, it's your decision to make, not mine," Janessa insisted, her voice taking on an edge. "Which is something I pointed out to your father." In a rare show of impatience, Janessa dragged her hand through her hair. "I love you, Garrett. I just don't want you to resent me a year or two down the road when you realize how much you gave up to be a member of the Church." She let out a sigh. "You have to make this decision for you, not for me."

His eyes softened, and he reached for her hand once more. "I'm making this decision for both of us, but if you weren't here, I would still make it for myself."

"Even if it meant losing your family, maybe even your country?"

Garrett nodded somberly. "Even then."

* * *

The site for the new temple was twenty miles inland. It would sit up on a hill, overlooking the main road leading to it as well as the Mediterranean Sea in the distance. When Garrett and Janessa arrived, a crowd of Church members was already gathering around the groundbreaking site. Several photographers and reporters were also in attendance.

Though a security sweep had already taken place, Garrett's bodyguards checked the area a second time before one of them opened the door. Garrett's automatic smile widened when he saw Tim standing outside of the vehicle.

"It's about time you got here." Tim grinned as he accepted Garrett's outstretched hand.

"I'm here now." Garrett returned his smile and turned to Janessa. "This is Tim O'Donnell, the friend I told you about from law school."

Janessa's smile was warm and welcoming. She reached out and shook his hand. "I'm so glad to finally meet you."

"Me too," Tim said, his eyes shifting back to Garrett. "So how did things go with your parents?"

Garrett understood his meaning perfectly and shook his head. "As expected."

"Garrett, I'm sorry." Tim laid a hand on his shoulder. "I really hoped they would understand."

"The jury's still out as to the consequences. But let's not worry about that right now." Garrett motioned up the hill. "You said you wanted to meet your prophet. There's no time like the present."

"You didn't tell me the prophet was going to be here." Janessa's eyes widened as Garrett took her hand.

Garrett leaned closer and spoke softly. "You didn't ask."

"What was I thinking?" she said wryly and fell into step with him.

Flanked by two bodyguards, Garrett expertly led them through the crowd and past the reporters for the brief ceremony. The prophet addressed those gathered, inspiring the members in this tiny country to appreciate the new opportunities the temple would bring them.

As Garrett listened to the words spoken and considered his family's reaction to his impending baptism, he could only wonder how much worse last night's conversation would have gone if he had also disclosed his plans to marry Janessa in the temple, a building his family would not be permitted to enter.

* * *

"They might still show up," Tim commented as Garrett glanced at the door for the fifth time in as many minutes.

"I don't think so." Garrett took his seat on the cushioned chair in the front row.

A minor act of deception had helped clear most of the guests from the building. To make it appear that they were leaving, Garrett and Janessa had moved to the back of the church building, and a few minutes later their limousine drove away as though they were inside. In reality, they had hidden in a classroom for a few minutes while they waited for the guests to leave.

Only a handful of people still remained in the building, and all of them were now gathered in the small font room. To Garrett's delight, the branch president had informed the prophet of Garrett's impending baptism, and he had been able to stay to witness the event. Janessa sat on one side of Garrett and reached over to give his hand a comforting squeeze as the branch president stood up to conduct the meeting.

The branch president offered a short talk about baptism and confirmation, after which Tim entered the baptismal font with Garrett. As he stepped into the water, Garrett's mind raced with all of the possibilities and the many outcomes of this step he was seconds from taking. Then he glanced up and saw the prophet's calm smile. His eyes then darted to Janessa and the tears glistening in her eyes.

He closed his own eyes as Tim began the baptismal prayer. The moment he was submerged beneath the water, he felt a peace unlike any he had ever experienced. When he stood once again, he looked up to see Janessa smiling down at him.

When it came time for Garrett to be confirmed a member of the Church, the Spirit filled the room as Tim laid his hands on Garrett's head. The prayer he offered spoke of many things, including how Garrett would come to rely on the Holy Ghost as he helped lead his country in difficult times as well as in prosperity.

Hope leapt in Garrett's heart, and he prayed his father would allow him the opportunity. When the prayer concluded, Garrett looked up to see his mother and brother. Stefano's eyes met his briefly before he reached for the doorknob and escorted their mother into the hall.

A mixture of emotions rushed through him—disappointment that his father wasn't present, surprise that the rest of the family had come, and, as he glanced at Janessa, hope for the future.

chapter 26

"Where's Tim?" Janessa stepped next to Garrett on the terrace as darkness settled over the village below.

"The branch president gave him a ride to the chateau so he could settle in," Garrett told her. "He wasn't sure he wanted to be around my father quite yet."

"Does your father know Tim is the one who gave you the Book of Mormon?"

"I don't think so, but Tim didn't want to take any chances." Garrett shrugged. "He knows we're returning tomorrow anyway."

"It's great that Tim could come for your baptism," Janessa commented, noticing the fatigue in his eyes. "How are you feeling?"

"I'm relieved that my father hasn't kicked me out yet." He tried to keep his voice lighthearted but couldn't quite pull it off.

"I think that's a good sign," Janessa agreed. "I imagine it will take him some time to come to terms with your decision."

Garrett nodded as he looked out over the water. "I wish my family could understand what it was like when I was confirmed a member of the Church. I had the most incredible feeling."

"The Spirit in the room was very strong," Janessa said as she laid a hand on his arm.

"Yes, but it wasn't only that." Garrett turned now to face her. "When Tim spoke of my service to my country, I felt this new sense of obligation, like it's my responsibility to protect Meridia from the world."

"You've always had that responsibility."

"Not like this." He shook his head. "I wasn't born to rule, nor have I ever had the desire to be king. In that moment though, I felt like the fate of Meridia was in my hands—not my father's hands, not Stefano's, but mine." Garrett glanced back at the palace.

"Perhaps it is." Janessa reached for his hand. "You have a gift now that they don't have. Maybe you felt that impression because there will be times when the Lord will direct you in a way that isn't what your father or brother would choose."

Garrett sighed. "I didn't expect to feel this weight."

"All I can tell you is to pray about it," Janessa suggested. "If there is something you are meant to do, the Lord will help you know what it is."

Nodding, Garrett turned to look over the Mediterranean Sea once again. He stared for a moment before he realized what he was staring at. "Do you see that?"

"What?"

"Is that a boat down there?" Garrett pointed to a dark spot in the water midway between two of the port authority posts. "It's running dark."

Janessa struggled to see the faint wake in the moonlight. "Do you think it's smugglers?"

"Why else would a boat be out there without lights on?"

"I'll get a phone," Janessa said, quickly turning to go inside. A moment later she returned with Stefano, who held a cordless phone to his ear.

Stefano passed the phone to Garrett. "The port authority is already on the line."

Garrett took the phone and gave the port authority the location of the boat headed out to sea. From where they stood, he could see a government vessel move to intercept and a second port authority boat take up the chase.

"It's trying to get away." Garrett handed the phone back to Stefano and headed for the palace. "I'm going down there."

"I'm coming with you." Janessa started after him.

"Wait." Garrett slowed for a moment. "I need you to get a message to your navy. Our latest reports showed one of your destroyers right outside our territorial waters. We may need it to help us."

Janessa sighed, reaching for the phone Stefano held out to her. "At least take your cell phone with you so we can get in touch with you."

"I have it." Garrett nodded and turned toward the garage.

"I'll come with you," Stefano told him.

Janessa headed for her room to retrieve her phone directory. She made the call to the local fleet commander and was surprised when she met resistance.

"I'm sorry, miss, but I'm not authorized to divert a US vessel into Meridian waters without permission from the Meridian government."

"I am calling you at the request of Prince Garrett of Meridia," Janessa told him. "I was assured that our military would help Meridia in any way possible."

"This sounds like an internal matter," the commander returned.

"This boat may be involved with the embassy bombing," Janessa told him, shifting tactics. "We can't afford to let it get away."

"I'll have to call Washington for authorization."

"There's no time for that," Janessa insisted, her mind whirling. "What if the king of Meridia were to request your help directly? Would that give you the authorization you need?"

"Well, I guess it would."

"Just a minute." Janessa strode down the hall to King Eduard's office and rapped on the door. The king opened it a moment later, surprise lighting his eyes.

"Your Majesty, would you please tell the US Navy fleet commander that he has authorization to enter your waters in pursuit of a suspected smuggler?"

King Eduard's eyebrows rose at her request, but he reached for the phone and waved Janessa into his office. When he spoke, his tone was commanding and authoritative. "This is King Eduard Fortier of Meridia. To whom am I speaking?"

Janessa sighed in relief as the commander gave his name and rank to King Eduard.

"Commander, you were just speaking with Janessa Rogers, my son's fiancée. I would appreciate it if you would note that any request from her is to be treated as a request from the royal family of Meridia."

Janessa's jaw dropped as he continued.

"Now, are you able to assist us in this matter?" King Eduard listened to the commander go through standard procedure. With a sigh, the king moved to unlock a drawer in his desk and then rattled off an authorization code to verify that he was indeed the king of Meridia. Once the verification process was complete, he nodded. "Good. Now I'll give you back to Miss Rogers."

Janessa took the phone, struggling to keep her composure. Still standing in the king's office, she gave the commander the last known location of the boat in question and also Garrett's cell phone number so that he would be in direct contact with the most reliable source. After receiving assurances that the US destroyer was indeed being diverted to assist them, Janessa hung up the phone.

"Are you going to tell me what's going on now?" King Eduard asked, motioning for Janessa to sit down.

"I'm sorry, Your Majesty." Janessa sat down and took a deep breath. "While Garrett was out on the terrace, he noticed a boat running dark. Assuming that it might be involved in a smuggling ring, he and Stefano called the port authorities to intercept it. When it headed for the open sea, Garrett asked me to engage the US Navy to help."

"And one of your commanders was slow to cooperate," King Eduard stated.

Janessa nodded, still reeling over his instructions to the commander to treat her as a member of the royal family. Could he have already come to terms with Garrett's decision, or was his request simply for his convenience during her stay? Reluctantly, she tried to push her personal thoughts aside and deal with the matter at hand. "I'm sorry to have put you on the spot like that. I didn't want to take the chance that we would lose a valuable lead."

The king leaned back in his chair and studied her openly. "I'm surprised you came to me for help after our talk this morning."

"As I said earlier, I'm here to help keep your family safe."

He smiled at this as though she had just shared her deepest secrets. "Have you always worked well under pressure?"

"I don't know." She considered. "I've always been quick to react to situations, though I'm not sure that's necessarily a good thing."

"Your assistance since your arrival has been exemplary," he started. "Though I'm still not sure how I feel about my son marrying a spy."

"I've never thought of myself that way." Janessa fought the urge to fidget, wondering how he had discovered that the engagement was real.

"What, then? You're employed by the Central Intelligence Agency, an organization known for spying."

Janessa sighed, grasping for the right words. "Meridia utilizes various organizations to obtain information for its protection, correct?" When the king nodded, she continued. "That's all I do. I try to uncover the threats against my country and the country where I live. When I'm successful, I feel like I'm helping keep people safe."

"Are you ready to give up that part of your life to marry my son?" Eduard asked now.

"Forgive me, Your Majesty, but how did you know we're really planning to marry?"

"I'm not blind, and more particularly, neither is the queen." He waved a hand absently as though brushing away an insignificant detail. "We only had to see you together to know where you were headed." He leaned forward and pressed on once more. "Do you understand your career will be over the moment you marry Garrett?"

Nerves jumped in her stomach as she considered the enormity of what he was saying. If Garrett was permitted to remain part of the royal family, she really would have to give up everything to marry him, not only her job but also her country. Janessa took a steadying breath before answering. "My future career plans would depend on what role you allow Garrett to have in your family. Besides, I have always been taught to put family first."

The telephone interrupted any response the king might have made. Janessa started to excuse herself, but the king motioned for her to remain where she was. The conversation only lasted a few minutes, and the king's expression remained unreadable.

He hung up and looked at Janessa. "It seems our countries work well together. With the help of your Navy, our port authority has boarded the vessel in question."

"Did they find anything?"

"Millions of dollars in stolen artwork."

"What?" Janessa shook her head in amazement.

"Garrett said at least one of the paintings was part of the exhibit in Bellamo."

"Is he sure?" Janessa's eyes widened. "That exhibit just opened Saturday. We weren't informed of any theft."

"If the theft occurred while the paintings were being shipped to Meridia, we never would have known if a forgery were put on display."

"How often do the museums here participate in exchanges like this one?"

The king paused as he made a quick mental calculation. "Between the museum in Bellamo and the one here in Calene, I would say five or six times a year."

"Alberto Manero, the gas station owner, deposited money into his offshore accounts at odd intervals. Art may not have been the only thing being smuggled through the port in Calene, but that would explain most of the money."

"And the embassy bombing?"

"I don't know. Garrett and I think the bombing may have been the smugglers' attempt to keep the US Navy out of Meridian waters." Janessa stood. "I'll call and see if my agency has had any luck in tracing those deposits."

The king nodded. "In the meantime, I would like to get this naval base issue resolved as soon as possible. One of our destroyers will be returning tomorrow afternoon to our naval base in Bellamo after being away for several months. I think it would be appropriate for you and Garrett to welcome the crew home."

"I would like that very much."

"Perhaps I will invite that commander to join you. I think he may appreciate a tour as well." A hint of sarcasm laced his voice.

Janessa's smile was instant. "I think that's a wonderful idea. We can thank him for his assistance tonight."

"Exactly."

chapter 27

Garrett listened to the museum director's report, but his eyes were on the two paintings in front of him. The forgery was good—so good that only an expert would be able to detect any differences. Even an expert would be unlikely to identify the forgery without being requested to go through the authentication process. These two paintings were just a sample of the artwork that had been stolen from this particular exhibit on loan from the Louvre. Three other paintings had also been taken and replaced with clever forgeries.

So far no one had been able to determine exactly when the switch had been made, but one thing was certain—the originals had made it all the way to Meridia. Whether they were stolen during transport or after they arrived at the museum was a question no one was yet able to answer.

The two men apprehended by the port authority had been identified, but they were not revealing any information. One of the men was Italian, the other French. Neither had a previous criminal record, nor were they suspected by Interpol of any major crimes.

"Regardless of when the pieces were stolen," Garrett finally said, "whoever took them had access either during transport or after they arrived."

"I'm afraid so." Pierre Dumond nodded. "I wish I could tell you that this was a clever theft, but I think it must have been an inside job."

"Security will need a list of everyone who has had access since the paintings came into our possession, including the security team who oversaw the transport."

"Yes, Your Highness." He bowed. "I will have that information sent over right away."

Garrett glanced at his watch. "I'd like a copy of your report as well."

"Of course." Pierre nodded. "Your Highness, may I also suggest that the art expert examine the paintings in the palace and the chateau?"

Garrett turned to look back at Pierre. "Do you think that's necessary?"

"Until we can determine how the artwork is being stolen, I think it is prudent to examine everything that uses our transportation system."

"You're right. Please let Martino know when that can be arranged."

Isabel Dumond stepped through the door as Garrett moved to leave. Today her model-thin form was clad in a short dress of deep violet. "Your Highness. I thought I saw your car outside."

"Hello, Isabel," Garrett greeted her.

"Did you come to look over the exhibit?" Isabel stepped closer, sliding a hand into the crook of his arm. "I'd be happy to show it to you."

"Thank you, but I'm late for a meeting." Garrett took a step away, relieved that Isabel didn't hang on. "Perhaps another time."

"Of course." Isabel smiled at him and watched him go.

* * *

Janessa stepped into the foyer of the chateau dressed in a simple cream business suit. She and Garrett had arrived earlier that morning and, at King Eduard's personal invitation, a member of the US Navy was expected to accompany them on their tour.

She looked up as Garrett and another man approached. Garrett wore his dress uniform, but the other man was dressed in a suit rather than a military uniform. Garrett stepped forward to take her hand. "You look perfect."

"Thank you. I could say the same for you." Janessa turned to face the man beside him.

"Janessa Rogers, this is Paul Hardel, the secretary of the United States Navy."

Janessa extended her hand, surprise crossing her face. "Secretary Hardel, I'm sorry I wasn't informed of your arrival."

"Our president wants this naval base matter settled, and it seems the king agrees," Secretary Hardel told her.

"I hope an arrangement can be made to everyone's benefit. The assistance from the navy last night was certainly very much appreciated by the Meridian government," Janessa commented.

"My fleet commander asked me to extend his apology. He wasn't aware of your position with the royal family," he said.

"An apology isn't necessary," Janessa insisted, though she had to fight back a smile as she considered how the commander from the night before must have felt when the king's voice came over the line.

On the ride over to the base, Garrett gave the secretary a brief overview of the base's history and capabilities. Moments later they disembarked from the limousine at the naval base. Though the base was secure, Janessa still checked the position of Garrett's bodyguards before moving forward to greet the officers designated to meet them.

After a few introductions were made, they toured the portion of the base that was largely unused. Buildings that had previously housed military families stood in various stages of disrepair. The housing units that had been built to replace them were now located on the other side of the base, and the money budgeted to tear down the old buildings had been needed elsewhere.

Garrett shared some of these details with Janessa and the secretary, and Janessa was pleased by the depth and sincerity of the secretary's questions. Before they left, Garrett stepped out in front of a large crowd consisting of the men who had just returned home and their families. After giving the expected speech, Garrett worked his way through the crowd, shaking hands with many who had come to see him.

A small contingent of reporters and photographers continued to snap photos as Garrett led Janessa and their guest back to the limousine. Once seated inside, the secretary immediately picked up his copy of Janessa's proposal and began skimming through it. A moment later, he looked up at Garrett.

"How favorable is your government to granting the US access to this base?"

"We find it the most credible solution to suit both our needs," Garrett said. "Outfitting a portion of our base to accommodate your Navy would appease the environmental societies here in Meridia, and, contrary to our original assumptions, the security risks would be significantly lower than if you were to construct a new facility."

"If both of our governments agree, how soon could construction begin?" Secretary Hardel asked.

"Within a matter of weeks." Garrett lifted a shoulder. "I believe once our militaries agree on how to handle security, construction could begin immediately."

"In that case, I would appreciate an audience with your father to finalize our proposal," Secretary Hardel stated.

"I'm certain that can be arranged. If you're agreeable, you and I can work out the basic details when we get back to the chateau. We can then set up a formal meeting with my father."

Secretary Hardel nodded. "The sooner the better."

A delivery truck was parked beside the chateau when they returned. Commander Peters stood with a clipboard in hand as he checked off the equipment being unloaded.

Janessa turned to Garrett. "I want to oversee the installation of the new sensors. I have my cell phone if you need me."

"I'm sure we can handle it from here," Garrett assured her. As Janessa moved to greet Commander Peters, Garrett motioned to the front door. "We can meet in the library, and I'll have our cook send in some lunch."

Secretary Hardel took a moment to watch the activity at the back of the truck before turning to follow Garrett inside. "Is it really a good idea for her to be openly involved in your security?"

"I keep asking myself the same thing," Garrett admitted. "I'm afraid she doesn't trust anyone else to do the job right unless she's watching over their shoulder."

* * *

"Let's try this again," Janessa said into her cell phone as Paolo led her mount out of the stables already saddled for her. She flipped the phone closed, stepped into the stirrup, and swung herself onto the bay gelding. "Thank you, Paolo."

"You need to bring that young man of yours riding. It has been too long since he has been able to ride for pleasure."

"I'll see what I can do." Janessa grinned at the mention of Garrett.

Paolo handed her the reins as Tim appeared leading another mount.

"I didn't realize you were back from the naval base," Tim told her casually as he swung himself up on his horse. "Do you mind if I join you?"

Janessa gave a shrug, not sure how much Tim knew about her real reason for coming to Meridia. As she looked at him, she realized she wasn't sure what his reasons were for being here either. Not for the first time, she caught a flash of awareness and intensity in his expression that just shouted *Cop*. Deciding that it wouldn't matter if security was tracking two riders or one, she nodded in agreement. "That's fine."

Following a path similar to the first time she had tested the new security, Janessa rode through the hillside with Tim following closely behind her. This time she penetrated closer to the chateau before turning back and crossing over the line of sensors once more. Anticipating that the tide was low enough, she headed down a path to the beach.

With a nod to the guards stationed on the beach, Janessa led Tim through the previous blind spot, hoping that the security office was now aware of their presence. She guided her horse down the beach until she was right next to the chateau. Then she pulled her cell phone out of her pocket and turned to Tim. "I promised to check in."

She pressed speed dial for Levi's cell phone. "I just wanted to let you know I'm down at the beach."

"If our sensors are correct, you are approximately fifty yards from the edge of the swimming pool," Levi told her. "We now have an overlap between the two types of sensors of approximately five hundred yards."

"Excellent." She looked up at the chateau, noticing Garrett and Secretary Hardel sitting on the terrace. "I'll see you in a little while."

She hung up and slipped the phone back into her pocket. With a wave to Garrett, she nudged her mount onward and headed for the stables with Tim following behind her. They took a few moments to cool down their mounts and then headed for the terrace.

At their approach, Garrett and Secretary Hardel stood. Garrett and Tim exchanged barely perceptible nods just before Tim was introduced to the secretary.

After they all exchanged pleasantries, Tim told Janessa, "I'm going to head inside and get cleaned up. Thanks for letting me join you."

Janessa nodded, suddenly suspicious that Tim's presence at the stables was not coincidental. She brushed her observation aside for the moment as Garrett motioned for her to join them. She took a seat and waited for the men to do the same. Janessa looked up at Garrett and smiled. "I hope your day has been as successful as ours."

"The new sensors worked?" Garrett asked.

She nodded. "At this point, I think we can assure your father that the chateau is as secure as the palace, at least for now."

"Where did you receive your training in security?" Secretary Hardel asked.

"I sort of picked it up along the way," Janessa said vaguely. She was certain that the secretary knew she was working for the US government, but she wasn't sure she should divulge more information than necessary. "How are your negotiations progressing?"

"Very well," Secretary Hardel said, glancing at Garrett as he nodded in agreement. "As soon as we can finalize the security details, I believe we will be able to reach an agreement everyone will be happy with."

Garrett tapped a finger on the arm of his chair, considering. "Have you met Commander Peters?"

"I don't believe so." The secretary shook his head.

"He's the US naval officer that was overseeing the new equipment that arrived today. He's been very helpful in assisting us with a security problem here at the chateau. I don't know if his schedule will permit it, but it might be wise to have him meet with our security personnel," Garrett suggested. "Since he is already here, the meetings could be kept low profile."

Secretary Hardel nodded. "I'm sure we can make Commander Peters available to meet with your military for the next few weeks."

"I can make arrangements for him to stay on the base," Garrett told him.

Janessa stood, motioning for the men to remain seated. "It sounds like you gentlemen have everything well in hand, so if you'll excuse me, I'm going to go upstairs and wash up."

"Don't take too long," Garrett suggested. "Patrice said something about chocolate mousse for dessert tonight."

"I'll hurry." Janessa grinned.

chapter 28

The next day, Garrett and Janessa stood in Janessa's sitting room looking over a handwritten list. "I'm sorry, Janessa, but I can't imagine any of these people being involved." Garrett studied the list of his close friends, a list he had helped compose.

"I don't know where else to look." Janessa stood beside him and stared at the names. "Whoever planted that bomb knew you well, and it was likely someone familiar with the chateau."

"Maybe we should concentrate more on people who know the chateau," Garrett suggested. "It's possible that someone noticed me pulling my car keys from my pocket as I walked to the garage sometime in the past."

"Then it could be anyone who has been a casual guest while you were staying here."

He nodded, noting the fatigue and worry on her face. Though it wasn't yet noon, she looked exhausted. "You aren't getting enough sleep."

"I know." Janessa sighed. "But the threats keep coming, and the gala is a little over two weeks away." She motioned to the file on her coffee table and sat down on the sofa. "I'm still working on the employee lists, but so far everything checks out. There's a high turnover rate with the caterers, so that's going to be the biggest challenge, trying to keep up with them."

Garrett nodded as he sat beside her. "Pierre Dumond, the museum director, narrowed the list down to three people besides himself who had access to the artwork at the times the stolen paintings could have been switched."

"How many other thefts have been identified?"

"Only four so far. Two of them we already knew about. One was recovered during an arrest by Interpol in Paris two years ago, and another was discovered missing by an art expert in Cairo. The other two were both from the National Gallery of Art in Washington, D.C."

"Had all of them been loaned to the museum in Bellamo?"

"No. The first painting was on loan to the museum in Calene. That theft was detected almost three years ago."

"Which coincides with Manero's bank records. What we really need are the records of everyone who had access to all of the artwork in question. If this has happened at both museums here, I would have to think that the switches must be taking place during transport."

"The investigators are looking over the security and employment records for the past three years for both museums," Garrett told her. He leaned over and gave her a quick kiss. "I have to get back over to the naval base, but I should be back before dinner."

"Do we have plans tonight?"

"I was hoping for a nice quiet dinner. Just the two of us."

"Sounds perfect."

* * *

Janessa stepped out of her room and was surprised to see Levi approaching. "Is something wrong?"

His hand tightened on the file he held, and his eyes darted to it before he looked back at her. "We received another threat. I thought you should see this right away."

Janessa's pulse jumped in her throat, too many images leaping to her mind, but she held out her hand.

Levi handed her the envelope, his voice low as he spoke. "Janessa, this isn't like the others."

She nodded, bracing herself against the possibilities. Slowly she opened the file and gasped. The images were similar to the other threats and yet so different. Like the others, words had been cut from newspapers to create the phrase "The Americans will be the death of the royal family." This time, however, the photos were not from the newspapers, but bright, glossy photographs manipulated to create the frightening images.

A photo of Janessa wearing an evening gown was in the center. The photo had been altered so that she was holding a smoking gun—a gun aimed at Garrett. Surrounding her image were photos of the members of the royal family, each one manipulated to show a horrific death.

Janessa took a shallow breath and then slowly drew a deeper one. "These photos were all taken the night of the gas station fire."

"That's what I thought." Levi nodded. "I checked out the list of photographers that were there that night. Unfortunately, all of these photos are on the internet. The magazine *Societé* has them on their website. Anyone could have printed them off."

"Another dead end." Janessa shook her head in frustration as she fought the wave of nausea that flowed through her.

"The police have already started trying to trace everyone who has accessed *Societé's* website since these photos were uploaded, but it sounds like there may be too many to narrow down the possibilities."

"Let me know if they find anything."

Levi nodded as he started back down the hall.

Janessa walked back into her room to put this latest threat with the others she had collected since her arrival. As she placed the thick file back into the safe in her room, she tried to fight the sinking feeling that her engagement to Garrett—whether fake or real—might be the greatest security risk of all.

* * *

After her meeting with the caterers, Janessa returned to her suite to do some research. She pulled up the internet site for *Societé,* the upscale society magazine that focused on the prominent citizens in Meridia and the surrounding countries. As she studied the photos on their website, she took note of those in attendance. Cynthia Renault was in many of the photos, reminding Janessa of a Hollywood starlet accustomed to being in the limelight.

Unable to find anything of significance, Janessa clicked through the website to find a list of the magazine's photographers. When she reached the editorial page, her eyes widened. The managing editor was Alfonzo Renault. Curious to see if he was related to Cynthia, Janessa dug a little deeper. After a few minutes of searching, she came across an article about the Renault family—Tomas, the owner of *Societé* magazine, with his two children—Alfonzo and Cynthia.

When she did another search and came across another image of Cynthia Renault, her mouth fell open. Beside an article dated today were several photos of Garrett with his arms around Cynthia. The surge of jealousy lasted several long minutes before she could bring herself to think logically. The photos had been taken on a yacht, but Janessa couldn't think of a single day since her arrival that Garrett would have had time to go out on the water like that, much less with another woman.

As she looked closer, she could see the subtle differences between the man she had spoken to hours before and the one in the photo. His hair was a bit longer now, his skin not quite so tanned. Surely these photos must have been taken when Garrett had dated Cynthia years ago, but why were they suddenly surfacing, and who was trying to make it look like Garrett was being unfaithful?

She stormed out of her room, not terribly surprised to see Tim down the hall. Every time she turned around he seemed to be coming around a corner. She nodded a greeting and quickly turned toward the back staircase. She needed to get out for a while and clear her head. She jogged down the stairs, oblivious to everything until she heard the click beneath her foot and froze. It was then that she noticed Max sitting at attention and Alan squatting down by the door.

"Don't move," Alan commanded in a quiet voice.

Slowly Janessa shifted her gaze to Alan. "I guess I found what you're looking for," she managed as she swallowed hard.

As Tim started down the stairs, Alan caught his eye and held up a hand to stop Tim's forward motion. "Go tell Martino to evacuate the chateau. Everyone needs to use the main entrance."

"What's wrong?"

"I think Janessa just found another bomb."

"Oh, no," he breathed before turning to race back up the stairs.

Terrified, Janessa tried to maintain a calm tone. "Can you see how it was planted?"

"There's got to be a loose floorboard." Alan skimmed his fingers lightly over the wooden floor. "This area was clean when I checked it out late last night."

Janessa's mind raced. "One of the caterers could have slipped away when they were loading up."

"Right now it doesn't matter much who did it." Alan gently pulled up a loose board that was directly in front of Janessa.

Tim appeared beside Alan with Levi. "What can we do to help?"

Alan glanced at their feet and then up at both men. "Levi, give me your shoes."

Levi didn't hesitate as he reached down and pulled both shoes off and squatted down to hand them to Alan. "Here."

Alan took one shoe from him and used it to brace one side of the floorboard up. Then he used the second shoe to brace the other side of the board. He dug a flashlight from the tool belt he typically wore and shined it beneath the board. "It's active."

"I already figured that out," Janessa managed. "Tell me something I don't know."

"Basically, we're dealing with a grenade-type explosive. When you stepped down, your weight knocked loose the pin that kept the bomb stable." Alan turned to Levi. "Go get me some tweezers. There's a pair of rubber-tipped ones in the toolbox in my room."

"I'm on it," Levi agreed and raced in the opposite direction.

Tim edged closer to Alan. "Can you see the pin?"

"Yeah." Alan shifted the flashlight from the explosive to the subflooring, where a metal pin lay in the dust. "But I'm going to need some help to get it back in."

Levi returned a moment later with tweezers in hand. "Here you go."

"Okay, let's get this done." Alan instructed both men about what he needed them to do. Tim sprawled out on his stomach on one side of Alan so he could hold the explosive steady while Levi sat on the other side and aimed the flashlight at the tiny piece of metal that could save Janessa's life.

Carefully, Alan reached beneath the board and used the tweezers to extend his reach and grasp the metal pin. He then shifted so he could insert it back into the explosive. "Okay, everyone hold real still." Alan's voice was calm despite the trickle of sweat now visible on his forehead.

"Wait!" Janessa urged. "Are you sure there aren't any booby traps like the last one?"

"It looks clean," Alan told her. "Trust me. We'll get you out of this."

Slowly, Janessa nodded her head and closed her eyes. She could hear the rustle of the breeze outside, she could smell the mixture of cologne from the men trying to save her, and she could feel her heart pounding. A million thoughts rushed through her mind as she faced the reality that this breath might be her last.

"Got it." Alan's voice broke through, and she slowly opened her eyes. "Everyone clear out of here before Janessa moves."

Janessa watched Levi and Tim reluctantly move to a safe distance while Alan remained sprawled on the floor with his hand beneath the floorboard. "What about you?" she asked.

"I'm going to make sure that it doesn't reengage," Alan told her. "Slowly take a step back."

Janessa nodded and took a deep breath. Carefully, she slid one foot back and then the other. Relief surged through her whole body as she exhaled heavily, and Tim and Levi moved forward once more.

"Let's get you out of here," Tim said, taking Janessa by the arm.

"What about the bomb?"

"I'll help him with it," Levi told her, squatting down as Alan began removing the tape that held the explosive in place. "You go get some air."

Reluctantly, Janessa nodded. She let Tim lead her out the terrace doors, vaguely noticing the servants clustered near the kitchen entrance.

"Are you okay?" Tim asked gently.

Janessa shook her head. "I know you're here to watch out for me, but I need a few minutes alone." She motioned to the beach. "I'm going to take a walk down by the water, but I'll stay in your line of sight, okay?"

Surprise lit his eyes, but he nodded. "I'll wait here."

With a nod, Janessa moved toward the sea.

chapter 29

Garrett glanced down at his watch before exiting the museum. In his hand he held the latest report on the art thefts. The task of finding someone who had access to the artwork at the time of each theft would be time consuming, and he hoped their security forces were up to the task.

He approached the waiting limousine, surprised to see more reporters than usual gathered nearby. Still focused on the information in his hand, he let his security detail keep the press at bay as he stepped into the limousine where Enrico was waiting. As soon as Enrico settled into the driver's seat, he turned to look back at Garrett through the open window.

"Your Highness, another bomb was found at the chateau," Enrico told him, his eyes dark with concern.

"What?" Sheer panic rushed through Garrett. "Was anyone hurt?"

"No, sir, but there's something else." Enrico handed Garrett a stack of newspapers and magazines through the window. "Martino asked me to obtain these for you."

Garrett's eyes widened when he saw the photograph of himself on the front page of the tabloid Enrico had given him. In it he was standing aboard his private yacht, his arms wrapped around Cynthia Renault. He vaguely remembered the outing nearly four years ago, and if he wasn't mistaken, this exact picture had appeared in a newspaper a day or two afterward.

He flipped to the next newspaper, annoyed to find similar photos with Cynthia. The headlines consistently insinuated that he was secretly seeing this woman while engaged to Janessa. He looked up at Enrico. "Has Janessa seen these?"

"I believe so, Your Highness."

"Take me home."

Enrico nodded as Garrett closed the window between them.

* * *

Janessa stood on the beach watching the last of the sun's rays glisten off of the Mediterranean. Her hair hung loose, the breeze pulling at the ends as the air began to cool. She wanted to be alone, but she knew she was far from it.

Activity was still buzzing at the chateau, where the most recent bomb was being loaded into a vehicle from the naval base, where it would be taken to be analyzed for fingerprints. Tim stood above her in the gardens, a silent sentry watching over her. Unfortunately, he wasn't the only one. Several photographers and reporters were parked outside of the chateau gates. She didn't have to look to know that several had their telephoto lenses aimed in her direction.

Never before had she considered what it would be like to crave solitude and not be able to find it. Could she really live like this, with the press always hovering around a corner? Would her relationship with Garrett be able to withstand the strain of the exaggerations and purely fictional stories the papers would undoubtedly create when they couldn't find anything better to print?

Tears threatened as she realized it didn't matter. Whether she could learn to live with the intrusion was no longer an issue. As long as she was paired with Garrett, he was in danger. Even after this current threat was eliminated, there would always be extremists whose anti-American sentiments would threaten both their peace and their safety. She chastised herself for not facing this reality sooner. A tear spilled over and rolled down her cheek unnoticed. If she truly loved him, she had to leave him and this place.

Her heart broke neatly in two as her dreams shattered amidst the crashing waves and the mournful cries of the seagulls. The Meridian temple would be built, Garrett would eventually find someone else to love, and she would go on, year after year, wishing for what could have been.

She wiped at her eyes before glancing back up at the press corps. She considered having the guards chase them away, but she imagined that they would leave on their own once they found there was nothing new to report. As she turned back toward the water, the thought came clearly into her mind: The press was camped outside the chateau because they were expecting something to report.

If Garrett truly had been unfaithful, no one would expect Janessa to remain in Meridia. They were waiting for her to leave, she realized. Questions tumbled through her mind as she tried to analyze the situation without tying her emotions to the problem. Those recent tabloids were likely not just the mean trick of an ex-girlfriend. It seemed that someone was worried that Garrett's engagement to an American would translate into stronger ties between the US and Meridia. But what if that wasn't the real issue? Or what if that was only part of it? Could her presence be perceived as interfering with the smuggling operation?

She caught a glimpse of the limousine approaching, and her thoughts turned to the man within. Would he understand why they couldn't get married? She uttered a quiet prayer, begging for strength as she saw Garrett descend the steps to the beach.

He closed the distance between them, but before he could reach for her, Janessa nodded to the crowd that had formed on the road. "We have an audience," Janessa began.

"Nothing in the papers is true," Garrett told her without preamble.

"I know that." Janessa sighed. "But I'm concerned that several of the articles quoted Lady Renault. Why is she lying about having a relationship with you?"

"She has long aspired to marry a prince. I can only think that she considers you the reason I'm not interested in her." Garrett shrugged. "I wish I could say this was the first time, but she has caused problems with other women I've gone out with as well."

"These articles might be coincidental, or maybe Cynthia is somehow involved with the other problems we've encountered." Janessa tried to sound professional but didn't quite manage it. "Someone is going to great lengths to get rid of me one way or another."

"I heard you found another bomb." Garrett couldn't hide the worry in his voice.

Janessa closed her eyes and banked down on the panic rushing through her. She took a deep breath and forced herself to say the words. "I have to leave here. This isn't going to stop until I'm gone."

"You aren't the type to run away," Garrett insisted, his voice clipped. "What's really going on here? I already told you that nothing is going on between me and Cynthia."

"I can't live like this!" Janessa shouted, her words carrying on the wind. With some effort she managed to lower her voice, but the emotions didn't fade. "As long as we're together, someone will be trying to hurt you. I can't spend the rest of my life wondering when someone is going to make it past security, always wondering if this will be the day that some security guard informs me that a bomb or assassin succeeded in taking your life."

"Janessa, these types of threats exist in all countries, including your own. You have to keep them in perspective," Garrett insisted. "Rarely does anyone succeed in following through."

"Then explain to me why we've disarmed two bombs in the space of a week!" Janessa shook her head. "Maybe it would be different if I wasn't American . . ." Her voice trailed off, and she twisted the engagement ring off of her finger. "I can't change who I am any more than you can. I wish I could."

Garrett just stared at her as she pressed the ring into his hand. "Please tell me this is for the press's benefit."

"I'm sorry, Garrett." Janessa shook her head as tears threatened once more. Quickly, she turned and walked away.

* * *

The suitcases were loaded, the royal family's private jet prepared. Janessa descended the front steps of the chateau and entered the waiting limousine. She took her seat in the back as was expected, barely aware of Tim sitting in the seat across from her. She fought the urge to look out the back window as Enrico started down the drive.

"Are you okay?" Tim asked as soon as they cleared the chateau gates.

"I will be," Janessa said, praying that her words were true. She hoped the ache in her heart would subside eventually, but at the moment she couldn't imagine that even time would erase the hurt and regret.

"If there's anything I can do . . ." Tim's voice trailed off.

"Just be a friend to him," Janessa asked, struggling to keep the emotion out of her voice. "He's going to need someone to lean on, and you understand him best right now."

Tim nodded. "I'm going to stay in the States for a couple of days, but Lauren and I will be back in time for Garrett's priesthood ordination."

"I hope he keeps the gospel in his life," Janessa said softly. As tears threatened once more, she stared out the window at the country she had come to love as much as her own.

chapter 30

King Eduard's private jet ascended into the air as dozens of reporters looked on. The limousine that had delivered Tim and Janessa to the plane now pulled away and headed back to the chateau. Enrico drove for ten minutes before he finally spoke.

"Are you okay back there, signorina?"

Janessa sat up in the back seat, grateful for the tinted windows that hid her from the outside world. "Yes, thank you," she answered. "I hope your daughter enjoys her trip to Washington."

"She has never seen your country before," Enrico told her. "She is excited to have the opportunity."

"It was kind of her to help us out," Janessa commented. She had sent a letter for Tim to deliver to her sister, Mary. While she couldn't give her sister details, she thought she could trust Mary to pretend that Janessa was staying with her over the next few days. She lifted her eyes to meet Enrico's in the rearview mirror. "Do you think anyone could tell it wasn't me?"

Enrico shook his head. "With the wig, my daughter looked just like you."

"In that case, let's see if we can be as successful sneaking me back into the chateau."

"With pleasure."

* * *

Garrett stood beside his balcony door in the darkness. A swath of light spilled into the living area from the lamp in his bedroom, but he didn't notice. The last of the reporters had left an hour earlier, after determining that Garrett wasn't going to make another appearance. When Janessa departed, he had stood on his balcony and watched her go, his heart breaking as he thought of her words on the beach. Knowing she was going to continue on in her security responsibilities did little to ease his pain.

He couldn't understand how he had come to need her so quickly any more than he could understand her reasons for breaking their engagement. Surely she understood that the alliance between their two countries would progress regardless of their personal relationship.

Though Garrett knew Janessa didn't believe the newspaper articles, his father had insisted he address the press as though Cynthia had been the reason for her departure. Sounding upset took little effort as he spoke with the newspaper editors who had printed the tripe. Unfortunately, Cynthia had given several interviews insisting that she had been involved with Garrett since his return from the United States.

Though he hated the "he said, she said" scenario, his father's press secretary issued an official press release detailing the age of the photographs used with the articles. Along with Garrett's side of the story would be the news that despite the falsehood of these allegations, Janessa Rogers had returned to the United States.

In the meantime, his father's press secretary would use his sources to find out who had pushed the story in the first place and why Cynthia Renault was lying.

Garrett thought of Janessa's reaction to the articles and shook his head. She had never doubted him. She hadn't fallen prey to the pettiness of the press, but her fears for his safety had driven a wedge between them that he didn't understand. Why was she suddenly so sure that her presence was the cause of their problems? Couldn't she understand that his safety meant little if he had to spend the rest of his life without her?

With a sigh, he moved into his bedroom. He needed answers, answers he couldn't find by himself. Kneeling down by his bed, he bowed his head and poured out his heart to his Heavenly Father. Was Janessa the woman he was destined to marry? Who was trying to come between them and why? He continued to ask the questions, hoping and praying that the answers would be revealed to him. But the answers he searched for eluded him as he stood and looked out the window at the brilliant stars overhead. And yet, despite his confusion, a new sense of peace washed over him, a sliver of hope reminding him that his destiny was still his to control.

Though the chateau was outwardly at rest, Martino and the staff had been busy all evening. After Janessa's departure, Martino had met with all of the staff members, reminding them of their privacy agreements and the security issues of keeping the affairs of the chateau and the royal family confidential. Martino had also reviewed the new security procedures, which would remain in effect for the next several weeks. No longer would outsiders be permitted anywhere without an escort.

Janessa's belongings were moved into the suite across the hall just in case the paparazzi were aware of which window was hers. Unlike the rooms she had previously occupied, her new living space was actually an apartment, complete with an office and a small kitchenette.

When Garrett heard the car drive up, he fought the urge to meet Janessa at the stairs. Instead he waited several minutes until he was certain she would be alone. He knocked on her door twice before she cautiously opened it. He slipped inside without a word and closed the door behind him.

He studied her for a moment, concerned at how pale she looked. "What you said on the beach—you couldn't possibly mean it."

"I do mean it, Garrett." Janessa leaned against the back of the sofa. "If I stay, I might as well be the person holding a gun to your head. It's like Rominez all over again."

"Who?" The name rang a bell, but he couldn't place it. He assumed it was from a past assignment that had gone bad.

"It doesn't matter." Panic flashed in her eyes before she managed to control it. "I'm sorry, Garrett. I can't be with you knowing that my mere presence will put you at risk."

"Janessa, I love you." Garrett stepped forward and took her hand in his. He ignored her resistance and pushed on. "Nothing matters to me more than being with you. Can't you understand that?"

"I can't live like this." She blinked hard. "I just can't. One way or another, I'll be leaving after the gala. If it's too hard for you to have me here, I can ask Director Palmer to send a replacement. At this point, it won't matter, since I'm no longer visible to the public."

Garrett shook his head vehemently. "I don't want you to go."

"We don't always get what we want," Janessa said softly. "Please don't make this any harder than it has to be."

The pain in his chest became unbearable. "Martino will check in with you tomorrow to see to your needs. Patrice also knows that you're here. I believe she has already stocked the refrigerator for you."

"Thank you." Janessa nodded somberly.

Without another word, Garrett left the room with the shattered pieces of his heart.

* * *

Alan lingered by Prince Garrett's living quarters. His knock had gone unanswered, and he had little doubt as to where the prince had gone. Enrico had informed him of Janessa's arrival, and now he could only wait to do something he rarely did. Interfere.

Janessa hadn't told him that she was in love with Prince Garrett, but he had known her long enough that he didn't need to hear the words. All he had to do was look at her. He also knew that the breakup on the beach wasn't just for show. Janessa was hurting, more than he had ever seen her hurt before.

When the prince came out of Janessa's room, Alan realized that she wasn't the only one in pain.

"Your Highness, could I have a minute of your time?"

"Can it wait until morning?"

Alan shook his head. Patiently, he waited as Prince Garrett's swirl of emotions melted into resignation.

Garrett opened his door and motioned for Alan to follow him inside.

"I believe you were informed of the explosive we discovered today," Alan began as soon as the door was closed.

Garrett nodded. "Enrico mentioned it."

"Did he tell you how it was found?"

This time Garrett shook his head, puzzlement flashing in his eyes.

"Your Highness, Janessa found it the hard way." Alan's voice was low as he struggled to keep his own emotions in check and fight back the guilt.

"What do you mean . . ." Garrett's voice trailed off as Alan's meaning became clear.

"My dog had already identified the problem. I was trying to locate where the explosive device was hidden when Janessa came down the stairs." Alan took a deep breath. He wasn't going to be able to stem the guilt after all. "I didn't see her coming until it was too late. She stepped on the bomb and activated it just as she noticed me."

Garrett's face paled, but he nodded for Alan to continue.

"It was a crude land mine of sorts planted in the floor inside the private entrance." Alan lifted a hand and waved away that detail. "I've known Janessa for a long time, but I've never seen her this shaken up. She knows that if we hadn't found the bomb when we did, it's doubtful you would still be here."

Garrett's breath shuddered out. "This is twice she almost died trying to protect me."

"If she didn't think you still needed protection, she wouldn't be here," Alan commented. "I thought you should know."

Garrett nodded as Alan reached for the doorknob. He thought of Janessa's comment a few minutes earlier and asked, "Can you tell me about Rominez?"

Alan stared at Garrett for a moment as he considered the security implications. Realizing that most of the information had already been printed in newspapers, he let out a sigh. "Miguel Rominez was a drug dealer turned informant in Venezuela. He had a huge estate that was supposed to have the best security known to man, and he insisted that he would be safe there.

"Janessa and Levi kept pointing out problems, but the higher-ups didn't listen." Alan shrugged a shoulder. "In the end, Rominez was assassinated right in front of his fortress. A close friend of ours was on protection detail and died right beside him."

"Janessa was there when it happened?" Garrett asked.

Alan nodded. "Yeah, she was there."

chapter 31

Janessa scrutinized the employee lists as she moved across the room. She turned away from the large mirror hanging on the wall to avoid seeing the puffiness under her eyes and the lack of color in her cheeks. The food Patrice had left for her in the refrigerator had been left largely untouched. When Janessa did think to eat, she couldn't seem to decide what she wanted, so she didn't eat anything at all.

She didn't want to cry anymore, but tears always seemed to be just beneath the surface. The what ifs were killing her, one memory at a time. What if Garrett wasn't a prince? What if they were from the same country? What if they caught whoever was behind the latest bombing attempts? With a shake of her head, she reminded herself that even once the current threats were eliminated, Garrett would always be in danger as long as he was paired with an American.

Her stomach grumbled, but she ignored it, instead trying to concentrate on the list of service employees once more. She had been at it so long she could already recite the names, but something was nagging her and she couldn't put her finger on it.

Only a day and a half had passed since she had snuck back into the chateau, and already she craved the outdoors. Levi had stopped by the day before to give her an update. The investigation into the most recent bomb had not revealed anything that she didn't already know. Except for those living at the chateau, only the caterer's staff had been present at the time the bomb had been planted.

Security levels had once again been heightened, and Levi had ordered some additional surveillance equipment to be installed in the interior of the chateau. Janessa prayed that all of their preparations would thwart any further attempts against the royal family, but still she worried.

She set the employee lists aside and picked up the schedule for the upcoming week. A number of luncheons and small dinner parties would take place beginning at the end of the week and continuing on until the day before the gala that was still two weeks away. Thankfully, Patrice and her staff were taking care of the food for the smaller events. The only deviation from this plan would be if Patrice was once again shorthanded in the kitchen and requested help from the catering service.

Janessa started across the room once more, her mind turning to the day she had helped out in the kitchen. Just as she was considering how she might send for Patrice, a knock sounded at the door. She pulled the door open a crack, sighing with relief when she saw Patrice standing in the hall, a basket in her hand.

"Come in, Patrice." Janessa ushered her inside and closed the door behind her.

"I brought you some lunch and a few more things to stock your kitchen." Patrice set the basket on the table and pulled out the plate she had fixed for Janessa. Her eyes narrowed, and she fisted her hands on her hips. "You aren't eating."

"I'm fine," Janessa insisted as she motioned to a kitchen chair. "I actually wanted to talk to you."

"I can only stay for a minute," Patrice told her, but still she sat.

"Patrice, the day when two girls were out sick, do you know what was wrong with them?" Janessa asked.

"They said it was some kind of stomach virus," Patrice answered. "Personally, I think it was something they ate. They went out to dinner the night before and were sick by morning."

"Did anyone know they were going out to dinner?"

"Everybody," Patrice told her. "They go out to eat at the same restaurant every payday."

"You told me that day you didn't call in help from the caterers for security concerns. Do you have any specific reason not to trust their employees?"

"I don't like the way those people work." Patrice hesitated a moment before confiding in Janessa. "I feel like I have to watch them all the time. They get lost looking for the bathroom or take forever to return when I send them out to serve." Patrice gestured with both hands. "I just don't trust them."

"Is there any way to find out who would have been sent to help out the day of that luncheon two weeks ago?"

"Lilia might be able to find out for you. Her mother is one of their cooks."

"I'd appreciate it if she could get me those names, preferably without anyone realizing she's looking for information."

"I'll ask." Patrice nodded as another knock sounded at the door. Patrice stood and motioned for Janessa to stay where she was. She peeked out the door and then opened it wide when she discovered Martino on the other side. Turning to Janessa, she said, "Eat your lunch. I'll stop by and check on you later."

"Thank you." Janessa watched Patrice leave, sidestepping some packages in the hallway. She stepped forward as Martino wheeled in several boxes.

"These just arrived from the United States," Martino told her. He unloaded the boxes in the office and then handed a small box to Janessa. "Prince Garrett also asked me to give you this."

Janessa took the box, trying to ignore the way her stomach jumped at the mention of Garrett's name. When she discovered a cell phone inside the package, she looked up at Martino. "I don't understand."

"The prince said that he heard you could no longer use your phone since you were worried someone might pick up the signal. This one has a secure connection to everyone in the royal family. The numbers have already been programmed into the phone's memory."

"Thank you, Martino."

"His Highness asked that you call him at your earliest convenience." Martino stepped to the door. "Please let me know if you need any assistance with your packages."

"I will." Janessa nodded, torn between whether to call Garrett first or find out what had just arrived. Garrett won. She had not spoken to him in almost two days, and she missed him more than she had thought possible. Just the thought of hearing his voice sent a shiver of anticipation down her spine.

"I can do this," she muttered, even as she reminded herself that their relationship was purely professional now. Working up her nerve, she found his number in the phone's directory and made the call. A frustrated sigh escaped when she reached his voice mail. "Garrett, I just wanted to thank you for the phone. I guess I'll talk to you later."

She hung up and moved into the office. Her desk had been set up to look out the window facing the naval base, and a daybed had been situated on the opposite wall. Just inside the door was a worktable, now laden with the three boxes that had just been delivered.

Janessa pulled the first box into reach and grabbed a pair of scissors from her desk. Ripping open the top, she discovered a new fax machine. Pleased, she moved the box to the side and opened the next one. This time she uncovered a STU-III, a telephone that would allow her to communicate securely with other members of the US intelligence community. The two machines together would allow her to send and receive secure faxes as well as communicate securely on the telephone.

The last box was the largest of the three. Inside were several smaller boxes, which Janessa discovered held the surveillance equipment Levi had requested. She was still poking through boxes when her new cell phone rang. Abandoning her new toys, Janessa hurried to the other room to answer it.

"Janessa?" Garrett's voice came over the line. "I'm sorry I missed your call. I was in a meeting."

She heard the strain in Garrett's voice and asked, "What's wrong?"

"What's right?" Garrett muttered. "I just met with my father and his chief of internal affairs. The only person who had access to all of the paintings in question was the museum director in Bellamo, Pierre Dumond."

"Are you sure?" Even though Janessa knew he was a suspect because of his access, she had also met the man. Everything in his demeanor shouted integrity.

"His access code was used on the day one of the paintings was stolen, he was working on the exhibit in Calene when the first theft occurred, and he had access to both of the others." His voice was weary as he continued. "The investigators think he might also be involved in the bombing at your embassy."

"Why would they think that?"

"His ex-wife was an American. She left him when their daughter was young, and apparently she ended up with most of their assets," he told her. "They think he has been holding a grudge against Americans ever since."

"I'm sorry, Garrett." She closed her eyes, wishing Pierre Dumond were the only thing she was sorry about. "I never thought it could be him."

"Neither did I," Garrett admitted. "He is being brought in for questioning, so my father and I will be detained for another day or two. Stefano will be escorting my mother to the chateau tomorrow morning. Mother said she'll check in with you when she arrives."

"Thanks." Janessa gripped the phone as she added, "Be careful."

"I will," Garrett agreed before hanging up the phone.

She closed the phone and moved to the window. Rather than pull the curtains back, she looked through the sheer white fabric. The Mediterranean looked so peaceful with only a single sailboat visible on the water. She could no longer see the road from her window, a precaution to keep the paparazzi from seeing her. As she watched the sailboat in the distance, she realized that from a boat a photographer with a telephoto lens could probably see right into her window.

Anxiety overwhelmed her once again as she chafed against the inability to go where she wanted when she wanted. She took a deep breath and then another one, reminding herself that this situation was only temporary. She moved back into her office and set about hooking up her new phone and fax machine, grateful that her suite had a private phone line to accommodate her new equipment. She barely had everything in place when the phone rang.

She lifted the receiver, surprised to hear a woman's voice on the other end. "Going secure?"

"One moment." Janessa opened her desk drawer where she had hidden the key for the phone. She inserted the key and turned it before responding, "Going secure."

The line distorted for a moment and then cleared.

"Is this Janessa Rogers?"

"That's right."

"This is Katie from finance. Director Palmer asked me to call you with some information," she told her. "We finally managed to trace the money deposited into Alberto Manero's accounts. The funds were all initiated from a bank account in Hong Kong. Our sources have confirmed that the account belongs to Byron Heuse, a well-known art dealer in Paris."

"You're positive?" Janessa asked.

"Oh, we're sure," Katie told her. "There's something else though. When we looked at the other disbursements from that account, we were able to trace several other sets of payments."

"Do we know who received the other payments?"

"Not exactly. Each time a payment went to Manero, similar payments went out to two other people. One person we still don't have any information on, but the other is traceable to a numbered account in the Cayman Islands. There isn't a name on the account, but one of our sources tells us that the owner is a member of Meridia's ruling council."

"Are you sure?" Janessa grabbed a pad and pen, finally sitting down at her desk.

"Our information supports what our source has told us. We have tracked deposits to Meridia, but we haven't been able to figure out who on the ruling council the accounts belong to," Katie said.

"Send me whatever you have, and I'll see if the Meridian authorities can help us on this end."

"I have the documentation in front of me. If you're ready, I'll fax it right now."

"I'm ready. And Katie, thank you for your help."

"I'll let you know if we find anything else."

Janessa turned the fax on to allow it to receive and then set down the hand piece. If someone on the ruling council really was involved, then everyone in the smuggling ring likely had access to all of the proceedings in Meridia, as well as updates on the negotiations regarding the naval base.

With a sigh, she picked up her cell phone once again. This time, instead of calling Garrett, she pushed the button for his father.

"Your Majesty, this is Janessa. I hope I am not disturbing you, but I have some information I thought you should be aware of."

"Just a moment." King Eduard spoke to someone in the background and a moment later came on the line. "Sorry about that. You said you had new information?"

"Not all good, I'm afraid," Janessa began. "My agency has confirmed that the payments to Manero came from Byron Heuse. He's an art dealer in Paris. They have also identified similar payments to two other individuals. One they still don't have any information on, but the other they have tracked back to Meridia. My source feels strongly that those payments were being made to a member of the ruling council."

"Who?"

"We don't know yet." Janessa picked up the fax off of the machine and scanned through the information. "From the documentation I've received, it looks like all three recipients have been receiving payments sporadically for the past three years. Can you think of anyone who might have started coming into some money around that time?"

"The members of the ruling council are well paid for their service to Meridia, but generally they are independently wealthy long before they attain such positions," King Eduard told her.

"Does the ruling council have to be informed before a final agreement for the naval base is signed?"

"Yes," he told her. "They have already given their initial approval to negotiate with the United States, but the location would have to be voted on."

"You said that Lord Tratte was opposed to the US Navy's presence here."

"Yes, he has been the most vocal member in opposition," the king told her. "I will have a list composed of all the members who have expressed reservations about allowing your Navy into our waters. Perhaps our intelligence staff can identify the recipient of some of that money."

"Thank you, Your Majesty." Janessa sat back down at her desk. She studied the fax copy of Byron Heuse's photograph. Perhaps Mrs. Manero could determine if he was one of the three individuals her husband had been meeting with, as well as narrow down who on the ruling council was involved.

chapter 32

"I don't know." Mrs. Manero sat in her sister's kitchen and looked over the photos spread out on the table in front of her. Her grief had been replaced by anger as she considered her husband's activities. Now she was determined to help the authorities find out who had turned her life upside down.

Prince Garrett sat across from her along with the chief detective on the case. The detective's voice was calm and soothing when he spoke. "Take your time."

Garrett watched the older woman slide one photo off to the side and then shift her gaze to another. Of the dozen photos on the table, one was of Pierre Dumond; one was of the art dealer, Byron Heuse; and six were of members of the ruling council who had voted against the US presence in Meridia. The four other photos were random police file photos.

Mrs. Manero skipped over Byron Heuse's and Pierre Dumond's photos without a second glance, instead focusing on over three of the photos of older members of parliament and one of the random photos. Finally she pointed to one of them. "I never saw the face of the other man, but I think this was one of the men meeting with my husband."

"Are you sure?" Garrett asked, leaning forward to confirm his suspicions. The photo she had chosen was of Lord Tratte.

"Yes, that's him." She nodded, staring down at the photo. "I remembered thinking that he looked familiar, but I don't think I've ever met him."

"You have been very helpful, Signora Manero." The detective stood and collected the photographs. "Please let me know if you remember anything else."

Garrett gave her a nod and added his thanks as he and the detective left the house. "Now what?"

"I'll have Lord Tratte picked up and brought in for questioning," the detective told him. "If you could have his bank records subpoenaed that would help speed up the investigation. With a request directly from the royal family, I should be able to get them within a few hours."

"I'll take care of it." Garrett shook the detective's hand. "Please keep me informed of your progress."

"Absolutely."

As soon as Garrett was back in his car, he instructed the driver to return to the palace. He had buried himself with work for the past several days to keep from thinking about Janessa. He thought about her anyway. After closing the window to give himself privacy from the driver, Garrett called his father to give him the news. Then he called Janessa to give her an update as well, though he knew it was just an excuse to hear her voice.

"I'm glad you called," she told him. "I'm starting to go stir-crazy."

"Hopefully you won't have to hide out too much longer," Garrett told her. "Mrs. Manero identified Lord Tratte as one of the men who met with her husband. She said that she never saw the face of the other man, so it is quite possible it was either Pierre Dumond or Byron Heuse."

"Which still leaves the woman," Janessa told him.

"Dumond is already in custody and is denying any involvement. Maybe Lord Tratte will be more cooperative."

"We can hope."

* * *

"I think I have what you're looking for." Patrice set a bag of groceries down on the kitchen counter and turned to face Janessa. "Lilia's mother has the names of the servers who would have been sent to help at the luncheon you asked about. It was a husband and wife team, Elina and Roberto Lumere."

"Have they ever helped you before?"

Patrice nodded as she started unloading the groceries. "Roberto is the one I especially don't like to have help, but it seems he is always the one they send."

"He's the one that takes forever when he serves?"

Again she nodded. "Brenna mentioned that he has gotten lost a few times when he has been in our service. Last summer she found him in the library. He claimed to have taken a wrong turn when he was looking for the bathroom."

"That does sound odd," Janessa agreed, stacking the canned goods in a cabinet. "Have you ever seen him bring anything into the chateau or take anything out?"

"Actually, that was the other thing that always bothered me. Everyone else from the caterers comes already dressed and prepared to work. Roberto always arrives in street clothes and then changes once he gets here." Patrice shook her head. "It's irritating to have to find him someplace to change and store his bag."

"How big is his bag?"

"It's one of those bags for hanging clothes." She held out her hands to gauge the size. "When it isn't folded up, it's rather large."

Janessa considered this new information.

"By the way, the art expert arrived this morning," Patrice told her. "He is studying all of the paintings here at the chateau."

"Who asked him to do that?"

"Signore Dumond. Apparently he made the arrangements before he was arrested." Patrice put the last of the food into the refrigerator. "Martino will be coming to retrieve the paintings in here to be examined as well."

"Thank you, Patrice." Janessa turned and looked at the seascape on her own wall. Could the forgeries have spread to the chateau?

A short while later Martino arrived to retrieve the artwork from her room.

"Has the art expert discovered any forgeries?" Janessa asked.

Martino nodded, his eyes serious. "He has discovered three so far."

"Was one in the library?"

Martino's eyes widened. "How did you know that?"

"Lucky guess," Janessa told him. "I would like to see a list of the forgeries and their locations when he is done examining all of the artwork. I think we have a lot of work to do before the luncheon on Friday."

* * *

Garrett and Stefano looked through the two-way mirror at the man who had once been their father's most trusted advisor. Throughout the interrogation, Lord Tratte maintained that he had done nothing wrong, insisting that the Americans had framed him because he was so openly opposed to their naval base in Meridia.

The interrogator had not yet informed Lord Tratte of how he had come to their attention but rather had allowed Tratte to assume that he had been identified through his bank records. With this strategy, his motives became more and more apparent.

"Don't you understand?" Lord Tratte asked the interrogator, assuming a superior attitude. "With the Americans here, Meridia will lose its autonomy. We will be just another port for sailors to get drunk and cause trouble. King Eduard has lost his perspective on the long-term effects this decision will have on our country."

The interrogator nodded in understanding. "So you are concerned with preserving our way of life."

"Absolutely. First it will be a US naval base, and then it will be high-rise hotels and condominiums. Our coastline will be cluttered with tourists, and the king will be forced to increase funding for the local police and the port authority."

"Do you often go out on the water?"

"Rarely." Tratte shook his head. "I much prefer looking at the water to being on it."

"I see. Well, that would explain why you don't own a boat." The interrogator flipped through his notes, taking his time before looking up. "But that being the case, why would you frequent Alberto Manero's gas station?"

Tratte narrowed his eyes. "I don't understand."

"Alberto Manero, the man who owned the gas station that caught fire last week," he read from his file. "His gas station only provided gasoline for boats, not automobiles. I just wondered why you would go there every month if you didn't have a boat."

"You must be mistaken," Lord Tratte said now. "I don't know anybody by that name."

"That really is odd." The interrogator stared him down, watching as his face paled slightly. "Why would you meet with him the first Tuesday of every month if you didn't know him?"

"I refuse to answer any more of your questions without my lawyer present."

"That can be arranged." The interrogator gave a curt nod and left the room. A moment later, he entered the viewing booth where Garrett and Stefano had been watching.

"Sounds like you have him on the ropes," Stefano told the interrogator. "If he's asking for his lawyer, you know he's worried."

He nodded. "It doesn't hurt that the financial records are supposed to arrive tonight. My sources say that his father squandered much of the family's fortune, and when he died several years ago, Lord Tratte found himself with debts that were well beyond the family's ability to pay."

"His longtime hatred of the United States must have helped him justify his involvement with the embassy bombing. The real question is whether he will identify the others involved."

"That may take some time, especially if he was responsible for the fire that killed Manero," the interrogator told them. "If he thinks he is going to take the fall for something he didn't do, he may come forward with more information, but I expect that he is still justifying his actions."

"Let me know if you get anything else out of him," Stefano instructed.

As soon as Garrett and Stefano were alone, Garrett turned to his brother. "What do you think the chances are that he set that fire at the gas station?"

"Tratte doesn't strike me as the type to get his hands dirty, but it's possible. He did serve a few years in the military, so he probably had the expertise needed." Stefano shrugged. "I keep wondering why Manero was killed."

"I have to think that either he wanted out or someone was afraid he would talk," Garrett suggested. "The night of the gas station fire,

Manero was supposed to have his monthly business meeting, yet his body was the only one we found at the scene."

"That may solve the first part of the puzzle. Now we just have to figure out who the third person involved was."

"And find Byron Heuse before he recruits replacements."

chapter 33

Later that week, Garrett watched through the limousine window as his father's private plane landed at the airport. As soon as the aircraft came to a stop, his driver pulled forward and parked next to it. A moment later, Garrett watched Tim O'Donnell escort his wife, Lauren, down onto the tarmac.

Heedless of the reporters that had been constantly following him since his arrival in Calene, Garrett stepped out of the car to greet his friends.

"When you said you would take care of our travel arrangements, I thought you meant that you would send us a couple of plane tickets." Lauren moved forward and gave Garrett a hug.

"The plane was in Washington anyway," Garrett commented as he shook Tim's hand.

"Well, we appreciate it," Lauren told him, avoiding mentioning the reason the plane had ended up in Washington in the first place. She climbed into the back of the limo and waited until Tim and Garrett were settled before she asked, "Are you going to tell me what happened with the American girl? Tim won't tell me anything."

Garrett turned to Tim. "Did you tell her I got baptized?"

"Yes. And I'm so happy for you! But how did you manage to keep this juicy bit of info from the press?" Lauren asked incredulously. "Nothing has been in the newspapers at all about you being associated with the Church."

"Believe me, that hasn't been easy."

"What about the girl? Is there any hope you'll get back together?"

Garrett shook his head. "I may need a miracle on that one."

Tim studied him for a moment. "I hope it turns out the way you want."

"So do I."

* * *

Janessa leaned over her worktable where she had spread out the museums' security logs. Since Garrett had told her of Pierre Dumond's arrest, something had been nagging at her. She couldn't reconcile the man she had met with a thief, and she definitely couldn't see him involved in an organization that would kill to obtain its objectives. She also couldn't understand why he had sent the art experts to the chateau to discover more forgeries unless he was innocent.

If she looked at the evidence like a prosecutor, the case was tight. Dumond had been in the right places at the right times to steal the works of art in question. His access code had been identified as the only one used in three of the thefts.

From a defensive point of view, no one had seen him take anything from the museums. His lifestyle had not changed significantly over the past several years, and none of the money filtering through the numbered account in the Cayman Islands could be traced to him in any way. Withdrawals from the account had been made in person over the years, mostly in cash, but no one in the bank could ever recall seeing Dumond.

Another thing that bothered her was the Tuesday meetings. Passport records had indicated that Byron Heuse, the art dealer, had not been in Meridia on any of the dates in question. Logically, that meant that Dumond had been the other man present, yet Signora Manero had said that the other man was younger than Lord Tratte. Dumond was actually a bit older than Tratte.

She peeked out the door of her office into the living room when she heard her door open. Queen Marta entered, followed by Prince Stefano.

"How are you holding up, dear?" Queen Marta asked as Janessa moved into the living room.

"A little stir-crazy, but other than that I'm fine." Janessa motioned for them to sit down.

Stefano nodded at her office as he sat. "I see you are still working hard."

"I just can't believe that Pierre Dumond is guilty." Janessa shrugged her shoulders. "If someone else managed to get his access code, he truly may be as innocent as he says he is."

"Securing his access code would not be an easy feat," Stefano told her with an air of authority. "The access codes are changed every six months. Three different codes were used in the thefts, all belonging to Dumond."

"Enough about that for the moment," Queen Marta interrupted. "I'm afraid we still have a lot of details to see to for the upcoming festivities. Patrice told me that you needed to speak to me about the caterers."

Janessa nodded. "I think some of their personnel are switching the paintings here at the chateau."

She went on to explain about Patrice's observations and the plans to increase the surveillance areas in the chateau.

Stefano's dark eyes sharpened as he considered the possibilities. "So most likely the caterers are bringing in the forgeries with their uniforms and then sneaking the originals out in the hanging bag Patrice mentioned."

"Right. The man, Roberto Lumere, is our main suspect, but when the police went to his home to question him, he and his wife weren't there." Janessa shrugged. "Of course, there is also the possibility that a guest has been orchestrating the thefts for the past several years."

"Pierre Dumond has been a frequent guest since he took over the museum in Bellamo," Marta said now, concern and regret filling her voice.

"Yes, but he has been here for nearly ten years. The thefts didn't begin until three years ago," Janessa pointed out. "I can't find anything in his background that indicates a significant change that would cause him to abandon his integrity and start a life of crime."

"Garrett is supposed to be sitting in on the interrogations today," Stefano told her. "Maybe the detectives will have some luck in uncovering some new information."

Stefano stood and leaned over to kiss his mother's cheek. "I need to get back to Calene. If all goes well, we will see you tomorrow."

"Just as long as you are here for the welcoming luncheon," Queen Marta told him. As soon as he left, she turned back to Janessa. "Now, why don't you tell me what is really happening between you and my son."

Janessa's jaw tightened, and she knew she couldn't talk about this, not yet anyway. "I'm afraid I'm not destined to live in your world."

"Nonsense," Queen Marta said.

"I'm sorry, Your Majesty, but I really don't want to talk about this, please."

Marta studied her a moment and gave a subtle nod. Her tone was compassionate as she said, "I want you to know that I would gladly welcome you to our family, and my husband has come to feel the same way."

"Thank you, Your Majesty."

With a brisk nod, the queen changed the subject. "Now, bring me up to date on the preparations for the gala, and we'll see what still needs to be done."

* * *

Friday morning Janessa met with Levi after he made a final check of the new security equipment. Alan and Max had already completed their sweep of the chateau, and they were now positioned at the front gate, where all vehicles would be inspected before proceeding forward.

Shortly before eleven o'clock, Janessa moved into the security office so she could help monitor the video feed from the chateau's security cameras and the new surveillance equipment that had been placed around the kitchen, dining room, and parlor.

Once she was satisfied that all of the monitors were functioning properly, she called Martino. "When is King Eduard expected to arrive?"

"Any minute," Martino told her. "The queen should also be arriving within the next ten minutes."

An alarm went off in her head. "Where is the queen?"

"She went into Bellamo about two hours ago. She said something about checking on the dessert menu."

"Has anyone heard from her since she left?" Janessa fought the rising panic.

"No, signorina."

"Call Enrico," Janessa instructed. "I want to know exactly where the queen is."

"Of course," Martino agreed, his normally formal tone softening with concern.

Behind her, Levi stood abruptly. "What's going on?"

"The queen went to the caterers two hours ago to finalize the dessert menu, but Patrice took care of that last week." Janessa pressed the number for the queen's cell phone, her tension rising. "She's not answering."

"How do you want to play this?" Levi asked.

"Start a location trace on any calls made from the queen's phone just in case," Janessa said as her phone rang.

Martino's voice was filled with anguish when he gave her the news. "Enrico is not answering his phone. Neither are the queen's bodyguards."

Janessa hung up her phone and looked at Levi. "Enrico and the guards aren't answering. Call the police and send them to the caterers, and get me some backup. You just became command central."

Heedless of who might see her, Janessa raced out of the chateau to the garage. She grabbed a set of keys out of the case on the wall and clicked the lock button to figure out which car they belonged to. She had just cleared the gate when she saw a limousine approaching. Realizing it was Garrett, she picked up her phone and pressed speed dial.

Garrett picked up on the first ring. "I just saw you drive by. Where are you going?"

"I'm going to the village." Urgency filled her voice. "Your mother left a couple of hours ago. I'm sorry, Garrett. No one told me she was leaving."

"I don't understand," Garrett said. "Where did she go?"

"The caterers." Janessa took a deep breath. "Garrett, I'm worried. She and Enrico aren't answering their phones."

"I'll meet you there as soon as I can."

"Garrett, hurry."

chapter 34

Queen Marta tapped her pen on the notepad in front of her. She had spoken to the florists, the caterers, and the musicians. Everything was ready. Janessa and Patrice had done an adequate job filling in for her preparing for the gala, and over the past few days she had been able to finalize the last details over the phone.

The extra security had been somewhat burdensome, but at times these things couldn't be avoided. She had hoped to find out what had transpired between Janessa and Garrett, but to her knowledge neither one had confided to anyone what had caused both of them to be so on edge. All she knew was that if the tension didn't ease soon, someone was going to snap.

The call from the caterer had come at the ideal time. She had been looking for an excuse to get out of the chateau for a while, and a drive to the village had been the perfect opportunity. She hadn't planned on taking quite so long, but it had seemed silly not to check on the other details while she was there. Besides, she knew that the staff at the chateau had everything under control for the upcoming luncheon.

She looked out the window, expecting to see the Mediterranean. Instead, all she saw were trees. Surprised that they hadn't arrived at the chateau by now, she pressed the button to lower the window that separated her from the driver.

"Driver, where are we?"

"We'll be arriving shortly, Your Majesty."

Marta's eyes narrowed when the driver turned his head enough for her to see his profile. This was not the same man who had driven her into the village. "Where is Enrico?"

"He wasn't feeling well. I am his replacement."

Marta thought back to when she had entered the limo, wondering how she hadn't noticed the change before. She remembered the window between her and the driver being up when she had entered the limo, which wasn't unusual, but she recalled that one of the caterers had opened the door for her and helped her inside instead of her driver. Suddenly uneasy, she glanced behind her, surprised to see that her security detail was not following them.

Marta took a calming breath and forced an air of authority into her voice. "We've been driving for twenty minutes. We should have arrived by now."

"The road to the chateau was blocked by an accident. We are circling around to come in from the other side."

With that, the driver closed the window between them. Queen Marta's eyes widened with shock. The window between her and the driver was always to remain in her control. The fact that he had closed it without her instructing him to do so was a complete breach of etiquette. She replayed her meeting with the caterers, now realizing how odd it was that the owner had not been there but had instead left two of her servers in charge.

Concerned that everything was not what it appeared to be, she retrieved her cell phone from her bag. She noticed that she had forgotten to turn the ringer back on after her meeting and quickly dialed her husband's number. Relief flowed through her when she heard his voice.

"Don't worry, darling. We are pulling up to the chateau now."

"Was the road blocked?" Marta asked, her heart racing.

"What road?"

"Eduard, something is wrong." Marta fought to maintain control. "My driver said that the road to the chateau was blocked and that he is going the long way."

"Where are you now?"

"All I see are trees." She shifted to look behind her, unable to even identify what direction she was traveling in. "I was in Bellamo. We left about twenty or thirty minutes ago."

"Everything is going to be okay," Eduard assured her, though she could hear the strain in his voice. "I want you to keep this line open, but don't let your driver know you're on the phone."

"Eduard, I love you."

"I love you, too." Eduard's voice wavered. "I'll see you soon. Now hide your phone, but keep it turned on."

"Okay."

Marta started to put the phone back in her purse when suddenly the limousine came to a screeching halt. She fell forward, crying out as the back door was yanked open and a man leaned inside.

"I'll take that." He grabbed the phone out of Marta's hand and held it up to his ear. "If you want to see the queen alive again, it's going to cost you fifty million dollars. I'll be in touch."

"Now, I think it's time we got reacquainted." He slid into the back seat with the queen as her eyes widened with recognition. A moment later they were on their way once more.

* * *

Two police cars and an ambulance were already at the caterers when Garrett arrived just moments after Janessa. Enrico was sitting on the curb, and an ambulance attendant was examining a wound on the back of his head.

"What happened?" Garrett asked as he rushed forward to where Janessa was standing beside two of the police officers.

"I am so sorry, Your Highness." Enrico started to stand, but the ambulance attendant held him in place and shined a light in his eyes. The attendant looked up at Garrett, his expression serious. "We need to get him to the hospital."

As Garrett nodded in agreement, a police officer moved forward. "Someone hit him from behind and tied him up in the storeroom." The officer hesitated a moment before dealing the worst of the news. "I'm sorry, Your Highness, but the limousine is missing, and no one has seen the queen since she arrived in town earlier this morning."

"Where are her guards?" Garrett asked, his lips pressing into a thin line.

"Three of them are inside being treated by the paramedics. It appears that they were drugged." The officer hesitated a moment before adding, "I'm sorry, but the other guard was already dead when we arrived. It appears he was shot in the back."

Garrett let the reality seep in. His mother's guards had been neutralized, and she was being held hostage by men who clearly would stop at nothing to get what they wanted. He couldn't contemplate what they might want just yet. As waves of fear and frustration rolled through him, he raked his fingers through his hair and closed his eyes against reality. He anticipated the call he must now make to his father, not sure he could voice the words. He pulled the phone from his pocket, surprised when it rang and his father's number was listed on the caller ID.

"Dad—"

"Garrett, your mother has been kidnapped."

"I know." Garrett took a deep breath. "We are at the caterers where she was abducted."

"The ransom is fifty million dollars." The king's voice was hard, and fury vibrated through the line. He relayed the information his wife had given him, as well as the fact that she had been heading inland.

Garrett turned as he heard a car drive away, and his eyes widened when he saw Janessa speeding away.

"Garrett, come home now," King Eduard commanded. "I want you at the chateau."

Not wanting to argue, Garrett simply said, "I'll talk to you in a few minutes."

Garrett hung up and then turned to the ambulance attendant that approached.

The attendant's voice was serious when he spoke. "Your driver is showing signs of severe trauma. Is there anyone we should call?"

"I'll take care of it." Garrett signaled to one of the police officers as the attendant crossed to the ambulance. "Please go to the chateau and escort Patrice Saldera to the hospital. She's my driver's wife."

"Of course, Your Highness."

With a nod, Garrett returned to his car. Trying to push aside his concern for Enrico, he ignored his father's request and headed away from the chateau.

* * *

Janessa took the curve as fast as the car would allow. Her cell phone sat on the seat next to her on speaker with Levi on the other end. She couldn't think about what the queen was going through right now. She had to stay focused on the task at hand—finding her.

She had seen Garrett's frustration, the helplessness he had tried so hard to fight when they had discovered that his mother was missing. She hated herself for adding to his aggravation by leaving him behind, but she assured herself that she had no other choice. She couldn't put Garrett in danger or allow his presence to jeopardize his mother's safety. She had to do what she knew best, and that was to work with the US military, not the Meridian authorities.

A trace of a call made from the queen's cell phone had narrowed down her position, as had the antitheft device on her limousine. Unfortunately, the cell phone had remained silent for the past fifteen minutes, and the limousine had come to a stop, probably abandoned.

"How close am I?" she asked Levi, who was tracking her movements through the car's antitheft system.

"Take your next left. Your ride is waiting in a clearing about two hundred yards away."

She whipped around the corner, skidding to a stop a mere twenty feet from the waiting Navy helicopter. Grabbing her cell phone, she ran to the vehicle, lowered her head, and hurried to climb inside. She took a seat and strapped herself in, pulling her headset into place as the helicopter lifted off of the ground.

"Do you have the last known location?"

"Yes, ma'am." The pilot's voice came through the headphones. "ETA five minutes."

* * *

Lauren O'Donnell sat quietly in the chateau library, feeling as helpless as King Eduard and Prince Stefano appeared. Tim had left just minutes after Garrett drove off, and Lauren was trying desperately not to think about the possible outcomes. She didn't want to intrude at such a difficult time, but the silence was driving her crazy. "I can't believe we haven't heard anything."

King Eduard stood rigidly in the corner of the room, but he turned and gave a brief nod in agreement. With a glance at his watch, he turned to Stefano. "Garrett should have been here by now."

Lauren immediately averted her eyes to the floor. She didn't know where Garrett was, but she knew that he had called Tim and asked him to meet him somewhere. She had been battling with herself whether or not to disclose this.

From across the room, Stefano picked up on her body language. "Do you know where he is?"

"I don't." Lauren shook her head. "But . . . I don't think he's coming back to the chateau. He asked Tim to meet him somewhere."

"Where?" King Eduard demanded.

"I'm sorry. I don't know."

Before the king could press further, Martino opened the door, his eyes wary. "I'm sorry to interrupt, but the guests have started to arrive."

"We'll be in shortly," King Eduard informed him.

"Father, you can't be serious," Stefano insisted anxiously. "We can't go forward with the luncheon. What if we get a call from the kidnappers?"

"We can't let our guests know that anything is wrong." The king moved to the door. "Take a few minutes to compose yourself. Then I expect you to come downstairs and entertain our guests. If anyone asks, your mother and Garrett aren't feeling well and won't be able to attend today."

As soon as he left, Lauren turned to Stefano. "How can he be so calm?"

"He isn't." Stefano sighed. "But he's right. We have to appear as though nothing is wrong. It's all we can do right now."

chapter 35

The limousine was abandoned on the side of the road. Janessa instructed the copilot to relay the coordinates to the local authorities as the pilot continued onward. The road wound through the trees for several miles before there were any crossroads. Calculating that the kidnappers could only be about fifteen minutes ahead of them, the pilot conducted a wide sweep to look for any vehicles.

When they found none, he continued forward again following the main road.

Anxiously, Janessa stared out the window, hoping and praying that she would see something that would point them in the right direction. She sighed, wishing she were back at the chateau watching from the security room. She had dreaded watching the single women trying to gain Garrett's attention at the luncheon, but she would trade that scenario for her current situation in a heartbeat.

At least she had the satisfaction of knowing that Cynthia Renault had been taken off the guest list after lying to the press about her relationship with Garrett. Still, Janessa expected that Isabel Dumond, the museum director's daughter, would have been at Garrett's side for the entire event.

Her eyes narrowed as she thought of Isabel. What if she, and not her father, had orchestrated the thefts? With Lord Tratte and Pierre Dumond in custody, everyone was assuming that they had apprehended everyone involved except for the woman who had been with them at the meetings with Alberto Manero. If Isabel really was guilty, one of the men who had attended the meetings was still at large along with her.

Janessa pulled the mouthpiece of her headset to her lips. "Can you patch me through to the security office at the chateau?"

"Just a moment," the copilot said. He instructed her on how to switch to the external frequency, and a moment later she was speaking with Levi.

"I need to speak with Prince Garrett."

"It will take me a minute to get him up here," he told her. Janessa could hear him place the call to summon Garrett to the security office.

Nearly two minutes passed before Levi came on the line once more. "Prince Garrett isn't here."

"What do you mean he isn't there?" Janessa asked, panicked.

"He never returned from the caterers." Frustration sounded in Levi's voice. "I'll call his cell phone and run a trace on his car." He paused for a moment and then said, "Wait a minute. Prince Stefano just got here. He wants to talk to you."

Stefano's voice came on the line. "Where are you?"

"In a chopper, searching the area near the abandoned limo. Do you know where Garrett is?" Janessa asked, afraid to think of where Garrett might be right now. She closed her eyes, praying for guidance, wishing for some way to solve this nightmare before anyone got hurt.

"We don't know. Apparently Tim is with him, but my father is not happy that he went off on his own," Stefano admitted. "Janessa, please tell me what I can do to help get my mother back." His voice was pleading, and she could hear him struggle for control as he spoke again. "Please."

The sincerity in his voice forced her back to the task at hand. "Can you find out from Pierre Dumond who his daughter Isabel hung out with? Also see if he knows whether she was often gone on Tuesday nights."

"You think Isabel was using her father's access codes?"

"I do. It's possible that she's the woman who was meeting with Manero." Janessa kept her eyes on the ground below.

"Keep this line open. I'll call right now," Stefano agreed quickly.

* * *

Garrett's Porsche screeched to a stop in the parking lot at the naval base. He was barely out of the car when he saw Tim approaching with Commander Dan Peters. "Are you ready?"

Dan nodded. "We have everything you asked for. But I still don't understand why you're so sure the kidnappers would take her out to sea."

"It's the only thing that makes sense," Garrett responded as he fell into step with the two men as they headed for the dock. "There are too few roads leading out of Bellamo for them to think they could get away. The best way to slip past the authorities would be by boat."

"I hope you're right," Tim said as he stepped onto the speedboat Dan had prepared.

"Do we have any idea where Janessa is?" Garrett asked as he followed Tim aboard.

"You haven't told her what you're doing?"

"No. I want her as far away from the action as possible."

Dan shook his head, silently communicating his disapproval. "Last I heard she was on a Navy helicopter. They're searching the road where we lost track of your mother's cell phone signal."

"What about the limousine?" Garrett asked.

"It was abandoned."

"Let's go then," Garrett said, moving to take the wheel himself. He started the motor as the other men cast off the lines. With a prayer in his heart, he headed out to sea, hoping that logic would combine with inspiration to help him find his mother safe and sound.

* * *

"We're here, Your Majesty."

Marta struggled to open her eyes against the bright light spilling into the back of the van. Her hands and feet were bound, and a gag prevented her from responding.

The man she recognized from the caterers moved forward to release the bands on her feet and then pulled her from the van. He held her up as voices drifted toward them.

"Are you sure about this?" a woman asked. "Shouldn't we keep her alive until after we get the money?"

"Don't worry," a man answered. "We'll have the money before you get clear of the tourist traffic anyway."

"Call me when the funds are transferred," the woman replied. "As soon as I receive your call, we'll finish up the job."

The voices were vaguely familiar, but Marta didn't think about that now. She struggled against the man holding her arm, reality closing in on her. They were going to kill her. No matter what money was paid, her fate had already been sealed. Knowing that she was fighting for her life, she nearly managed to break free as the man dragged her down a gangplank to a waiting sailboat.

"That's enough now." The man gripped her arm harder, and Marta yelped with pain. "Things will be a lot easier on you if you cooperate."

She dragged her feet and tried to scream, but the gag muffled the sound. The heel broke off one of her shoes as she struggled futilely to stop her forward motion. Clearly frustrated with her, the man finally gripped her around her waist to carry her on board. Marta kicked her feet but only managed to catch her foot on the dock's railing.

"That's enough!" the man roared at her. He set her down on the deck of the sailboat and took both of her arms to give her a good shake. Impatiently, he dragged her through a doorway and down a flight of stairs. Her eyes didn't have time to adjust to the darkness before she was pushed into a room below deck.

The queen's eyes widened with terror when the woman came into view holding a syringe.

The expression on Isabel's face could only be described as smug as she spoke. "You've caused enough trouble."

Marta whimpered as she again tried to struggle free. Her fight took on a new urgency as Isabel moved closer, but none of her efforts could stop the needle from sliding under her skin. The drug took effect immediately, and Marta's vision blurred until there was nothing but darkness.

chapter 36

Eduard sat in the parlor, his head in his hands. The last of their guests had left shortly after three, finally concluding the longest luncheon he had ever attended. Now that they had survived the pretense that all was well, there was nothing to do but wait. He hated waiting.

Stefano stood by the terrace doors, staring out at the road. Lauren sat across from the king, quietly waiting for any news. No words of comfort were spoken, as none would be accepted. Silently, they each uttered their private prayers. Only time could give them what they wanted, just as time could steal that which was most precious. No more calls had been received from the kidnappers, but Eduard had instructed that the money be available for when the time came to negotiate.

Never before had Meridia paid a ransom, and that precedence warred within him now. No amount of money was more important than his wife's life. If it came down to a choice, Eduard was afraid he would be the first to pay.

For thirty-five years, Marta had been his anchor. She worked tirelessly each day, always putting his well-being and the happiness of their sons above all else. So many times she had been his sounding board and his voice of reason when he had a significant decision to make. This was the first time since he had ascended the throne that he had been faced with a crisis without her by his side.

The fact that one guard had been killed brought home the very real fact that the kidnappers didn't place a high value on life. Even now, Enrico was fighting for his life in the local hospital. According to the latest report, the doctors were still trying to determine if surgery would be necessary to relieve the pressure building up on Enrico's brain.

Hurried footsteps sounded in the hall, and Martino rushed into the room, a telephone in his hand. "Your Majesty," he said as he held out the phone.

Eduard took the phone, closed his eyes, and took a deep breath. "Hello?"

"Fifty million dollars," the voice said. "You will wire transfer the funds to the Grand Cayman National Bank."

Eduard picked up a pen and scribbled the account number down on a pad of paper. The voice was being electronically distorted, so there was no way for him to identify the speaker. "I want to speak to my wife," he finally said. "I need to be certain that she is okay."

"Pay the money or she dies. You have four hours."

Eduard slowly held the phone out as the line disconnected.

"Well?" Stefano asked urgently. "Is she okay?"

"I don't know," Eduard said wearily. "I just don't know."

* * *

The helicopter circled around a series of crossroads. Janessa could feel time running out, and she felt helpless as she kept her eyes on the ground searching for anything remotely suspicious. She was trying to keep her thoughts positive, but if they didn't find the queen soon, they would have to deal with the ransom demand. She knew what the percentages were on successfully negotiating the release of hostages, and she didn't want to entertain the possibility of being on the losing end of those numbers.

Knowing that Garrett was out there on the water looking for his mother made it that much more difficult for her to concentrate. Levi had informed her that Dan Peters was with him, but Janessa would have preferred for him to be safely back at the chateau. With a prayer in her heart, she continued to stare at the terrain below.

Stefano's voice came back on the line, frustrated and impatient. "Pierre Dumond couldn't recall any specific friends that Isabel has associated with consistently over the past few years. All he could tell me was that she is gone almost every evening, including Tuesday nights. He also said she has been doing a lot of sailing lately."

"Sailing," Janessa repeated, her memories tumbling over one another. "So Garrett has the right idea. The kidnappers may be trying to get away by boat."

"Hold on a minute. Levi wants to talk to you," Stefano interrupted.

A moment later Levi came on the line. "I think we've got something. A ransom call came in. We traced it to six miles southwest of your location. I already notified the local authorities. They will stop any vehicles in the area."

"Got it." Janessa quickly switched frequencies and gave the location to the pilots. Switching back, she spoke to Levi once more. "Have you heard from Garrett?"

"He hasn't checked in for some time. I'll call his cell phone and give him an update."

"Thanks." Janessa shifted forward eagerly. Below her she could see two police cars racing along the street. She pressed a hand to the window as the helicopter made a sudden turn and a plain utility van came into view. Excitement and trepidation coursed through her as the pilot found a spot along the road where he could land. He maneuvered to bring the helicopter directly in front of the van, effectively blocking its path.

The driver slammed on the brakes and made a sudden U-turn. The van traveled only fifty yards in the other direction before a police car cut it off. The second police car pulled up right behind the first, and the officers quickly drew their weapons and moved to secure the driver.

To Janessa's surprise, a woman was pulled from the van, but it wasn't Isabel. Instead, it was a woman Janessa remembered from the caterers, presumably Elina Lumere. Janessa pushed open the helicopter door and approached the van with the naval officer that had been sitting beside her. She glanced in the front of the van to find it empty. She then moved to the back as one of the policemen yanked open the rear doors. Janessa stepped forward, stunned as her eyes swept over the interior. She closed her eyes against what she saw. Nothing.

She moved forward to look for any sign that the queen had been inside just as her cell phone rang. She answered it to find Garrett on the other end.

Garrett skipped any preamble and immediately asked, "Did you find her?"

"Garrett, she isn't here." Weariness filled her voice as she looked once more at the empty van. "I'm so sorry. The driver was one of the women who worked for the caterers. We didn't come across any other vehicles when we were flying overhead. I don't know where she could be unless they took her by boat."

"I'm already out on the water looking for her."

"I think Isabel Dumond may have been the woman meeting with Manero. If I'm right, she's who we need to find."

Determination filled his voice. "I'll find her."

* * *

"How can we tell which one it is?" Dan Peters asked, looking out over the half dozen sailboats currently in view. He had taken over the boat's controls ten minutes before so Garrett could focus on the boat traffic unhindered.

"It's not that one. There are kids playing on the deck." Garrett shifted his binoculars to study the other nearby boats.

"Only those two are flying Meridian flags," Tim commented as he studied two boats to their starboard. One was cutting across the little bay, and the other was angling toward the open sea.

Garrett pointed toward the one moving out to sea. "Head for that one."

Dan turned the wheel and increased speed. Beside him Garrett inhaled sharply.

"What's wrong?" Tim asked.

"I think that's Isabel." Garrett continued to study the thin woman at the wheel with her dark hair streaming out from underneath a ball cap.

"Then that's the one."

* * *

"We should have heard something by now," Roberto Lumere said anxiously as he came topside. He still wasn't sure he should have agreed to this kidnapping scheme. It was one thing for him and his wife to use their jobs with the caterers to switch forgeries for real paintings inside the royal chateau, but the prospect of being involved with the queen's death was quite another matter—one that left his stomach queasy.

Isabel glanced down at her watch. "Maybe your wife decided to skip out with the ransom."

"That's not funny." He scowled. "We have plans for our share of the money."

"I have plans myself," Isabel commented lightly.

"I thought your only plans were to become a princess."

She shrugged one shoulder. "It takes a great deal of money to live alongside royalty. Now that the American has left, perhaps Garrett will come to his senses."

"You don't really think that you can buy yourself into the royal family, do you?"

"I don't need to buy my way in," Isabel said confidently. "Once the queen is gone, the royal family will need someone to play the role of hostess. With my close association with the family, I'm an obvious choice. A little more time with Garrett, and I'm sure everything will fall into place." Her tone turned haughty. "I would love to see my mother's face when Garrett and I announce our engagement."

Roberto wondered what drove her more, her hatred or her greed. "Was your mother really that horrible?"

Her eyes narrowed, and her tone filled with venom. "She took all of my father's money, left him to struggle to make a life for himself, and never once tried to contact me after she moved back to the United States."

Realizing too late that he shouldn't have broached the topic of her mother, Roberto swiftly changed the subject. "Hurry up and get out of this tourist traffic. The sooner we make the drop, the better."

"Why don't you go downstairs and get ready?" Isabel suggested. "We'll be clear in a few minutes."

Begrudgingly, he moved below deck as a speedboat approached pulling a water-skier behind it.

The driver of the other boat took a path parallel to them, and the sailboat rocked as it hit the speedboat's wake.

"Tourists." Isabel shook her head. A moment later, she heard foot-steps behind her and turned just in time to see a gun barrel pointed at her head. She stared at the gun several long seconds before she looked up at the man who held it. Her jaw dropped when she realized it was the man who had just been waterskiing beside them.

The speedboat came back around with several people on board holding weapons aimed at Isabel. She could only gape at Garrett when he climbed aboard.

"Where is she?" Garrett demanded.

"I don't know what you're talking about." Isabel attempted an innocent look but failed miserably.

Already Garrett was headed below deck as Tim secured Isabel's hands. A pistol in his hand, Garrett pushed open one door to reveal a stateroom. He did a quick search only to find the room empty. He then turned and saw the man down the hall only a second before a shot was fired.

Garrett dove into the room he had just searched as bullets whizzed down the hall. He could hear a door open, and he cautiously peeked out the doorway. His eyes widened when he saw the man dragging his unconscious mother out of the room, holding a gun to her head.

"Drop the gun and go back up those stairs or your mother dies."

His heart pounding, Garrett evaluated the man in front of him for about two seconds. The man swallowed hard and panic shone in his eyes. Slowly, Garrett let his gun drop and stepped into the hall with his hands spread out to the side. "I just want my mother back."

"Go on." The man waved the gun in his direction briefly, his hand shaking as Garrett backed down the hall and he moved cautiously forward.

Garrett sensed someone behind him as he reached the stairs. "Please, just let me get her to the hospital, and no one will get hurt."

The man shook his head, wordlessly moving forward. He dragged the queen with him, using her body to shield his own as Garrett ascended the stairs. With a prayer in his heart, Garrett stepped out into the light and moved back as the man followed him.

Garrett didn't worry about where Tim and Commander Peters were, nor did he take the time to see that Isabel had already been moved to their speedboat and tied up. He concentrated only on the man in front of him. The man's eyes shifted to the speedboat as he backed up to the railing.

"Get back on your boat, and maybe I'll let your mother live."

Panic shot through Garrett as he considered what the man was demanding. "I'm not leaving without her."

"You don't have a choice." He pressed the gun firmly to the queen's temple, the muscle twitching in his arm. A second later, Commander Peters emerged from his hiding place on the far side of the boat and squeezed off a single shot. He hit his mark, the bullet penetrating the kidnapper's forehead.

Before Garrett could rush forward, the man fell overboard, taking the queen with him. "No!" Garrett shouted as he raced to the side of the boat and leaped into the water after them. He saw his mother facedown in the water and quickly stroked to her side and turned her over. He wrapped an arm around her, taking the time to find that she had a weak pulse. He then pulled her to the side of the boat, leaving the kidnapper's body floating behind them.

"Is she okay?" Tim asked, reaching down to help Garrett lift his mother into the boat.

"She's been drugged." He climbed into the boat and looked past Isabel, who was tied to a seat, instead motioning to Dan, who was now standing at the wheel. "We've got to get her to a hospital fast."

Tim helped Garrett situate the queen on the rear bench. Dan, who was already on the radio requesting a medevac helicopter, put the boat in gear and turned toward land.

Garrett sat on the bench, resting his mother's head in his lap. He closed his eyes, praying silently. *Please let her be okay.* He heard Tim move toward them, draping a towel over the queen. Garrett looked up into his friend's eyes. "Will you give her a blessing?"

Tim nodded. As he prepared to add his own prayers to Garrett's, a helicopter sounded in the distance.

chapter 37

The private waiting room was nearly full as King Eduard stood silently by the door. Security outnumbered the family and friends who were waiting anxiously for news of the queen's condition as well as Enrico's. Patrice and her family had already been informed that Enrico had a ruptured blood vessel, and they were all praying that the surgeon would be able to repair it.

Dan Peters had taken custody of Isabel and was dealing with the task of turning her over to Meridian authorities. No one had any doubt that she would spend the rest of her life in prison, but they didn't care about that now. Their only concern was for the health and safety of those dear to them.

Garrett glanced across the room where Tim was sitting quietly with his wife and found himself envious of what they had together. He kept expecting to see Janessa walk through the door, but so far he hadn't heard from her. Dan Peters had promised to bring her up to date after he finished reporting to the local authorities, but Garrett was starting to wonder if he should go outside so he could use his cell phone and call her himself.

His thoughts were interrupted when the doctor walked in.

"How is she?" King Eduard asked urgently.

"She's going to be fine," the doctor said with relief. "I want to keep her here for a day or two until all of the drugs are completely out of her system, but she is responding remarkably well to treatment."

"Can I see her?" Eduard asked.

"For a few minutes."

Garrett and Stefano followed their father down the hall into their mother's room. She was sleeping peacefully, and already her color had improved from when Garrett had first found her. As Eduard sat beside his wife's bed, Stefano tapped his brother's shoulder and nodded toward the door. Silently they left the room together.

* * *

Janessa pulled into the garage, turned off the engine, and let her head fall back in surrender. They had nearly been too late. She kept going over her actions in her head, second-guessing every move, every decision she'd made since she had found out the queen was missing. She still wasn't sure what she should have done differently, but she knew she should have done better.

After the helicopter pilot dropped her off to pick up her borrowed car, she had swung by the hospital to check in on Queen Marta and Enrico before heading back to the chateau. She had missed Garrett and Stefano by a few minutes, but she had been able to see the king long enough to be assured that the queen was indeed going to recover.

She had also spent a few minutes with Patrice, who was still waiting to see Enrico. Patrice had been informed that the surgery had been successful but that it would take Enrico some time to fully recover. Despite the fact that her husband would be in recovery for a couple of hours, Patrice refused to leave the hospital until she saw for herself that he was going to be okay.

Janessa thought of the guard who had lost his life. Though she didn't personally know the man, she felt the emptiness deep in her stomach that came with an unexpected death. She knew firsthand what it was like to lose a coworker in such a way, and the other guards would undoubtedly have some grieving to do in the months to come.

Wearily, Janessa opened the car door and stepped out. She couldn't remember the last time she had been so physically and emotionally exhausted. Guilt was still eating at her that the queen's security had been inadequate and that Marta had managed to leave the chateau in the first place without Janessa's knowledge.

She started toward the door, turning when she heard a sound behind her. She turned a moment too late to prevent Eric Hennero from gripping her arm. The young councilman no longer looked interested in idle small talk about sailing. Instead his dark eyes hardened as he pulled Janessa closer. "Well, it seems you didn't leave town after all."

She flashed back to her first meeting with Hennero. "It was you." Janessa's voice was deceptively calm as her eyes swept down to see the gun in his hand. "You were the other man meeting with Manero."

"Very good." He nodded. "It seems Prince Garrett chose you for more than just your looks." He glanced down at her left hand, and his eyebrows lifted. "Don't tell me you really broke off your engagement over a few silly photographs."

"Cynthia was involved too?" Janessa asked even as she tried to comprehend her situation.

"Not in the way you think." Hennero let out a harsh laugh. "She was so sure you would leave if she could make you jealous that I gave her some suggestions as to how she might pull it off. I never realized it would work so well."

Terror gripped her, and she chose her words carefully. "I was a bit preoccupied this morning. I must have forgotten to put on my ring."

"Yes, that must have been difficult for you, finding out that the queen was gone." Hennero nodded in understanding. He pulled her with him toward the car she had just climbed out of and reached into her purse to retrieve her cell phone. "Now, I need you to call Prince Garrett. Tell him to meet you here in the garage."

"Why would I do that?" Janessa shook her head.

"Because if you don't, I'll kill you. Eventually I'll get another opportunity to get to Garrett or Stefano." Hennero's voice softened. "I don't want to hurt anyone. I just need some money so that I can get out of the country and start a new life."

"What makes you think the royal family will pay a ransom?"

"I know the bank in Bellamo already had the money ready to pay for the queen. Prince Garrett can just go in and have the funds transferred while I keep you in the car for insurance. When my bank confirms the transfer, I'll let you both go." He held out the phone once more. "Now, make the call."

Janessa watched as he set the phone on speaker and then pressed speed dial for Garrett. When Garrett answered, she tried to keep her voice calm. "Garrett, could you do me a favor?" She continued before he could answer. "I left my engagement ring in my room this morning, and I was hoping you could run it down to me. I'm in the garage."

She heard a slight hesitation and hoped he realized that something was wrong. It would be obvious she was on speaker, but she could only hope he wouldn't comment on the oddity of the request. Fortunately, his voice sounded perfectly normal when he asked, "Where are you going?"

"I wanted to visit your mother, but I didn't want the press to see me without my ring. You know how important appearances can be."

Another brief pause. "Are you going to be back in time for dinner with Mr. Rominez?"

"I'm planning on it," Janessa said, relief flooding through her. She didn't know how much Garrett knew about the Rominez assassination, but she was sure now that he knew something was wrong.

"Go ahead and pull up in front of the main entrance, and I'll bring your ring," Garrett suggested in a subtly commanding tone. "I'm headed out to the stables anyway."

"Okay, I'll see you in a few minutes," Janessa said and then watched Hennero end the call. She looked at him now, hoping to stall. "This family trusted you. Why would you steal from them?"

"For the money, of course." He laughed. "Unlike my partners, I was smart enough to take my payments in cash. If Tratte and Manero hadn't panicked and bombed the embassy, no one ever would have known a thing."

Just keep him talking, Janessa thought to herself. "And the fire at the gas station?"

"Manero was convinced someone had seen him on the night of the bombing. He was falling apart." He motioned for Janessa to take her place behind the wheel of her car. "It was only a matter of time before he started talking."

"But why set bombs here at the chateau?" Janessa slid into her seat, praying for guidance.

"You know what they say about a woman scorned."

"Isabel?" Janessa's eyes widened as he slammed her door shut.

"With some help from Tratte." Hennero climbed into the back seat, keeping the gun trained on Janessa. "After all, we couldn't have an American for a princess, now could we?"

"Apparently not," Janessa agreed numbly.

* * *

"It's got to be Councilman Hennero," Levi said as he stood in Prince Garrett's sitting room. "He's the only person the guards didn't record leaving."

"At this point it doesn't really matter who it is." Garrett finished pulling on his riding boots and stood anxiously. "Are you sure those bullets will penetrate the car doors?"

Levi nodded. "I've seen them work before."

"Are you ready?" Tim interrupted, tugging at Garrett's riding jacket himself to make sure Garrett's bulletproof vest wasn't visible.

"Yeah." Garrett nodded, habitually picking up his cell phone and slipping it into his pocket. "I just hope this works."

"Me too. How good are these snipers of yours?"

"They'll hit their target," Garrett said, not sure if he was trying to reassure himself or his friend.

Tim stepped toward the door and turned back to face Garrett. "They'd better."

* * *

Janessa gripped the steering wheel, her breathing coming in shallow bursts as she pulled up in front of the chateau. She closed her eyes, praying that Garrett would keep a safe distance. For the first time in her life, she couldn't see a way out. If she refused to cooperate, Hennero would just wait until Garrett went to the garage to abduct him. With his mother in the hospital, there was little doubt that Garrett would use his car within the next twenty-four hours.

He knows something's wrong, she reminded herself. She thought of Garrett's reference to Rominez and wondered how much Garrett knew. Rominez was the ultimate example of how the best security could fail. She prayed that this wouldn't be one more such example. Still, the mention of Rominez's name made Janessa feel certain that Garrett knew they were in danger.

She looked up as the front door opened, and a new wave of panic enveloped her when she saw Garrett step outside. "No," she whispered to herself without realizing she had spoken.

The voice from the back seat was quiet but firm. "Just do what I tell you, and no one will get hurt."

Janessa watched him coming toward her. She didn't notice his subtle analysis of the car, only the way he seemed completely at ease as he strode toward her. When he reached into his pocket, she swallowed hard. Surely he hadn't really brought her the ring!

What would happen if she tried to drive away? Would Hennero be able to get a shot off at Garrett, or could she possibly get far enough away that he could flee to safety before it was too late? She reached forward to put the car in gear just as she heard her cell phone ringing.

She gasped, and her movement stopped immediately. Her heart raced as she tried to listen for any sound from the man crouched behind her seat. He still had her phone, so she had no way of answering it, but Garrett was so close he would wonder why she didn't reach for it. Suddenly, she realized who was calling. She turned her head back to look at Garrett, realizing that his hand was still in his pocket, the same pocket where he normally carried his own phone.

With a subtle movement, she tilted her head toward the back seat. Garrett took another step and nodded to his right. Then suddenly gunfire erupted.

Hennero made a strangled cry, and Janessa screamed. Garrett started forward, but Tim and Levi rushed out of the chateau, and Tim grabbed Garrett to keep him back. As Janessa pushed open the car door, Levi aimed his gun at the floor of the back seat. She pushed out of the car, refusing to look at the now lifeless body behind her.

The moment Levi signaled it was clear, Garrett pulled free of Tim's grasp and rushed forward to Janessa. He took her by the shoulders, his eyes scanning her as though making sure she was still whole. Then without a word, he drew her close and just held on.

chapter 38

Janessa stood beside her sister's hospital bed and stared at the new life in the bassinet beside her. A few days had passed since she'd left Meridia, but for now she tried to focus on the present. She reached down and gently caressed her niece's tiny fingers. "She's beautiful, Mary."

"I never thought I could love someone so much," Mary said softly. When Janessa lifted her eyes to look at her, she continued. "Of course, I thought the same thing when I got married."

"Did you ever wonder if you were supposed to marry Kevin?"

"Not really." Mary shook her head. "I prayed about it because I was supposed to, but I always knew I was making the right decision. The love I felt for Kevin was so huge, I couldn't imagine walking away from it."

Somberly, Janessa nodded. She understood now what it was like to love so deeply, but instead of experiencing the miracles that could come from it, she had only heartache. As the baby started to fuss, Janessa lifted the tiny infant and handed her to Mary before making an excuse to leave. She knew that many more family members would be arriving shortly, and she wasn't ready to face them yet.

As she moved out of the hospital, she thought back to the day of the queen's kidnapping. Her stomach clenched every time she thought of Garrett walking toward the car where Hennero was waiting for him. Her relief had been so huge when he had pulled her into his arms that she probably would have agreed to anything in that moment. The moment hadn't lasted, however, interrupted almost immediately when a call had come from Director Palmer.

The US ambassador to Meridia had used his connections to have her called home, citing the queen's kidnapping as one of several reasons for her removal. She knew that his reasons were flimsy at best and that Garrett could have intervened to keep her in Meridia until the gala, but she had been guilt-ridden enough to think that perhaps it would be best if she was no longer at the chateau. She knew it had been cowardly to leave while Garrett had still been occupied with the authorities about Eric Hennero. She just didn't think she could handle saying good-bye.

By the time she arrived at CIA headquarters, Levi and Alan had already sent their reports, each of them citing several examples of her successes while in Meridia. Janessa wished she could have believed their words to be true, but for each incident she could find something that she should have done differently. She didn't even want to think about her part in helping Hennero get within shooting distance of Garrett.

For the first time in her career, she felt like a failure. She still couldn't believe that the queen had left the chateau without her or Levi being aware of it. That mistake had made the kidnapping possible, and, despite Janessa's efforts to help locate the queen, ultimately it had been Garrett who had gotten the job done.

She had gone over the scenarios again and again in her head, always reaching the same conclusion. She should have trusted Garrett instead of turning to the US military for help. Repeatedly she had seen how well their countries could work in tandem, but when it mattered most, Janessa hadn't trusted her Meridian counterparts. More specifically, she hadn't trusted them to keep Garrett safe.

The birth of her niece that morning had given her a much needed distraction. It also made her yearn for something she had thought she could live without. A family of her own. With a heavy heart, Janessa climbed into her rental car. As she started driving around the Maryland side of the beltway, she looked up to see the Washington DC Temple come into view. Remembering her sister's comment about prayer, she took the exit, hoping that within the walls of the majestic structure she could find some peace of her own.

* * *

Garrett stood outside the simple townhouse that had a pink sign hung on the door announcing "It's a girl!" The gala would take place tomorrow, but the event no longer held any importance for him. For the past week, all he'd been able to think about was finding Janessa. She had left Meridia a week before, and all of Garrett's attempts at finding her had failed. His calls to her sister's home had gone unanswered, and everyone at the CIA was either unwilling or unable to give him any information about her current whereabouts.

He didn't know why Janessa had left so suddenly, and for the first time since he'd learned about the gospel, he found his faith truly lacking. He felt a sense of panic when he thought about going through life without her. If Janessa was praying to the same God, why wasn't she receiving the same answers? He had spent hours on his knees, but the answers weren't getting any clearer as the days wore on.

He had hoped to gain some insight to what his future would hold when Tim had ordained him to the priesthood the previous Sunday, but no inspiration had come. His day had been brightened in an unexpected way, however. To his surprise, his father had attended his ordination and had requested to speak with him privately following it.

Though Eduard had asked that Garrett keep his religious preferences as private as possible, he informed his son that their family relationship was more important than their religious preferences and that he hoped Garrett would continue in his role as an active member of the royal family. Garrett's first instinct had been to share the good news with Janessa. A feeling of hollowness had filled him, and the thought of going through each day without her was unbearable.

Despite the sympathy offered by his friends and family, he found he couldn't talk about it to anyone. He didn't know how to explain to those close to him that he couldn't talk *about* her; he needed to talk *to* her.

Janessa had played a huge part in saving his mother's life. He had read the medical report. Had Garrett arrived even five minutes later, his mother might not have survived. Janessa had given him that five minutes and more by recognizing that his mother was missing before it was too late. He still wasn't sure how Janessa had identified Isabel Dumond as the insider at the museum rather than her father, but that tidbit of information had also helped save time during their search.

Finally unable to stand it any longer, Garrett had taken his father's plane and flown to Washington to find Janessa himself. Following his instincts, he had come straight to her sister's house. He glanced back at his guards, who had accompanied him to the US, and motioned for them to stay by the car. Taking a deep breath, he climbed the three steps to the front door and knocked.

He could hear voices inside, and then the door swung open. Though the woman standing before him was taller than Janessa and her hair was light brown, he could see the resemblance immediately. "You must be Mary."

Mary glimpsed the hired limousine parked at the curb and the four guards flanking it. Slowly she nodded. To Garrett's surprise, she didn't make any offer to invite him in, instead shifting to more fully block the door.

"I'm sorry to intrude, but I'm looking for Janessa. I hoped she might be here."

"Do you really think this is a good idea? You trying to work things out with her?" she asked directly in a straightforward way that closely resembled her sister's. She crossed her arms and gave a little shake of her head. "Have you even considered how much Janessa would have to give up to live in your world?"

The truth of her statement struck a chord, and memories of his years at Georgetown flashed into his mind. "It's not easy living in my world, but I hope she is willing to try."

"But do you understand that she would have to walk away from her work, even her country, to be with you? Do you understand how difficult that would be for her?"

Garrett's shoulders sagged as he let the truth of her words seep in. He didn't try to hide his disappointment as he considered that what he wanted most might not be best for Janessa. "I only want her to be happy." He debated whether he should leave but couldn't bring himself to do it. Instead he found himself blurting out his feelings to this complete stranger. "I know life with me won't be easy, but I love her more than anything. I don't think I can bear going through life without her, and I will do everything in my power to make her happy." Desperation hummed through his voice as he added, "Please let me talk to her."

"I would," Mary started, compassion showing on her face, "but she isn't here."

"Where is she?"

"She went to Meridia." Mary smiled mischievously as she added, "To the gala."

* * *

Everything was ready. The ballroom was decorated, the musicians were in place, and the food was ready to be served. Security guards were posted at the front gate, along with the dog that would provide an extra layer of defense. Several US naval officers were also present to augment security, a kind of thank-you to the king for signing the new agreement to grant the US Navy access to the base in Bellamo.

Pierre Dumond had been released following his daughter's arrest, though he was still struggling with the realization that his daughter had been harboring such an intense hatred against her mother and the United States. Byron Heuse, the art dealer behind the smuggling ring, had already been apprehended in Paris. Hopes were high that the threats against Meridia would finally cease.

Music drifted through the open terrace doors to where Janessa stood looking out over the sea. The water in the swimming pool rippled behind her, only tonight the moon was dark. Three weeks before, Janessa had stood in this very spot when Garrett had asked her to be his wife. Now she didn't even know where he was.

Garrett's family had been evasive as to his whereabouts, and she was beginning to think that he had changed his mind about wanting to marry her after all.

The day her niece was born she had spent hours walking around the temple grounds trying to find some sense of what her future held. As she had sat down on the edge of the fountain and stared up at the majestic Washington DC Temple, she had noticed an elderly couple walking out the door. Though both of them struggled with the basic task of walking, the man crossed the stretch of pavement to the handicapped parking and drove his car as close as he could to the front of the temple. He then struggled to get out of the car so that he could open his wife's door and help her settle inside. Then the woman smiled, her face filled with love and appreciation for her husband.

The possibilities in her own life had bolted through her in that moment. If she walked away from Garrett, she could very well be living her life alone. Going back to Meridia and facing her fears might give her what that elderly woman had. Love. Absolute, unwavering love.

Janessa's thoughts were interrupted by the sound of footsteps approaching. She turned to see the king step beside her.

"The gala is beginning. What are you doing out here?" Even though Eduard's voice was somewhat commanding, Janessa sensed he was asking as Garrett's father rather than as the king.

"I needed some fresh air," Janessa managed.

"I assume you heard that Pierre Dumond was released and that the real criminals are now behind bars."

"Martino told me." Janessa nodded. "I didn't think Signore Dumond was guilty, but then there were times I didn't know what to think," she admitted.

"This has been a confusing time for all of us," Eduard stated. His voice was serious as he continued. "I have understandably been concerned about the consequences of Garrett joining the Mormon Church."

Janessa nodded but said nothing.

"It has always been difficult for Garrett being the second son," Eduard said now. "With royalty, a second son is often seen as being second in more ways than just birth order. Even though Garrett has never expressed any resentment that he wasn't born to rule, he has often struggled with his role within the royal family."

Janessa listened, afraid that the king was going to tell her that Garrett would not be allowed to continue as a royal.

"After what the family went through last week, I spent a lot of time thinking about what is most dear to me." His eyes darkened, and he drew a deep breath. "Regardless of his decision, Garrett is still very dear to me, and he will always remain so."

Blinking in surprise, Janessa managed to find her voice. "Are you saying you have decided not to disown him?"

Eduard nodded. "I am a lucky man to have a wife and two sons I can be proud of. If you decide to marry my son, I will be that much more blessed."

Swallowing hard, Janessa struggled to speak. "Thank you."

He gave her a curt nod. "Now, let's get you to the party."

Still uncertain of her role for the evening and her future with Garrett, Janessa let the king escort her to the ballroom.

* * *

Garrett stepped into the ballroom, where the dance floor was already crowded with couples and a feeling of celebration scented the air. He stood just inside the door for a moment, his eyes searching for Janessa. His mother spotted him first and crossed to where he stood.

She was beautiful in her evening gown, her tiara sparkling against her dark hair. A wave of gratitude washed over him as he considered the many miracles that had brought about her safe return. Holding a hand out to him, Marta drew him close and reached up to kiss his cheek. "Welcome home."

"Thank you, Mother." He looked at the dance floor once more. "The ballroom looks wonderful."

"For such a difficult time, things have turned out nicely." Marta smiled as she noticed her son's attention shift.

Across the room, Janessa stood near the doorway leading to the terrace. Her silver gown shimmered beneath the lights, and her fiery hair was swept away from her face, soft curls falling over one shoulder. She was speaking to one of her many acquaintances, and Garrett was once again struck speechless and motionless by her beauty and apparent social ease.

Marta gave her son a subtle nudge. "Go talk to her."

"What?" Garrett drew his attention back to his mother and tried to regain his composure.

Marta just smiled and reached up to kiss his cheek. "She'll make a fine princess. Good luck."

"Thanks," Garrett managed as he looked up at Janessa once more. This time their eyes met. He moved forward, a million thoughts running through his mind. She was everything he wanted, and he knew at that moment that if it took him the rest of his life, he was going to convince her that they could build a wonderful life together.

He barely broke stride when he reached for her hand and nodded to the door. She turned to follow him, uncertainty showing in her eyes. With her hand in his, Garrett led her outside. He greeted several of the guests as he continued down the terrace steps, but still he didn't speak to her. Silently, he continued down the path to the swimming pool.

Turning to face her, he realized he was completely vulnerable. Everything he hoped for, everything he wished for was tied up in her. He swallowed hard and finally asked the question that had been tormenting him for days. "Why did you leave without saying good-bye?"

"I thought it would be best." Janessa spoke softly, but she kept her eyes on his. Her voice was guilt-ridden as she spoke. "I'm sorry about everything that happened the day your mother was kidnapped. If I had done a better job . . ."

"What do you mean if you had done a better job?" Garrett asked, truly shocked to hear the guilt and blame she was carrying. "You helped save her."

She shook her head, her eyes dropping to the ground. "We both know that isn't true. I was supposed to help protect your family, and I failed."

"You didn't fail," Garrett insisted. "If you hadn't realized she was missing when you did, she wouldn't be alive today." He reached out and tipped her chin up so that she was looking at him once more. "You kept telling me that no security is perfect. Why are you being so hard on yourself for being right?"

Janessa gave a shrug that was meant to be careless, but he knew better.

He ran a finger along her jaw, his eyes staying on hers. "Why did you leave me behind at the caterer's that day?"

"I had a job to do, Garrett. Part of that job was to keep you safe, and I was afraid I couldn't do that if you were with me." She hesitated a moment before adding softly, "I realize now that was a mistake."

For the first time, Garrett smiled. "Is this why you came back? So you could apologize?"

"No." She shook her head as insecurity flashed in her eyes. "I came back because I wanted to see you again." She let out a shaky sigh. "I did a lot of praying and soul-searching, and I finally realized that there aren't any guarantees in life and that my fear shouldn't ruin our chance to be together." Even as she said the word, her shoulders stiffened. "Then I got back here and you were gone. I thought maybe you changed your mind."

Hope speared through him, and he shook his head in amazement. "I can't believe no one told you. I told my family not to disclose my whereabouts in order to avoid gossip—I didn't intend them to keep it a secret from you! I wasn't here because I was at your sister's house looking for you."

"What?" Her eyes widened.

"Mary looks a lot like you. She has your sense of humor, too." Garrett gave in to the urge to grin as he stepped closer. Then his voice thickened as he spoke once more. "I love you. Nothing is ever going to change that." Slowly, he drew the ring box out of his pocket. "Every night when I kneel down to pray, I ask for the same thing—that you will once again agree to be my wife." He took a deep breath and rubbed his thumb over her fingers. "I can't promise that my world will always be safe, and I know the press will intrude more than we want, but my life will never be complete without you in it."

Her eyes filled, a single tear spilling over as she struggled to find her voice. "I have spent the last week trying to convince myself that I didn't belong in your world. I was so sure I was doing you a favor by staying away, but I kept getting tripped up by the same problem. I love you too much to live without you."

"I love you, now and forever." Garrett slipped the ring on her finger and lowered his lips to hers. "Promise me you won't ever take this off again."

Janessa slid her arms around his neck as tears filled her eyes. "I promise."

about the author

Traci Hunter Abramson was born in Phoenix, Arizona. After graduating from Brigham Young University, she spent several years working for the Central Intelligence Agency. She then left the CIA to stay at home with her children and pursue her love of writing. She has written several books, including *Undercurrents, Ripple Effect, The Deep End,* and *Freefall.*

Next from Traci Hunter Abramson . . .

LOCKDOWN

Prologue

Riley Palmetta glanced at the classroom door when it opened. She didn't recognize the student who poked his head inside, so she turned her attention back to the professor. *Only one more week of classes,* she reminded herself as she battled another wave of senioritis. The birds chirping outside the window only served to remind her of the balmy spring weather.

Letting out a little sigh, Riley let her mind wander. With graduation just around the corner, she could almost taste freedom. Finals week would be rough, but then everything would be smooth sailing from there. She considered her struggles of the past four years—the part-time jobs, the internships, the endless studying, and the mountains of scholarship applications. "Free time" was still a foreign concept to her, but she looked forward to finding out exactly what it entailed.

She supposed she had always been driven, even in high school, when she had taken every advanced-placement class offered so that she could whittle down the time it would take her to earn her college degree. Her parents, neither of whom had attended college, still didn't understand Riley's inexplicable desire to succeed or her insatiable need to learn. More precisely, they couldn't understand that Riley actually liked making goals and working toward something.

In an attempt to keep her closer to home, her father had continually insisted that Oswell Barron University was too exclusive and too expensive, but Riley hadn't listened. The private university in Bainbridge, North Carolina, a small college town half an hour north of Durham, was everything she wanted in a school. Its size, location, prestige . . . even the scholarship opportunities had been a perfect match. Now, after four years of college, Riley was just a heartbeat away from collecting her engineering degree—and she had done it without a single penny of debt.

She glanced at her watch, already wishing the class was over even though they still had another thirty minutes to go. She turned her eyes back to the professor just in time to hear a hammering noise and see him drop limply to the ground. A moment later the noise repeated itself, and the boy in front of her slumped down onto his desk as screams echoed through the room. Riley looked up to see the slender, dark-haired man point his gun and shoot off another round.

This can't be happening! Riley thought as the girl beside her fell to the floor. Instinctively, Riley dropped down beside her. She couldn't believe her eyes. This man was actually shooting at them! Blood dripped onto the floor in front of her from the lifeless form sprawled over the desk—a lifeless form that had been planning to study with her tonight.

Her heart pounding, Riley squeezed her eyes shut to block out the horrifying images. She grappled with reality, her mind whirling. Suddenly, the gunfire stopped, and she heard footsteps in the hallway along with a panicked voice a few rows back.

She didn't even have time to lift her head to see who else had survived before another spray of gunfire erupted in the classroom. The smell of blood overwhelmed her, and she heard a little voice in her head tell her to play dead—that if she wanted to live, she had to appear as though she were among the fallen.

She kept her eyes closed as once again the gunfire momentarily ceased. Muscle by muscle she tried to relax. Perhaps this was just a bad dream, she thought to herself. Maybe she had dozed off again in class and at any moment the professor would wake her up. She didn't jolt when the next spray of gunfire began, which she considered a miracle in itself. It also proved what she didn't want to face: this wasn't a dream.

Chapter One

Two years later

Tristan Crowther drove through the historic section of Bainbridge as he headed for Oswell Barron University. Until today he had only seen the campus on television, and he was almost surprised by the peaceful setting as he pulled up near Sedgely Hall. He climbed out of his truck and glanced in the back, quickly checking under the tarp to make sure his gear had survived the trip.

He took the time to study the three-story structure in front of him as he approached. The stone was weathered and gray, the hard lines of the building making it seem somewhat formidable. Adding to the gloom was the knowledge that twenty-three people had died inside the walls of Sedgely Hall just two years earlier. He still remembered the helpless feeling that had washed over him when he'd heard the news.

But now he pushed those thoughts aside as his deep blue eyes scrutinized the building. The warrior in him evaluated the possibilities for entry and escape as he struggled to keep his objectivity. He might have been helpless to stop the massacre two years ago, but he could make a difference now.

The students and faculty of Oswell Barron University had spent the past two years trying to recover from the tragedy. Now, in an effort to prevent similar incidents from happening again, they were offering their campus as a training ground for law enforcement officers. Tristan was part of the task force that would help create the training course, which would begin in three weeks.